JARDIN'S GAMBLE

LAYLAH ROBERTS

BOOKS BY LAYLAH ROBERTS

Doms of Decadence

Just for You, Sir

Forever Yours, Sir

For the Love of Sir

Sinfully Yours, Sir

Make me, Sir

A Taste of Sir

To Save Sir

Sir's Redemption

Reveal Me, Sir

Montana Daddies

Daddy Bear

Daddy's Little Darling

Daddy's Naughty Darling Novella

Daddy's Sweet Girl

Daddy's Lost Love

A Montana Daddies Christmas

Daring Daddy

Warrior Daddy

Daddy's Angel

Heal Me, Daddy

MC Daddy

Motorcycle Daddy

Wilde

Sinclair

Luke

.

1

Thea Garrison had shit luck.

Fate was basically a bully and she enjoyed giving Thea constant wedgies. Sometimes, she even swirled her head in a dirty toilet.

Don't laugh. That nearly happened once. Although that had more to do with a three-day flu and a pushy six-year-old than bad juju.

Today was supposed to be awesome.

She had on her best outfit. Like all her other clothes, it was from the thrift shop, but the black pencil skirt and loose white blouse actually appeared brand new and hadn't needed altering. Which, with her boobs and butt was practically a miracle.

Plus, she'd actually gotten her brothers to school with time to spare and all their clothes on. This was no mean feat. Usually she screeched up to the curb with only a few minutes to spare, one boy with no shoes or the other wearing his shirt backward. Once, Ace hadn't been wearing any underwear. She'd just pretended not to hear him when he'd told her.

That had been the same day as her job interview. The one

she'd been certain she wouldn't get since she had very little experience. Luckily for her, Jardin Malone had run through so many personal assistants he hadn't had much choice but to give her a try. He wasn't an easy guy to work for. Uptight, blunt, and a perfectionist.

He was also hot as hell. Although she pretended not to notice, he was her boss after all.

Thea was determined to keep this job. It paid better than anything else she could get, plus she was good at it. She'd stuck at it for over two months now. Apparently, his lordship's previous personal assistant had lasted just a week.

Nothing was going to ruin today. Not those snobby-ass bitches at the boys' school calling her names behind her back. Not the fact she was basically an outcast at work because of her secondhand clothing and a car that should have gone to the great junk yard in the sky a long time ago.

She'd even thought she'd be early enough to splurge on a coffee and one of those sticky buns at the food truck.

Life had been looking pretty sweet. Until two minutes ago when smoke had started pouring out of her hood.

Attempting to ignore it, she kept driving. She was still fifteen minutes from work. It was early, so there wasn't too much traffic on the road. And she wanted that sticky bun. She could taste it.

"Come on," she muttered to herself, praying the smoke would magically disappear.

Might happen. Maybe.

If fate wasn't a bully and a bitch.

The car started to shudder. A horn honked at her, no doubt noticing the plume of smoke erupting from the hood of her car. Or maybe it was just that she'd slowed down to a crawl.

She hit her blinker and moved off the road onto the wide shoulder.

"Shit. Shit. Shit." She slumped forward, resting her forehead on the steering wheel. *Come on, Thea. Big girl panties. You can deal.*

She undid her seatbelt and climbed out of the car. After opening the hood and waving to clear the smoke from in front of her face, she stared down at the motor.

Fuck a duck.

Like she had any clue what she was doing. She reached for the cap where most of the smoke seemed to be originating from. Her skin instantly seared from the heat, and she snatched it back with a yelp of pain, holding the wrist with her other hand. Tears threatened.

Deep breaths, Thea.

You've had worse. This is nothing. Breathe.

The sound of an engine approaching had her pushing her injured hand behind her back. She'd learned early in life it never paid to show any weakness. She stared in surprise as a huge, black truck pulled up beside her tiny, beat-up car. This truck screamed masculinity. It was the type of truck a man would buy if he were trying to overcompensate for being small in other areas.

Her mouth dropped open as the door opened and one of the biggest, most rugged-looking guys she'd ever seen in her life stepped out.

Okay she was pretty sure he hadn't bought this truck to compensate for being overly small in other areas.

At least she sure hoped not or else there was something wrong with this world.

The guy was a giant. She barely reached five foot three and weighed close to a hundred and fifty pounds. This dude was at least a foot taller and twice as wide. He could probably bench-press her and not even get winded.

That was fucking hot.

Even hotter was the idea of him picking her up and pressing her against the wall while fucking her.

Down, girl.

"Hello? Hello, miss? You okay?" His voice was gravelly. Low. Sexy as fuck. He had on a black T-shirt and black jeans along with motorcycle boots that were . . . yep, black.

"Seems to be the theme," she muttered.

"Sorry? Miss, are you okay?" the deep voice asked again.

She continued to stare at him, taking in the ink that was revealed on his forearms, in swirling, green patterns. The trimmed beard, those piercing, blue eyes and jet-black hair.

Mama save me.

He frowned and stepped closer to her. Suddenly, he reached out and placed his palm over her forehead.

"Hey, what are you doing?" She stepped back, nearly tripping in her heels. She still wasn't comfortable wearing shoes this high, but she thought they made her legs look long and thin rather than short and dumpy.

He grabbed her arm, saving her from falling flat on her ass. Which would have been another injury to add to her still throbbing hand. That was going to be a bitch to type with.

"Careful there," he rumbled. He scowled down at her feet. "What the fuck are you wearing on your feet?"

"Shoes."

He rolled his eyes heavenward as though searching for patience. "Shoes, huh? Looks more like instruments of torture."

He wasn't wrong there. They were black stilettos with a series of straps that ran up her feet. They looked sexy as fuck, but comfortable they were not.

Didn't help that they were a size too small for her and by the end of the day they'd be pinching horribly.

Why had she worn them? Why hadn't she worn her perfectly comfortable, if boring, ballet flats?

Vanity. Pure and simple.

"There's nothing wrong with my shoes."

"You just about landed on your ass," he pointed out.

Not her finest moment, to be sure. "Because you tried to grope me!"

"Grope you?" He raised his eyebrows. "When did I grope you?"

"You touched my forehead."

"Seems we have different definitions of what grope means. I was checking to see if you had a temperature."

"What? Why?"

"Maybe because you were just standing there, staring at me, your cheeks flushed and your breath coming in sharp pants. Thought you might have been ill. Now I'm guessing it was . . . a hot flush?" There was heat in his eyes, mixed with amusement.

She folded her arms over her chest. His gaze dropped to the cleavage she'd unwittingly pushed up over the top of her shirt.

"Stop staring at me!"

Oh, like you don't like the interest in his gaze. Hussy.

His own arms crossed his chest. "Like you weren't eye-fucking me when I walked up?"

Oh, fuck. She could feel her face flaming hot. "You're right. I think I have a temperature."

His face clearly told her he thought she was a liar. He was so right.

Then his gaze flickered over to the raised hood of her car. She wasn't sure if she was grateful for that or not. Part of her missed that heated, amused gaze roaming over her skin. Her eyes dropped to his huge hands, just imagining him running them all over her. Cupping her breast. Squeezing her ass. Spanking her.

Jesus, Thea. Get it together.

She licked her lips.

"That fever still raging, huh?" he drawled, keeping his gaze on her car.

"Seems to be," she croaked.

After sending her another heated look, he headed back to his truck. Wait. Where was he going? Was he going to just leave her here?

She knew he was under no obligation to help her. And let's face it, most of her life people had walked away from her. But still . . . it seemed kind of rude.

Especially when she'd already mentally undressed him several times.

That kind of thing created a bond . . . well, it should have.

You're an idiot, Thea.

Disappointment flooded her. Not because she thought anything would come from her attraction to him. She was experienced enough to know that sexual chemistry could fizzle and die as quickly as it had begun. Just because someone got her blood pumping didn't make them good boyfriend material. In her experience it tended to be the opposite.

But instead of going for the driver's door and taking off, he moved around the back of the truck, opening it. When he returned, he held a small toolbox.

"Do you . . . do you know how to fix my car?" she asked hopefully.

"I'm a mechanic," he confirmed.

Elation filled her. Quickly followed by worry. What if he expected to be paid for his time? She'd need to offer something. Only she didn't have any cash, and even though she'd just been paid, she had bills coming out her butt.

Crap!

Okay, one issue at a time. Either way, she was going to have to part with some money to get her car fixed. If she had her way, she'd take it to old Joe who lived three streets over and took care of the neighborhood cars for a case of beer and a pack of cigarettes.

Of course, that could be the reason her car was now smoking, considering Joe had just given the motor a tune-up.

Awesome.

He grabbed a rag and undid that same cap. That would have been much smarter than just reaching for it with her poor hand, which still throbbed.

She pushed the pain to one side. She couldn't do anything about it then, and looking at it would just make it hurt worse.

"Can you fix it then? I'm going to be late for work." She didn't want to sound rude or ungrateful, but she really had to get to work. Her boss hated tardiness.

She was certain that if he had his way she'd live at the office. He practically did.

"Unfortunately, I can't."

"But I thought you were a mechanic." Maybe, like old Joe, he wasn't a very good one.

"Shame. Looks like he should be good with those hands," she muttered to herself.

"Excuse me?"

Her eyes went wide as she stared up into the handsome man's face. A smile curved at his lips as his eyes danced down at her. "Did you just say I look like I should be good with my hands?"

"Nope, I didn't say that." Because that would be way too embarrassing.

The look he gave her told her he thought she was a complete and utter liar.

"Can't do it now, I'll have to get it towed back to my garage. It's not far from here."

She chewed at her lip anxiously. "Can't I drive it now and get it to a garage after work?"

"Not unless you want to blow your engine up," he replied. "And that I can't fix."

Shit. Shit. Shit.

She thought about her options. The car couldn't stay there, it would just get towed and she'd never be able to pay the towing fees and the fine. But if she let this guy tow it to his garage who was to say he was any good? Or that he'd charge a fair price?

She sighed. Only one option was clear.

"I'll get it towed myself. Thank you."

He gave her a skeptical look and shut the hood, turning and leaning his ass back against it. "I'm good at what I do, and I don't hike my prices." His gaze turned thoughtful. "Tell you what. I won't charge labor; you just pay for any parts that are needed."

"I couldn't ask you to do that," she said.

"You aren't asking, I'm volunteering."

She shook her head, feeling ashamed. "I don't need charity."

Reaching out, he tilted up her chin. That time she didn't flinch back. His blue eyes stared down into hers. "Go on a date with me then."

"P-pardon?"

"Payment for my labor. Go on a date with me. Unless you have a boyfriend?"

She blinked. "No, I don't. You're seriously going to tell me that in return for you working on my car for free you want to take me out on a date?"

"Yep."

Her gaze narrowed. "You're not going to insist on some fancy restaurant and order champagne and lobster then leave me with the bill, are you?"

Anger flashed in his gaze. Her breath caught. "Not sure what sort of men you've been dating, but when I take a girl out, I pay."

"So, not only will you be working on my car for free but you'll be paying for me when we go out? That doesn't seem fair."

"Everything always fair in your life?"

She snorted. "Rarely."

"Seems a fair trade to me. Few hours of work in exchange for a few hours of your company."

"This isn't a sex thing, is it?" she blurted out.

"Pardon?"

"You're not asking me out because you think I'll give you a blowjob in the restaurant bathroom? Because while I like sex, I'm really not that type—"

Her sentence was cut off as he placed his hand over her mouth. "I'm gonna stop you right there before you succeed in pissing me off," he growled at her.

He already sounded plenty pissed off, so it was probably a good idea he'd shut her up.

"I am not asking you to have sex with me. Okay, maybe trying to bribe you to go on a date was not my best move. But when I take a girl out, I pay and I do not expect anything in return. All right?"

She mumbled behind his hand.

"What was that?" he demanded, removing his hand.

"Most guys would," she told him.

"Well then those guys would be dicks and totally unworthy of your attention."

"You don't even know me," she whispered. "Why would you want to help me? Why would you want to take me on a date?"

He gave her a wicked smile. "Maybe I just enjoy saving damsels in distress. Gives me an ego boost."

"You need an ego boost?" She gaped at him. How could someone who looked like he did need an ego boost?

He burst into laughter. "Well, I don't now. Maybe we don't know each other. But that's what a date is for. Getting to know someone. And hell, maybe I'm just hard-up for some company."

"I doubt that," she said dryly.

"Look, I'll get your car towed. Got a buddy who will do it cheap. I'll work on it for you, when it's fixed, I'll give you a call and we can go on that date."

She cocked an eyebrow. "You'll hold my car prisoner until I agree to a date?"

"Damn straight." He winked at her and she couldn't help but smile back. He was charming and funny and gorgeous.

Why aren't you jumping at the chance to date him? *Because you're an idiot.*

She let out a deep breath. "It's a deal." She held her uninjured hand out to him. Her other hand was still throbbing painfully. Perhaps she was being stupid. For all she knew, he was going to take off with her car and she'd never see him again.

Yeah, right. Because your car is totally worth stealing.

He wrapped her small hand in his, gently squeezing. Dear Lord, there was something about such a big, strong man being so very careful with her that did something to her insides.

Likely there was something wrong with him. Maybe he snored. Or he didn't lower the toilet lid. Perhaps he did drugs. Or pimped out women.

Her breath whooshed out of her at the thought.

"Hmm, I'm guessing you're back to thinking I'm some sort of serial killer," he drawled.

"What? No!"

He grinned. "You're the worst liar."

She bit her lower lip. "Sorry."

"Would it help if I gave you my mama's phone number? She'd kick my ass if I didn't treat a lady right."

"I . . . I . . . no!" she squeaked out, completely horrified at the idea. Speak to his mother? On what planet would she want to do that?

He threw back his head with a laugh. "That was a joke. My mama and I aren't exactly on speaking terms."

Oh, that was sad.

"Okay, darlin'. Here's my card. Tell me your name and number and I'll put it in my phone." He drew his phone out.

Crap. Well. Here goes nothing. She rattled off her details.

"Thea, it suits you."

She wrinkled her nose. "Do you think?" She'd always thought it sounded too pretty to be her name. Too elegant and refined. Everything she wasn't.

He tapped his finger against her nose. "No bad thoughts about yourself allowed."

How the heck did he know? She gaped at him. But he didn't give her an explanation. He was too busy tapping away on his phone. "My buddy will get your car in twenty. You said you needed a ride into work?"

"I'll be fine. I'll get a friend to pick me up." A friend ... an Uber ... that was close, right?

He watched her suspiciously. But she went back inside her car and brought up the Uber app. It wasn't a cost she could really afford, but she'd take public transportation home. It would mean taking three different buses and walking for half a mile at night in her shitty neighborhood, but it couldn't be helped.

When the Uber was booked to arrive in five minutes, she looked at the card.

Carrick Arson.

Cool name. Carrick. He didn't look like a Carrick. She slipped back out of the car when he got off the phone. Grabbing hold of her bag, she locked up. "What shall I do with the keys?"

"I'll wait for my friend to get here."

She frowned slightly. "I don't want to hold you up."

He shrugged. "It's that or leave the keys under the tire, darlin' and there's no guarantee even this car will be here when Jack arrives."

She bristled slightly at the slur to her car. But hell, who was she kidding? It was only the truth. It was a piece of shit.

She sighed. "I don't know what to say."

"Thank you works. I mean; if you wanted to say thank you, Carrick, you handsome, gorgeous, sexy man, I wouldn't say no."

She grinned. "Thank you."

He held a hand to his chest. "Wounded."

A giggle escaped, surprising her. Laughter wasn't something that really existed in her world. Something inside her softened. This big, gorgeous, funny man had managed to make her laugh.

A car pulled up and she looked over. There was her Uber.

Carrick's eyes narrowed as he looked at the car. "Friend, huh?"

She shrugged.

Leaning down, he brushed his lips across her cheek. Then his mouth moved to her ear. "Just as well you're not mine. Or you'd be getting a red ass. Both for lying to me and for taking an Uber."

Crap.

"You've got a thing against Ubers?" she asked, ignoring what he'd said about giving her a red ass. He had to be joking, right?

Or was there something about her that screamed, spank me?

Dear Lord Thea. Chill.

"I'm not happy you'll get into a stranger's car but not mine."

She cleared her throat. "You are a stranger."

"Not for long. And then we will revisit this. That's a promise."

Thea had the feeling she was in far, far over her head. But a shiver of arousal went up her spine as she looked into his face. She saw the intensity in his gaze and nodded, incapable of speech. Then proving himself the gentleman he'd proclaimed to be, he walked her over to the car, opening the back door. She slid in.

The Uber driver turned to smile at her, blanching when he saw Carrick standing there, scowling at him.

Holy. Shit.

"Fasten your seatbelt," he rumbled.

She scowled. She'd been about to. Maybe. With a sigh, she did it up. He crouched down and grabbed hold of her chin, kissing both of her cheeks. "Have a great day at work." He turned to the Uber driver. "Drive carefully, anything happens to her, I'm holding you accountable."

"Carrick," she protested. Thing is, she wasn't sure if she was protesting the threat to the Uber driver or the note of possession in his voice.

She didn't know him. He didn't get to claim her.

Right, like you're putting up any sort of real protest.

"Text me when you get to work."

Before she could remind him that he didn't get to make demands on her, he closed the door and was walking away.

And man, he sure did fill out his jeans nicely.

IT TOOK everything he had to walk away and not drag her out of that car and over into his truck.

An Uber.

Was she freaking kidding him? Not only had she lied to him, but she was trusting her safety to some stranger?

Taking a deep breath in, he let it out slowly.

Easy, man.

Much as he'd wanted to go all caveman on her ass, he'd known he had to let her go. Throwing her over his shoulder and taking her back home wasn't the way to win her over. And he wanted that. He wanted her trust. Her desire. Her fire.

He'd immediately noticed the way her gaze had eaten him up as he'd walked toward her. It had amused him as she'd stood there, her mouth slightly open, pulse racing. He'd be lying if he said it hadn't boosted his ego.

Most women who saw him coming toward them would run the other way, not devour him with their eyes. He was a big guy and she was small. Curvy in all the right places, but still so fucking small. Delicate. Even though he'd never use his strength against a woman, she didn't know that. She should have been more careful. He frowned as he thought about her being that trusting with another stranger. One not as honorable as him.

Yeah, he'd pushed her into that date. And, no, he wasn't going to let her pull out. But he wouldn't want anyone else to do that to her.

Ah, well, after your date you won't let anyone else close to her anyway.

He wasn't sure what it was about her that called to him so strongly. But he wanted her.

And no one was going to get in the way of what he wanted. Not this time. Never again.

2

———

Jardin stepped into the outer office just as Thea started to lower herself onto her seat.

"You're late, Ms. Garrison," he barked. He felt a flicker of guilt as she startled, and her seat flew backward on its wheels. She teetered on her heels and he dove forward.

He might be an ass at times, but he wasn't about to let her fall flat on her butt. Grabbing hold of her waist, he steadied her.

Her waist was so tiny that his hands fit all the way around. His pulse picked up. He should never have hired her. It had been a stupid, impulsive decision. One made with emotion rather than logic. Something he prided himself on no longer doing. Emotion would be his ruin. Once, he'd let himself be run by it, and he'd lost everything.

Quickly, he drew his hands from her waist, still tingling. Need for her was a thirst inside him that would never be quenched. Because Thea Garrison was off-limits.

He'd hired her because he'd been desperate. He'd gone through more personal assistants than every other lawyer in the firm. Combined. He was a hard taskmaster. He knew that. Once, he'd had more give in him. More laughter. But that was all gone. All he had was work. And family.

And he dedicated his life to both. Allowing nothing to interfere.

Especially not a petite, gorgeous woman who wore ill-fitting clothes, had far too many shadows in her eyes and was definitely too young for him.

"I'm seriously rethinking these shoes."

He glanced down at the hideous things with a grimace. How did she even walk in those? And they looked to be too small for her, her toes poking over the edge of them.

If she were his, he'd have her in Louboutins. Those red soles would look sexy as hell. Especially as that would be all she'd be permitted to wear.

Focus. She's your personal assistant not your sub.

And she would never be his sub. He didn't take on untrained subs. Not anymore. Plus, she was his employee. He didn't mess with people he worked with. Although that soon wouldn't be a problem.

"You're fired. Get packed up and leave."

Her mouth dropped open and the blood left her face as she swayed, making him worry she was about to faint. He reached for her again, but she shocked him by slapping his hands away.

He blinked. She was normally so professional. It had surprised him considering her lack of experience. Part of him had expected her to be gone by the end of the first day. That she'd lasted two months shocked him. But he didn't have time in his life for mistakes. And he didn't suffer anyone taking advantage of him. Not again.

This is what he got for taking a chance on someone.

"You . . . you're firing me?"

"I'm sorry if I wasn't clear," he said smoothly. "Yes, you're fired."

"For being late?"

"Yes, for being late."

What wasn't clear about that?

Devastation filled her face, almost swaying him. But he couldn't allow it to. The New Orleans Malones didn't deal with emotion. They didn't like displays of affection and feelings. He couldn't remember ever seeing his parents kiss or hold hands. It just wasn't done.

Unlike his wild cousins, he wasn't given to letting everyone around him know exactly what he was thinking. His visits to Haven were now few and far between. Even though he was glad Alec and West had found women who made them happy, it was difficult for him to see. One evening at dinner, Alec had sat with his wife, Mia on his lap, feeding her bites of food, his hand rubbing her swollen belly as he watched her with affection.

His mother would have died of shock had his father dared to touch her like that. Let alone pull her onto his lap and feed her by hand.

It just wasn't done.

Of course, she likely wouldn't understand that Jardin was a Dom. She'd think he was perverted. She'd likely have disowned him. She'd been a cold, hard bitch, who'd never smiled in her life.

Mia rarely stopped smiling.

So why am I trying to emulate what my parents had? Maybe I should be more like the Texas Malones?

Dear Lord, there had to be something wrong with him. Had he really just thought that? His cousins were insane. It was just by some weird stroke of luck that two of them had managed to find women to put up with them.

How none of them had ended up dead or in jail was beyond him. Every time he visited, he risked his life. They'd been known to shoot at visitors. And just because he was family didn't mean he was exempt from that.

It had almost become a competition. He'd even seen money exchange hands. Assholes.

Damn, he missed them. It had been months since he'd been to Haven. Even if it did hurt, being there reminded him he was alive. The longer he spent in New Orleans, the colder he grew. The less invested in his life he became. The more the memories got to him, pulling him under, taunting him.

"But you don't even know the reason why I'm late," she said quietly.

"You're not ill. And I'm guessing no one died since you're not crying. I don't see what other excuse you can possibly have."

"My car broke down."

"And your phone was broken? Why didn't you call me?"

Surprise filled her face. "You would have helped me?"

Helped her? Of course he would have. No, wait. No, he wouldn't have. She wasn't his sub. Not his responsibility.

"I meant to call a cab," he explained coldly.

She blinked. And he worried for a moment that she might cry. Tears—her tears—might just break through the coldness. And he couldn't allow that. If he let her in, he was in trouble.

Because, deep down, the last thing he felt when he looked at Thea Garrison was cold.

Nope. She heated him from the inside out. When she was near, his hands itched to draw her closer. His ears begged to hear more of her sultry voice. His entire body leaned toward her. Wanting . . . needing to touch her.

And that is why he had to get rid of her. Thea was temptation wrapped up in a small, sexy package. It would be all too easy to get drawn into her web. He wasn't going to allow himself to fall for her.

So, he acted like she didn't affect him. Like she barely existed beyond work. He didn't ask her about her homelife, even though he worried about how threadbare her clothing appeared to be. He didn't express interest in her wellbeing, not even when she turned up to work with large, black circles under her eyes. He didn't care. Or, at least, he pretended not to.

Because he had to keep himself safe. From the moment he'd given into weakness and hired her, he'd been cursing himself.

Because he fucking wanted her. And for more than a quick affair. He wanted to wake up to those smiles in the morning and go to sleep with her curled next to him each night.

But it wasn't happening. She was his personal assistant, or at least she had been. She was way too young. Naïve. Innocent. They likely had nothing in common.

Nope. Best he stick to his asshole routine and get rid of her.

"I called for an Uber and I got here as quickly as I could. You see there was—"

"You called an Uber?" He glared down at her.

She frowned. "Yes. Why does everyone find that so objectionable? There's nothing wrong with taking an Uber."

"It's unsafe."

She threw her hands in the air. "How is it any less safe than taking a taxi?"

"Taxi drivers are vetted."

"Right, we both know that's not always the case. Anyway, as I was telling you there was this man—"

"What man? Where?"

An exasperated breath popped out of her and she placed her hands on her hips, glaring up at him, her toe tapping a tune out on the thick carpet.

"If you'd let me finish, I'd tell you."

Damn. How had he not seen this feisty side of her before? She always acted so professionally.

This was hot.

Back on track. Stop thinking about how hot she is. You're firing her, remember?

It shouldn't turn him on to have her scold him, and he couldn't understand why it did. He normally preferred subs who were obedient, who followed his every word to the letter. Brats had never interested him.

"There was a man who pulled up when I was broken down and offered to have my car towed and fixed at his garage."

"And you just let him?"

What was wrong with this girl? Was she totally naïve? How the hell had she survived as long as she had without someone taking advantage of her?

His hands clenched into fists at the thought.

"Well, it seemed like a good offer."

"He's likely stolen your car, taken it to a chop shop, and you'll never see it again."

"I could leave my car on the side of the road, keys in it, with a sign saying 'take me' on it and it would still be there in the morning," she said dryly. "Trust me, no one in their right mind would steal that heap of junk."

What kind of car was she driving around in? How was that safe? Why didn't she have someone looking after her? Making certain she was safe?

"Why didn't you call a family member?"

"Like whom?" She gaped at him as though that was a weird question.

"Like your dad. Don't you have a dad?"

To his shock, she burst into laughter. "Do I not have a dad? Jeez, how to answer that? Yes, I have a dad, but he isn't the sort of person you call when you're in trouble."

He didn't like the sound of that.

"I didn't have anyone to call who could help. But it took a while to, uh, negotiate getting my car to his garage. I did call and leave a message with Jenny, though. Didn't she give it to you?"

"No, she didn't." He stalked over to the intercom system. "Jenny!"

"Yes, sir?"

The other woman's silky voice grated on him for some reason. He'd seen the way she looked at him. Hungry.

Jenny walked into the room, her hips swaying. A predator looking for prey. Although her prey came in the form of a rich husband. Her dress was tight and way too short for a receptionist in a respectable law firm.

"What kind of outfit do you call that?" he snapped.

She faltered, giving him a surprised look. Then she glared over at Thea. He moved his gaze to Thea and caught her biting her lip in an attempt to hide her grin. Thought that was funny, did she?

Jenny had worked there for longer than Thea, but she didn't spend much time on a day-to-day basis with him. She probably thought her overblown fake looks gave her some sort of protection against the lash of his tongue.

That would backfire on her.

"This is Prada."

How the fuck did she afford Prada?

"I don't care." He waved his hand dismissively. "Why didn't you give me the message from Thea?"

The other woman looked over at Thea with a triumphant look, obviously thinking she'd gained the upper hand. "I never got one."

Thea gasped, an outraged sound. "Jenny, I spoke to you less than an hour ago."

"It's Jennifer," she said coldly. "And I never got your message. Sir, could I get you something? Coffee? Tea?"

The *me?* was silent but definitely implied. His gaze narrowed in on her. "Pack up your shit. You're fired."

"W-what?" Her eyes flickered from Thea to him. "You can't fire me! I didn't do anything wrong!"

"You didn't pass on an important message to me and you lied

and said you didn't receive that message. Grounds enough to be fired."

"I'll sue!"

"You do that. You'll need to find a rich boy-toy to afford a lawyer, though, won't you? Not sure how easy that's going to be for you."

"You-you asshole! How do you know she's not lying?" She swung her hand at Thea. "Or is that because she's fucking you? That gets her special treatment?"

He stared at Jenny. Just stared until she flinched under his unwavering, icy glare. "Get. Out. Now."

The other woman turned and fled, steady on her heels.

"You do realize you've just fired the two women who know how to make your coffee the way you like it," Thea pointed out dryly.

"You're the only one who knows how to make my coffee properly. She puts too much creamer in it. And you're unfired."

He turned away.

"Just like that?"

"Just like that. Now, make me some coffee and then we'll go over what I need from you this week."

SOMETIMES SHE WISHED she didn't need this job so much.

Most of the time she wished her boss wasn't as gorgeous as he was. Or as forbidding. Because the man was glacial. He didn't smile. He didn't joke. He didn't do warm or friendly. Except with clients. Then he was a very different man.

And if the gossipers around the water cooler were to be believed, he used to be warm. He used to be human.

Something had changed him. She had no idea what. And it wasn't her business. But she wished she could go back in time and stop it from happening. Because seeing him smile . . . she'd bet it was a hell of a sight. She bet it was beautiful.

With a sigh, she prepared his coffee in the break room. She turned right as Jenny walked into the room. For once, she didn't look perfectly put together. There was a smudge of mascara under one eye and a few pieces of hair had come free from her bun.

Thea might have felt bad that she'd lost her job if she hadn't been gunning for her from the day she'd been hired.

"I know you're fucking him," Jenny stated harshly. "That's the only reason he'd hire you. Although what he sees in a fat whore like you is beyond me. You should just fuck off back to the filthy gutter you crawled up out of, slut."

"Well, well, what is going on in here?"

The voice was deep. Commanding. With a Texan drawl. She nearly dropped the cup of coffee she held. That was all she needed. To burn herself with hot coffee. One burn was enough, thanks. Or worse, stain her clothes. It took her a long time to find this outfit. She didn't want it ruined.

She gulped as she looked over Jenny's shoulder to the man who stood there. He looked like sin dressed in jeans and a button-up, plaid shirt.

Jenny sneered at him. "Who are you? And what are you doing back here? This is for employees only."

"That so? Must have got turned around in this big ol' building," he drawled, laying it on thick. "Hard for someone from the country to get his bearings without no hills."

She choked on a laugh.

Jenny sniffed, obviously not understanding he was joking. She looked him up and down. "Are you sure you got the right firm? Jin, Stein, and Malone is a very exclusive law firm."

"Exclusive huh? Well, la-de-da. It's okay, I been counting up my pennies. Brought a whole jar of 'em with me."

She couldn't hold back her giggles any longer. The cowboy glanced over at her and winked.

"Stop laughing, you stupid cunt!" Jenny screeched.

"Whoa." The cowboy rubbed at his ear. "Got some good lungs on you."

"Fuck you!" Jenny screamed at him.

"Now, you see, I'm usually down for a good fuck, but I'm busy right now. Got to go talk to my cousin about a little job. And well, to be honest, you're not really my type. Bit too bony. And screechy. Now you, on the other hand," he looked Thea up and down with hunger in his gaze, "you most definitely are my type."

She could feel herself blushing bright red even though she didn't believe him. There was no way she was his type. She was pretty certain she wasn't anyone's type. But the conversation was definitely pissing Jenny off.

And that was pure gold.

The cowboy smiled at her. "Maybe after I've met with my cousin, I could take you out for an early lunch, darlin'? Got to be something decent to eat around here."

"What? Has everyone lost their fucking minds? How can you prefer a fat, ugly bitch like her!"

The smile fell off the cowboy's face. "I think it's time you left." He straightened and glared down at Jenny, who didn't have the sense to see that behind this one's smile lurked darkness. "You're starting to piss me off and you don't want to do that."

"What's going on in here?" a familiar voice demanded.

She winced as Jardin stepped up behind the cowboy. They were about the same height. The cowboy was maybe a bit wider in the shoulders. Both dark-haired and handsome. Even though they were dressed differently, there was something similar about them. And she wasn't talking about their looks.

It was like they'd both known pain. Darkness.

"Well, hello there, cousin," the cowboy said with a wide grin. His eyes danced with amusement. "I've come for a visit."

COULD his day get any worse?

Really? He'd woken up thinking it was going to be like every other day. Work. Work. Sleep. More work. Instead, it seemed like the universe had decided that today it was going to throw a whole bunch of obstacles in his path to strain his patience.

"Wait," Jenny said. "You're his cousin? You can't possibly be a Malone! You . . . you're not refined or rich." She ran her gaze dismissively over Maddox's clothes.

Oh, she was so mistaken.

"I'm not?" Maddox replied. "Huh, that's weird cause that's what it says on my passport."

Thea started giggling, and it was the sweetest noise Jardin had heard in a long time. His cock grew hard and he had to take a few deep breaths to calm himself.

"Shut up, you stupid bitch!" Jenny screeched.

Oh, hell no. He was not putting up with that. He stepped forward, around Maddox, who'd stiffened, right as Jenny reached out and shoved Thea. Thea flew back on those ridiculous heels of hers, toppling over onto her ass, the cup of coffee smashing to the floor.

A cry flew from her lips.

"Thea! Are you all right?" he asked pushing past Jenny and crouching down by Thea, who was sitting there, looking shocked.

"I . . . I think so."

"Don't worry, I'm sure your slut will be fine to service you tonight."

He stood, staring down at Jenny. She flinched, fear entering her gaze. Good, she should fear him. "I was willing to let you leave and that be the end of it. But you've pissed me off now. Don't expect to get a job in this town, hell, the whole state. I'll have you blackballed, and you'll find my reach is far and wide. If I were you, I'd go home now, pack up your pathetic excuse for a life and find some Podunk town in the middle of nowhere where you might be able to pick up some waitressing work because your life here is over."

"You sure told her, cousin. Couldn't have happened to a nicer bitch," Maddox said in a friendly voice, but his eyes were cold as he looked Jenny up and down.

She brushed past them all with a fake cry.

Jardin turned as Thea attempted to push herself up. She winced and he frowned.

"What's wrong? Did she hurt you? I'll fucking kill her."

He was all too aware of his cousin watching in interest, but he didn't care.

"Oh, no, it's not from her. It's just my hand."

"What's wrong with your hand?" he snapped.

"Uh, cuz, not that I want to tell you how to handle your personal or private affairs—"

Yeah, right. When didn't one of his nosy cousins like to butt into his business?

"But maybe you'd want to help her up before you start interrogating her?"

Damn it, he had a point.

Jardin held out his hands for her to take. Thea gave him a surprised look and only reached up with her left hand. He guessed she'd hurt her right hand. He helped her up, moving his hands to her waist to hold her steady.

"This is becoming a habit, huh?" she tried to joke.

He scowled down at her.

"What? You often get trapped by crazy psycho bitches then get rescued by a hot cowboy and his uptight cousin?" Maddox joked.

Jardin turned to scowl at him. "Watch your language."

Maddox held up his hands. "Just saying."

"You two really are cousins?" she asked, looking at them.

"Unfortunately," he growled. "What's wrong with your hand?"

Jardin laid out his hand, expecting her to immediately put hers in his. What he was not expecting was blatant disobedience. She put her hands behind her back and shook her head.

Maddox whistled. "Not something you experience every day, cuz. Good on you, darlin'. Make sure he doesn't wear his hand out too much on your ass later."

He whirled to his cousin, who had moved to the small kitchen and was looking through the cupboards for who knew what. With his cousins, you could never be certain of what the hell they were up to.

"Maddox!"

"Yeah?"

"She's my secretary, not my sub."

Maddox turned to give him a curious look. "Huh. Really?"

You cannot kill him. You cannot kill him.

"I'm not his secretary," Thea said.

"See, she thinks she's your sub too."

"I didn't say that!" Thea's eyes were wide, shocked. Did she even know what Maddox was talking about? "I'm his personal assistant."

Jardin didn't understand why that distinction was important. But he just sighed and gestured to the small table. "Sit. Show me your injury."

"It's fine."

"I didn't ask if it was fine. I told you to show me your hand."

"Oh, I'd do as he says, darlin'," Maddox warned. "That's his serious voice."

"He has a voice that isn't serious?" she asked, looking genuinely surprised.

Jardin ground his teeth together in frustration.

"He does. Shocking, huh? I mean, he's always uptight, but sometimes, he smiles," Maddox whispered that last part as he drew out a cloth and started cleaning up the coffee mess.

"No," she whispered back.

"If the two of you have finished with your comedy act," he snapped.

Thea gave him a guilty look but Maddox just grinned.

"Thea. Hand. Now."

With a deep sigh he didn't appreciate, she placed her right hand in his. He scowled as he took in her angry, red skin that sported several blisters, one of which had burst.

"What the hell! How did you get this? Your hand is burned!"

3

Jardin inspected her hand, trying to ignore the way his skin heated where it touched hers. Her hands were small and delicate. Like the rest of her.

Part of him wanted to bundle her up, tuck her away somewhere safe, and make sure she was treated like the precious thing she was.

The other part wanted to tie her to his bed and fuck her. Hard. Hot. Until she forgot her name, forgot everything except who she belonged to.

Mine.

Except she wasn't.

He needed to get his fucking head together. His scowl grew as he stared down at her injured hand. Maddox whistled as he cleaned up the spilled coffee. Jardin gave him a sharp look.

"Since when do you know how to clean?" He'd been in the bunkhouse Maddox shared with most of his brothers. The place was a pigsty. He'd gotten five steps inside before fearing for his health.

Of course, they'd all laughed like it was a big joke.

"Since Mia moved in and wrapped big brother's balls around her little finger."

"Maddox!" he snapped before rising to grab the first aid kit from under the sink. Thank God no one else was around at this time of day. That was all he needed to turn this into a total mess.

"What?" Maddox looked over at Thea, who was blushing. "I love Mia. It wasn't an insult to her. I'm glad she has him firmly by the balls. He was way too uptight before she came along. All 'Maddox stop getting into bar fights. And Maddox stop leaving your brothers tied up in the middle of nowhere without food, clothes, or water.' Total bore."

"You . . . you did that? To your own brother?" Thea asked, wincing as Jardin started putting burn cream on her poor hand.

"It was only once. Or, wait, maybe twice. And they both deserved it. But I've learned my lesson. Next time, I'll leave food and water." Maddox winked at Thea and she shook her head with a smile. It was obvious she thought he was joking. Jardin knew he wasn't.

"How did this happen?" he asked quietly. He was debating taking her to the emergency room. He glanced up at her.

She was biting her lip worriedly. She was wearing bright pink lipstick. She wore it every day. A shudder nearly moved through him at the thought of those pink-colored lips wrapped around his cock.

Easy, man.

"My car had smoke pouring out of the hood. So, I opened it up and foolishly reached in to undo the cap where the smoke was coming from. It was hot."

"Ouch," Maddox said sympathetically. "Darlin' as a general rule, if something is smoking, it's usually hot."

"Thanks for that lesson, Maddox," he said dryly. "Maybe you could go wait in my office?"

"Sure. I'll make sure that bitch has left without stealing any of the office supplies."

"No, just—"

But it was too late. He was gone. And he'd do whatever the hell he wanted anyway.

After slathering some burn cream on her skin, Jardin reached for a bandage and started wrapping her hand. "You should go to the emergency room."

"It's just a small burn. There's no point in waiting around for hours for a doctor who'll tell me to put burn cream on it."

She could have a point. But he still didn't like it. Didn't like that she was injured. Hurting. That she'd come to work like that and hadn't said a word.

"I don't think it needs to be covered," she told him.

He simply stared at her then resumed wrapping her hand. "You can't keep it wrapped up all day. It needs to breathe. Take it off every so often then reapply cream and put it back on. Do you have cream at home?"

"Hmm, oh, I think so."

He sighed and handed her the tube of cream. "Take this. There are other first aid kits around here. Just remember to order some more. I'll get a town car to take you home."

She stiffened, alarm filling her face. "Why? I'm not still fired, am I?"

Suddenly, he felt tired. In fact, it felt like he'd been nothing but tired these past few years.

"No, you're not still fired." He should say yes. Get rid of her. But the truth was, he wasn't sure he could do without her. Not just because she was the best PA he'd ever had. But because he'd fucking miss her. For the first time in years, he looked forward to coming to work because he got to see her.

So, what are you going to do about it?

Nothing. Absolutely nothing.

Coward.

"But you're going home. You can't work like that."

"I can." She got on her feet. "I'll be fine."

"You've got burns all along the palm of your hand and your fingers. How are you even going to type?"

"I'll use my other hand. It'll be fine."

He narrowed his gaze, his suspicions aroused. Why didn't she want to go home?

"Most people would jump at the chance to go home and rest for the day."

"Well, I'm not most people and I can't afford the day off," she countered.

That he could believe.

"It's with full pay."

Surprise filled her face, and he saw her think about it. Then she shook her head stubbornly.

Brat.

"Thea," he said in a low, warning voice. "It's not a request."

He preferred his women to defer to him. In and out of the bedroom. He liked to be firmly in charge. No matter where he was.

Her eyes flashed with defiance. His palm itched. He knew that if he ever took her over his knee it would be all over. And he wasn't just talking about his career, because she'd be in her rights to sue his ass for assault. It was about his inability to keep her at arm's length. To keep kidding himself that when it came to her, he didn't care.

"You're already down a receptionist," she pointed out in a reasonable voice, ignoring the fact she'd been given an order. He ground his teeth together. At this rate, he'd have no teeth left by the end of the month. "You can't afford for me to be off as well."

Fuck.

She had a point. But he didn't like it. He let out a breath. What was it about her that stirred the darker parts of him? Usually, he kept them better hidden. Most people probably saw him as the easiest Malone brother to deal with. The most reasonable.

Or at least they would have. Before the tragedy.

That's what the people in his social circle started calling it. *The tragedy.*

"Fine," he said. "But you call the agency and get a temp out here quickly. I don't want you doing both jobs."

"The other PAs will help cover the front desk."

No, they wouldn't. Not unless he ordered them too. They didn't like Thea and they would like to see her fail. Not that he'd let that happen.

You just fired her twenty minutes ago.

Like he'd actually meant it. Although, he should send her away. Maybe Maxim could use her services. Actually, no. There was no way he'd send her over to his younger brother. Maxim was flirt. He went through women like it was an Olympic sport and he was determined to get that gold medal.

"Fine. But if I see you using that hand, you're going home. No arguments."

"Yes, sir," she said impudently.

He just frowned at her as she turned on her heel and walked out. But his eyes lingered over her plump, firm ass in that skirt.

Shit.

When they returned to her office, Maddox was nowhere to be found. Thea walked out into the main reception area. He followed, groaning as he saw his cousin sitting at the front desk, his feet up on the desk, arms crossed behind his head as he spoke to one of the firm's biggest clients. Melanie Arnold was rich, smart, and a total bitch.

Fuck. Jardin was going to have to do some fast talking and groveling. Then Melanie threw back her head and brayed with laughter at something Maddox said.

"Well, that's unexpected," Thea muttered.

"Get that temp here now," he commanded, stepping forward with a smile and a hidden glare aimed at Maddox, who just gave him a shit-eating grin.

How had this day gone downhill so quickly?

4

Using her fork, Thea stabbed her salad with disinterest. The sun beat down on her shoulders. She probably should have chosen a shady area to sit in. Her hand throbbed with pain as she forced another forkful of the bland food.

"Argh, I'd be looking all sad and depressed too if I had to eat that rabbit food," a familiar voice drawled. Then a long-limbed body dropped down beside her. His scent reached out and teased her.

It was pleasant. But it didn't do things to her body the same way Jardin's did.

Or Carrick's had.

How could she find both of them so attractive? They were so different. One big and rough-looking but with a surprising sense of humor. The other refined and cold. With a sharp bite.

"It's not so bad," she said, peering down at her salad.

"Darlin', it's a few leaves of lettuce and carrots. Rabbit food. You need some real food. I'll get you some pizza."

"Pizza. I remember pizza," she replied wistfully.

"Sounds like you're in mourning, darlin'."

"I miss carbs. But they're not my friend. They go straight to my ass."

He peered down at her bottom. "Nothing wrong with your ass as far as I can see. You on some weird diet?"

"I wouldn't call it weird. But yeah, I'm not eating carbs."

"Why the fuck would you want to do that?" he asked incredulously.

"Um, to lose some weight." Isn't that why most people went on a diet? "Got to get rid of this fat ass somehow."

"If you were mine, I wouldn't let you diet or talk bad about yourself."

"Do you have a girlfriend?" she asked.

"Nope. I'm too young and hot to settle down."

She rolled her eyes, pretty sure he was older than her. "Uh-huh, well, let me give you a tip, women don't like being told what they can and can't do. That shit went out of fashion a long time ago."

He leaned back, sprawling on the stairs. It should have been uncomfortable, but he looked completely relaxed. He tilted his hat back and stared up at her with eyes that were piercing. Serious. They were eyes that saw too much.

She resisted the urge to shift around in discomfort.

"Did it? Where I come from, men look after their women. They put them first. Protect them. Care for them. And they also ensure their women know there are consequences for breaking the rules. For putting their health and safety in danger."

"Consequences?" *Shit. Why do I sound so breathless?*

"Uh-huh."

"Like what? They beat them?"

"Hell no. Any man who touched a woman like that would be run the fuck out of town, after being beaten soundly. We don't take kindly to anyone hurting women and children. All the women are protected by every man in Haven. It's a safe place."

Was he for real? Or was he making this stuff up?

"Every woman in town has a male guardian. Someone who watches out for her. Usually her husband, boyfriend, a male family member. The sheriff fills in if they don't have that. And every woman has rules to help keep her safe and happy and healthy. And if she breaks those rules, she gets punished. Now, if the sheriff is your guardian your punishment won't be the same as if your guardian is your husband."

"What would the sheriff do?" she asked curiously. This all sounded so bizarre.

"Dunno. Depends on what you did. He might give you a firm scolding."

All right. Didn't sound so bad.

"Aren't you gonna ask what a husband might do? Want to know what Alec would do if Mia put herself in danger?"

There was a note to his voice that told her she really didn't want to know. Yet, she knew she was going to ask.

"Alec?" she asked instead.

"My oldest brother. The stick-in-the-mud I was talking about earlier. Mia's his wife."

Okay, she was going to give in even though she felt bad for talking about Alec and Mia when she didn't even know them. "What would a husband do?"

"He'd spank her."

Her heart raced. "You're lying."

He grinned. A perfect grin with a row of white teeth. "Maybe I am, darlin'." He stood then leaned down. "Then again, maybe I'm not. Why don't you come to Haven next time with Jardin and find out?"

Her heart skipped a beat. Fuck, was she excited by that idea?

"Who knows? You might like it so much there you'll stay and find yourself a Haven man. Unless you're hoping my cousin might get his head out of his ass someday and see what's right in front of him."

"There's nothing between Jardin and me." Oh, but she'd thought about it. Every night since she'd started working there. But there was no way a man like Jardin Malone would ever look at her twice. Besides the fact he was her boss, he was one of *the* Malones. Rich and gorgeous, their family had lived in New Orleans for generations. She wasn't anywhere near his league.

"Well, then, there's nothing to stop you from coming to Haven, is there?"

The truth was, she was way more tempted than was healthy.

5

By the time the end of the day came around, Thea was exhausted. Trying to do everything with one hand was harder than it sounded.

She didn't see Jardin much for the rest of the day, he'd been in meetings all afternoon. Her brothers went to her neighbor's every day after school. Juanita was a godsend. Thankfully, the bus dropped them off not far from her house. Still, she felt guilty as hell about it. She wished she had more time to spend with them.

But she also needed money to buy them food and clothes. And growing boys needed a lot of both.

She got out of the town car that Jardin insisted she use to get home. She'd had it drop her off outside her neighbors' place, where the boys were. Fuck, her neighborhood was creepy in the dark. She walked quickly across the street, her gaze roaming her surroundings. It felt like someone was watching her.

Her instincts warned her to run. But she knew better. If someone were watching, it would be like dangling a red flag in front of a bull. By the time she reached Juanita's, her breath was coming in sharp pants and she was sweating.

Christ. Way to overreact to nothing.

She knocked on the door. Ella, Juanita's thirteen-year-old daughter answered. She had on way too much makeup and her clothes were several sizes too small. Hard eyes stared out at Thea before she turned and walked away without saying anything.

Thea got it. Living in this kind of neighborhood eventually sucked your soul. It could crush you. That was why she was determined to do better for Ace and Keir. She'd make sure they didn't end up in some gang or dead from an overdose before twenty. They were so smart they'd qualified for a scholarship to go to a private school. They were going to do something with their lives. Be better than she was.

The sound of the boys yelling greeted her, and they rushed down the stairs, brandishing fake swords, which were actually just large sticks, and horsing around. Diego, Juanita's youngest son, was with them.

"Guys!" she yelled. "It's time to go home."

"Aw," Keir said, turning with a pout. "Can't we stay? Diego's mom's making tacos."

And all they'd likely get at home was scrambled eggs and toast. She got it. She wished she had the time to make them proper meals. But she was already dead on her feet.

Juanita popped her head out of the kitchen. "Hey, chica. Get in here, take a load off."

"Hey, Juanita, thanks for having the boys. But we should get going."

"Stay for dinner."

The boys whooped and took off. Guilt filled Thea. Juanita had four kids. And while her husband had a job, they weren't much better off than Thea. Yet they always had extra food for whomever walked through their door. They were good people. They took great care of their kids and it was clear they loved each other. Thea often found herself jealous of the way Juanita's husband looked at her, like she was his whole world.

"Don't give me that look," Juanita told her. "There's plenty of food. Sal's working a double shift, so he won't be home until later. Sit. Tell me what's happening."

An hour and a half later, her belly full with good food and her heart lightened with friendship, she made her way down the street with the boys. She blamed her inattention on her sleepy state and that's why her danger radar didn't go off as soon as they stepped into the rundown house that their landlord took great pleasure in charging them rent for while never doing anything to fix up the place. And that included the holes in the roof that leaked when it rained.

She opened the door, ducking just in time as a fist swung at her face.

"Boys, bedroom. Now!" she screamed, backing away and blocking the next swipe at her face. At least he was only using his fists. One time, he'd greeted her with a baseball bat and broken her arm in two places. It still ached on cold days.

Spittle flew from his mouth as he screamed with rage. The fact that she'd managed to escape his meaty fists only stirred his fury. She dodged back as the boys raced out of the room. They knew what to do when the bastard got like that.

Get the fuck away from the psycho.

The stench of bourbon and piss filled the air, making her gag. Her dad was dressed in a holey, white wife-beater, pit stains under the arms. His jeans sagged off him. His muscle might be turning to fat and his body might be deteriorating from years of abuse, but he still had a good hundred pounds and a whole foot of height on her.

Plus, he was a nasty son of a bitch with zero morals.

"Where's my money, bitch!" His face was red, mottled.

She forced herself not run off. She couldn't escape him. Not with the boys in the house. She just had to keep him away from them, and survive as best she could.

He lunged out at her, his hand pulling back to crack across her face. She ducked and dove forward, tackling him. Her skin crawled where she touched him. And she only managed to push him over because he was already unsteady from hours of drinking before they'd gotten there.

She'd gotten rid of all the booze in the house, so he'd obviously brought it with him.

He roared and climbed to his feet as she shifted away. But her foot connected with the arm of a chair and she toppled over, unable to catch herself on the ridiculous heels she wore.

"I know you took it, bitch! I need my money!"

She had no idea what money he was talking about since he never had any. Other than what he stole from her, that was.

She scrambled backward as he made his way over to her, breath heaving from his chest.

"I want my fucking money." He reached down, grabbing her shirt and ripping the front, exposing her plain, cotton bra. His gaze fixated on her chest.

Her heart raced, fear making it hard for her to think. To react. He'd never touched her like that before. He'd bruised her, made her bleed, made her dream time after time of revenge, of escape.

But he'd never hurt her sexually.

Something shifted in his face. Something calculating.

"Maybe there's another way. Maybe I don't need the money. Maybe he'll take you instead." He started cackling as she stared at him in shock. Had he finally lost it?

"Yeah, 'bout time you paid me back after I fed and sheltered you all these years."

Yep, he'd lost it. Fed and sheltered her? She'd taken care of herself all these years. With no help from him. In fact, he'd been more of a fucking hindrance.

If it weren't for the boys, she'd have left a long time ago.

Reaching down, he grabbed her sore hand before she could stop him. "What's this? Got a little boo-boo?"

He squeezed until she screamed in pain. A satisfied smirk crossed his face. He wouldn't be happy until he'd exacted his pain. Using her other hand, she dug her nails into his wrist to try to force him to let go.

"Get the fuck away from me," she yelled at him.

He loosened his hold on her hand only to grab hold of her neck, pressing her to the floor. His hand tightened around her neck until she knew it would bruise, until dark dots danced in front of her eyes. She couldn't breathe. Shit! He was going to kill her!

"Pathetic bitch."

He let go of her. She lay still, gasping. She couldn't risk incurring more of his wrath. Not when she had the boys to think of. If anything happened to her . . .

He stepped back, chuckling to himself and stumbled over to where her purse was. She didn't even bother protesting as he searched around inside it, pulling out a twenty-dollar bill. She knew better than to keep anything more in there.

Her cash supply was hidden safely away from his greedy hands.

On his way out the door, he grabbed the nearly empty bottle of bourbon, drank the rest then threw it against the wall. It landed with a crash, but she didn't even flinch. Small price to pay.

Her entire body shaking from the aftermath, she used a chair to pull herself onto her feet. Her hand was throbbing, her throat ached. But he was gone. She tugged the ends of her shirt together. Great. Seemed her best outfit was now ruined.

After quickly checking on the boys, who'd followed her instructions exactly and hidden themselves under the bed with their tablets and headphones, which she'd had to work an extra job for months to afford. She managed to get them out, telling them it was bedtime. Without a word, they got into their pj's and got into bed.

Then she popped some painkillers before hopping in the shower. By the time she got out, her trembling had ceased and the throbbing in her hand was down to a dull roar.

After getting into her pajamas, she put some more cream on her hand. She'd leave the bandage off to let it breathe for a bit. Another blister had popped. She'd need to be careful not to let it get infected.

She examined her neck in the mirror. Fuck, was it going to bruise? She'd have to find something high-necked in her closet. This wasn't her first rodeo so she had a couple of possible tops she could use.

After checking on the boys, who were fast asleep, she slid into bed and grabbed her phone, surprised to find two voice messages. One from an unknown number. The other from her boss.

She played the one from the unknown number first.

"Hi, Thea. This is Carrick. From earlier. I'm the guy with your car." He cleared his throat and she had to grin at the note of nervousness in his voice. "Anyway, wanted to let you know I started working on it tonight. It's got a blown head gasket and worn disc brakes. Hopefully, it will be fixed by this weekend and we can go on that date. Anyway, uh, I'll call tomorrow night with an update. Sleep tight, don't let the bed bugs bite . . . Jesus, can't believe I just said that."

The call ended, and, despite the day she'd had, she found herself grinning.

Then she played the next message, tensing up, unsure why her boss would be calling.

"Thea. It's Jardin. Malone."

Her eyebrows rose. Her normally unflappable boss sounded almost unsure of himself.

"I called to tell you that I won't be in until ten as I'm meeting with Eric Henderson."

She frowned. Had he forgotten she did his schedule? She already knew this.

"Make sure you're in on time."

Thea rolled her eyes with a sigh. Be late one time . . . what about all the times she'd been early? Did they count for nothing?

"And, uh, make sure you put cream on that hand and get some air on it. Then bandage it again. Good night."

Well, that was weird.

6

———

S hit. Shit. Shit.

She placed her forehead down on the desk after ending the call with the school. After taking a bus to get the boys to school she'd gotten into an argument with one of the bitch moms. She'd had the fucking audacity to complain that Keir had been picking on her son during lunchtime. More like she was just bitter because Keir beat her little Arthur out for the top math prize last term. But all that had meant that Thea barely managed to get to work on time.

And now . . . shit. A fight? Her boys wouldn't have started a fight, right?

With all the violence they'd witnessed at home, most people would say it was inevitable. But she knew her brothers. They were good kids, despite all the shit thrown at them.

First things first. Taking a deep breath, she walked over to Jardin's office and knocked.

"Yes?" he called out.

She opened the door and peeked in. He was sitting at his desk, looking at some papers. "Um, Jardin you busy?"

Stupid question, Thea.

When he glanced up at her, the look on his face echoed her thought. Yep, she got it. He was always busy. The man was a workaholic. He never seemed to stop. She wondered what he was like at home. Whether he ever changed out of his ubiquitous suit. Not that he didn't look really good in a suit.

Really good.

But sometimes she wondered what he'd look like in, well, nothing at all.

Not the time, Thea.

"Are you well? You look flushed."

She could grab onto it as an excuse. Or tell him her hand was hurting. She was certain he'd let her have time off for either of those things. But she couldn't do that. She cleared her throat.

"Actually, I need to leave. See, my brothers have run into some trouble at their school. And I—"

"Are you their legal guardian?"

She wished she were. But she'd warned them against saying anything about their father until she was sure she was in a position where child services would leave them in her care. She needed a steady job and a better place for them to live. But once they were hers, then she wouldn't have to stay and suffer the asshole's abuse. She'd worn a high-necked, black shirt today, which also had long sleeves, to hide the bruises on her wrist and neck. It was going to be hot as hell on the bus going home since it wasn't air-conditioned like this building, but she didn't have much choice.

"Well, no, but—"

"Then let your parents take care of it."

"My mom has been dead for five years and my dad is, uh, busy." That wasn't a lie. She was sure he was busy drinking or sleeping.

"So are you."

"I have to go."

"Leave and you'll be fired." No anger. No irritation. His voice was tinged with ice.

"Fine. I'll quickly pack up my stuff. Thank you for everything." She turned away, cursing herself for that last part. Why had she thanked him? He'd just fired her. No doubt he'd blackball her like he said he would do with Jenny.

Idiot.

She'd reached her desk when he came thundering out of the office. "Excuse me?"

"Um, which part didn't you hear?" she asked, hoping it was the last part.

"The part where you said, 'Yes, sir,' and got back to work."

Her temper stirred. "You fired me."

"I'm always firing you!" he shot back. "You never leave!"

She wouldn't say he was always firing her. It'd only happened twice.

"Well, this time I'm going."

She picked up her photo of the boys. She didn't have a lot of personal stuff. Jardin reached out and snatched the frame back out of her hand, putting it on the desk.

Her hands went to her hips. "What do you think you're doing?"

"The photo stays."

"You hate that photo. You hate me having anything personal at work."

"And yet I've allowed the photo to stay these past two months. Just like you."

"You've allowed me to stay? Seriously?" Now she was getting angry.

"Seriously."

She knew this wasn't a good idea. Her control was shot. Worry over the boys. Over her father's cryptic words last night, it was all getting to her.

"I have to go. The photo is mine, and I'm taking it with me."

He kept hold of the photo and stared intently at her. "Why do you have to leave?"

"I told you! My brothers need me at their school."

"Why?"

She took a calming breath. *You cannot kill him.* "The principal just called. There was a fight—"

"Someone started a fight with them?"

It soothed something inside her that he immediately assumed someone else had started the fight. He didn't know her brothers, but it felt good that he gave them the benefit of doubt.

"The principal said they started it," she admitted.

He tilted his head to the side. "But you don't believe it."

"Keir and Ace wouldn't start a fight. But they would stick up for themselves or their friends. I have to go. I don't have time for this. I'll get my stuff later."

"No, you won't."

"Sorry?"

"Wait here. I'll get my keys."

She blinked. She couldn't keep up with him. "Keys?"

"Your car broke down, right? How were you planning to get to the school?" he asked impatiently.

"Um, I was going to take an Uber." A bus would be cheaper, but she didn't have the time to waste.

His jaw hardened. "Ubers aren't safe. You won't be taking one of those."

"Jeez, I never knew people were so biased against Ubers," she muttered.

"What?" he asked as he turned away.

"Nothing. Why would you take me? You just fired me."

"You're not fired."

"I'm not?" She rubbed at her forehead. He was making her head spin with his back and forth.

"No. Wait there."

He didn't waste time, returning with his keys. "Come."

She wanted to protest, but she really needed to get to the school. And having him drive her would be quicker than waiting around for an Uber. She followed him to the elevator and got in. He pressed the basement button.

"Are you really not going to tell me why you went from firing me one minute to giving me a ride the next? And what about your appointment with Mr. James at two?"

Withdrawing his phone, he tapped on it as the elevator opened at the basement level. This building was only a year old and no expense had been spared. The basement was clean and well lit.

She followed him as he started striding through the basement. He pressed a button on the fob in his hand and the headlamps on a car up ahead lit up. Thea gaped at the car she saw.

A Lamborghini? Was he serious?

Okay, so she knew he had money. But that was crazy. She'd never ridden in a new car before, let alone something like that. To her shock, he moved around to the passenger door and opened it for her.

"Are you getting in or have you changed your mind?" he asked.

Moving forward carefully, she slipped into the seat. Her hands moved over the buttery soft leather. He climbed into the driver's seat and turned to her.

"Belt," he reminded her.

She reached over and slipped her seatbelt on. "This car is gorgeous."

Jardin just grunted and started it up. Thea closed her eyes. She swore she just came a little.

"You okay?"

She opened her eyes as he backed out of the parking spot quickly.

Holy. Shit.

"Yep," she said in a strangled voice. "I'm good."

"Hmm. Where's the school?"

She gave him the address, waiting for him to say something asking how she could afford to send her brothers to that school, but he didn't say a word. As they exited the garage, he hit the call button on his phone. She half-listened as he moved his meeting with Mr. James, who was obviously a friend as well as a client.

When he ended the call, she turned toward him, taking in his strong profile. Dark hair that was neatly trimmed. He was clean-shaven and impeccably put together. Yet there was a darkness swirling beneath the civilized veneer, and it called to her.

Why couldn't she be attracted to some nice guy? Someone with a steady job, cute smile. Someone who would come home each night, complain about his co-workers, eat a simple dinner, and get up and do it all over again.

Why did she have to be attracted to the unattainable?

Argh.

"So, you didn't say why you changed your mind about firing me?"

He glanced over at her quickly then moved his gaze back to the road. "You want to tell me why you need to go to the school and not your father?"

No. She did not. And she got his message loud and clear.

"Fine," she said. "Guess we just won't talk. Probably better for everyone."

He cleared his throat. "You didn't fight for your job like you did yesterday. Why? Why did you just give in?"

"Have you ever thought that maybe you shouldn't have "fired" me over such small things?"

"Being late and having to leave during the day are not little things."

"Every other morning, I've been early. I've probably put in so much overtime, I could have a week off and still be in the positive.

I'm good at my job. I'm good with the clients. Yet you couldn't say yes when I ask to leave to go to my brothers' school because they're in trouble."

"You didn't ask."

"Pardon?"

"You didn't ask."

Huh. She hadn't thought of it that way.

"So, you'd have let me go if I'd asked?"

He seemed to think about that. "Likely not. But you also didn't give me the full story."

"So, let me get this straight. If I'd walked in and asked if I could have time off to go get my brothers because they were in trouble at school for fighting, you'd have let me go?"

"I'd probably still have told you to let your parents do their job."

"Like I said, my mom's dead." It was a wound that never healed. It hadn't even scabbed over yet. How could it when it was continually scratched at?

"And your father?"

"He doesn't factor in."

He grunted.

"Are you driving me there to make sure I'm telling the truth?" It was the only thing she could think of.

A look of surprise filled his face. "No. It didn't actually occur to me you might be lying."

"Then why?"

He tapped his fingers against the steering wheel. "You were prepared to walk away."

"Yes, well, you fired me."

"That's how I knew this was important to you."

She puzzled that through. Had he thought she was playing him? That if he'd pushed back, she'd have rolled over? Well, in a way she usually did. Although she preferred not to think of it like that.

"My brothers are more important to me than anything."

"Hmm." He pulled up outside the school. It was close to two in the afternoon. She rubbed her forehead tiredly, reaching for her belt as he climbed out and opened her door. He held out his hand. Surprised, she reached out to take it, forgetting it was her injured hand.

He grasped hold of her wrist and she flinched with a small cry.

"What the hell? Why does it look so swollen today? Why does it hurt when I touch your wrist? It wasn't burned."

"It's nothing," she said quickly, snatching her hand back and managing to climb out of the low-slung car without his help.

"We're taking you to urgent care after this."

"I'm fine," she told him, walking past him and moving quickly toward the office. The last thing she needed was to end up having to explain the bruising on her wrist that was very clearly finger marks.

Not happening.

She strode into the office, aware of him behind her. She thought she felt his stare, but when she turned to look at him, his gaze was on his phone. Unaffected. Uninterested.

Well, what did she expect? It wasn't his problem.

The receptionist looked up at her with a sneer. Yeah, she got it. Everyone there considered her trash, blah, blah, blah. She wasn't really in the mood for any of it.

"I'm here to see Ms. Mackerly," she said abruptly. "Thea Garrison."

As though the bitch behind the desk didn't know exactly who she was.

"Take a seat." The receptionist's gaze moved over to Jardin. "Can I help you, sir?" Her voice became far more deferential.

Thea clenched her jaw against her reply as she slammed down into one of the hard seats.

"No, you can't," Jardin replied, taking a seat next to her.

"Well," the receptionist huffed.

They sat there. Thea tapped her fingers against her thigh, wondering what the hold-up was. Jardin sat beside her, busy working on his phone, seemingly unconcerned about the fact they were wasting time. She knew what this was. A powerplay by the principal. But the thing was, she was using her brothers to piss Thea off. To make her feel small. And she wasn't going to put up with that.

She jumped to her feet. "This is ridiculous. I was called in. Why am I having to wait?"

The receptionist frowned at her. "Ms. Mackerly does have other things to do than just meet with you. Please sit down."

The door to the principal's office opened just as Thea opened her mouth to blast the receptionist and Ms. Mackerly stepped out. The older woman had pale blonde hair that was twisted back off her face. Her slim body was encased in a long skirt, white shirt, and a jacket. Her entire outfit probably cost more than Thea made in a month. But she didn't give a shit.

"Where are my brothers?" Thea demanded.

The principal looked her up and down. "Your father is absent again?"

"Where are my brothers?" she repeated.

"Come in."

Thea stepped forward and Jardin stood up to follow. She was kind of surprised. She'd thought he'd wait out there and finish whatever he was doing on his phone.

"Sir, if you'd like to wait out here, I'll be with you as soon as I can." Ms. Mackerly looked Jardin up and down, and a predatory sort of hunger filled her gaze.

Bitch.

Thea felt the ridiculous urge to tell her to get her eyes off her man. But he was her boss. He wasn't hers. Besides, the principal was probably his type.

"I'm not here for you," Jardin replied coldly. "I'm here with Thea."

The principal's eyes turned frosty and her mouth turned down. "Thea, as this is a family matter, perhaps you'd like to request that your friend wait outside."

"We're not friends," Jardin said before Thea could reply. Probably just as well considering what she would have said. "And I'm not waiting out here."

The principal was fuming, but she nodded stiffly. Thea stepped inside and her stomach instantly knotted as she saw Ace and Keir. Both of them looked a bit roughed up. Ace had a bleeding knee and Keir's shirt was ripped and he had a black eye. They were both covered in dirt and leaves. And they looked scared. But they were okay.

She rushed forward and got to her knees in front of them, wrapping her arms around them both. Normally, they'd push her off. Even at seven, Ace thought any affection from his older sister was gross. But this time, they both clung to her.

She forced herself to move back, ignoring the glare from the other woman who sat across the room.

Rosemary Pincher could kiss her ass. She was the same bitch she'd had a run-in with this morning, and it didn't surprise Thea to see her there with her son, Arthur.

"Are you all right?" She looked them both over, wincing. Fury bubbled under the surface. Why hadn't their injuries been seen to? Why were they sitting there, scared and in pain?

"If you don't mind, I've been made to wait long enough," Rosemary said in that nasally voice of hers. "Some of us do have things to do and now I need to take Arthur to his pediatrician and have him examined. That bill will be coming to you, Miss Garrison."

Oh, hell no.

Thea ignored the bitch behind her and looked at each boy in turn, waiting for their reply.

"We're okay, Thea," Ace whispered while Keir glared at Rosemary and Arthur.

She gave them both a small smile. "I'll take care of this, okay?"

"Unfortunately, there is little you can do, Miss Garrison," the principal said smugly. "Keir and Ace were fighting on school grounds. Two against one. We have a no-bullying, no-violence rule. One strike and you're gone. I have no choice but to expel them both."

Oh, and didn't that just make the bitch happy? She'd been waiting for her chance to get rid of the boys. To get one up on Thea.

"Is that so? Where was that rule when Arthur was bullying Ace every day?" she asked, standing and turning around so she stood in front of the boys, protecting them.

"My Arthur would never," Rosemary said, holding her hand to her chest.

"Your Arthur would, and did constantly."

"And where's your proof?" the principal asked.

"Where's yours?" Thea asked, glaring at the principal before turning her gaze to Arthur and his mother. "Jesus, he doesn't even have a scratch on him. And you're accusing my boys of attacking him?"

"We didn't, Thea," Keir told her. "He and his friends were picking on Ace. I stuck up for him and they attacked us."

"See. Keir has told you what happened." Thea knew the principal wasn't going to take their side, but she wasn't letting it go without a fight. The boys deserved to see someone sticking up for them.

"Well, it's his word against Arthur's," the principal said.

"So, Arthur is lying. Guess it's one strike and you're out," she said with false sympathy to Rosemary.

Oh, she knew it wasn't going to work that way. She wasn't stupid. Rosemary Pincher's husband was wealthy. She spent her days doing yoga and drinking almond decaf lattes. Keir and Ace were going to be thrown under the bus. But she wouldn't go down without a fight.

"Well, there are witnesses," the principal said. "They all agree Keir and Ace started the fight."

"That's not true!" Ace said. "It was Arthur! He's always saying things about Thea being white trash and a whore!"

Rosemary sucked in a horrified breath, slamming her hands over Arthur's ears. Like her ten-year-old son wasn't the one to speak the filthy words in the first place.

And Thea knew just where he would have gotten them too.

"Wonder where he heard that from, huh?" Thea asked.

"That's enough!" the principal said. "Miss Garrison, I have no choice but to expel Keir and Ace."

"You do have a choice."

Thea startled. She'd actually forgotten Jardin was there. Which was weird. She'd never thought that was possible. He was sitting in a chair at the back of the room, still tapping on his phone.

"Pardon?" the principal tried to act unaffected by him, but there was still that hunger in her gaze.

"You said you don't have a choice, but you do. You're choosing to believe this little thug and his pretentious bitch of a mother."

"Who are you?" Rosemary screeched. "How dare you speak to me like that! My husband—"

"Spends more time on the golf course than he does at home. I can see why." Jardin glanced up to give her an unimpressed look.

"Who are you?" Rosemary demanded. "Do you know my husband?"

"Not that well. I prefer to use a broker who doesn't scam money from his clients."

"How dare you?"

"No. How dare you?" He stood, slipping his phone into his pocket. "How dare you call Thea names and in front of your son, knowing he'll come to school and repeat them to her brothers? As far as I can see, we're done here. This boy is clearly the bully. Thea's brothers were sticking up for her honor." He turned to the principal. "Expel the Pincher boy and apologize to Thea and her brothers then we can leave. I might actually still get some work done today."

"Excuse me!" the principal said. "You do not tell me how to do my job. The only boys getting expelled are these two hooligans." She pointed to Keir and Ace.

Thea was still in shock at hearing Jardin stick up for her and her brothers that she hadn't been able to speak yet. But at those words she frowned and turned to blast the principal.

"My brothers are not hooligans. They—"

"Yeah, hi," Jardin interrupted her. She turned to glare at him. She couldn't believe he was making a call right now.

Although she'd cut him some slack since he'd been defending her. She couldn't remember the last time someone had actually done that for her.

Wasn't that sad?

"I'm at the Elite Boys Academy. Yeah, that's right." His gaze turned to the principal. "You remember my PA, Thea? Yeah, that's the one. Her brothers attend school here. We were called in because they were being picked on by Al Pincher's kid. That's him." Jardin's lips turned up into a cruel smirk.

Rosemary Pincher appeared confused. The principal was growing increasingly angry.

"That's it. The kid called her a whore and her brothers stuck up for her. But the principal is blaming Thea's brothers and wants to expel them. You got it. Thanks."

He ended the call. Then he turned to the principal. "You can expect a call from the board soon. Head's up, they won't be happy with you." He looked at Rosemary. "Don't ever talk about Thea or her brothers that way again." Then he turned to Thea. "Now, if we could go?"

The principal let out a shocked bark of laughter. "You can't be serious. You have no authority here."

"Actually, I've got far more power than you can imagine. And I'd start thinking up some good excuses for your decisions here if you want to keep your job.

"Are you threatening me?"

"Yes. Was I too ambiguous? I apologize. I am threatening you." Her phone rang. "There you are."

She turned slowly and picked up the phone. She was pale, in shock. Thea felt much the same way. Jardin was wielding his power like a sledgehammer. And he was doing it for her.

What was the feeling filling her? Gratitude? Relief?

Happiness?

"Hello?" The principal's tension eased slightly, and a smile flickered on her face. "James, how lovely to hear from you. What? No. Oh. Yes. I understand. Yes. But I . . . yes . . . sorry. Yes. Certainly, sir. Goodbye." She ended the call, looking ill. "What's your name?"

Jardin smiled. "I'm sorry, did I forget to say? I'm Jardin Malone."

Rosemary took in a sharp breath, looking ill. "You're a Malone?"

"Yes. I am a Malone. And your son insulted and abused people under my protection. As did you. And since you seem to know who I am, you know the Malones protect their own." He turned to the principal. "And seeing as one of my closest friends is the head of the board and the biggest donor to this school, I'm thinking you'll be treating Ace, Keir, and Thea with more respect, right?"

He didn't bother to wait for a reply, just turned and opened the door, walking out. A king assuming his orders will be obeyed. A dictator who had no fear of being stabbed in the back. Because no one would dare challenge him.

Something bloomed inside her. Attraction. Admiration. A slight tinge of fear. She'd always known he was powerful. That he could be ruthless. But she'd never seen that side of him.

"Thea?" She glanced down into Keir's concerned face. "What now?"

She puffed out a breath. "We follow him, I guess."

She didn't expect him to be waiting for them. After all, he had things to do. And it wasn't like he could give them all a ride in his two-seater car. But he was standing at the head of the stairs leading outside as they approached. The bell had just rung and kids were spilling out everywhere, but, somehow, they knew to give him a wide berth. When Thea and the boys reached him, he grabbed her uninjured hand and led her down the stairs.

She was dimly aware of all the stares from the mothers they were getting. Looks of admiration aimed at Jardin. Of jealousy aimed her way. Not that she blamed them.

When they reached his car, he turned. He shocked her by crouching down in front of the boys. "If you have any problems with this school, you tell me."

"That was so epic!" Ace cheered, grinning up at him. "You told off the principal."

"Who are you?" Keir asked suspiciously.

"I'm Thea's friend."

She didn't bother to point out he'd said they weren't friends earlier. She was still dazed, in shock. He stood, continuing to look down at them.

"Boys, this is Mr. Malone, my boss. These are my brothers, Keir and Ace."

Keir continued to scowl while Ace gave him a big grin, both of his front teeth missing.

He frowned down at her. "Are you well?"

"Umm. Yes. Just can't believe that happened." She was elated. But there was a part of her that was sad she couldn't fight her own battles, couldn't stand up for the boys herself. "She won't change her mind about us, though."

"Snakes never lose their venom," he agreed. "But there are ways of removing it. Don't worry." He reached up with his free hand and brushed his fingers over her cheek. The skin tingled in his wake. "I can't give you a ride home, I'm afraid."

"Oh, that's okay. We'll be fine. We can take a bus."

He frowned, sighing. "You're not taking a bus." He turned as a shiny, black town car pulled up behind him. He walked over and opened the door. "Inside, boys."

Ace whooped. Keir still frowned but that was nothing new for her suspicious nine-year-old brother.

Crap. How to tell him she couldn't afford to pay the fare for the town car? She couldn't. She sighed. She'd get in and have him drop them off a few blocks over. Poor guy had to make something for this trip.

As she slid by him, she glanced up at him. "Thank you, Jardin."

"You're welcome, Thea. By the way, the car is paid for. And I expect you at work on time tomorrow."

7

C arrick couldn't believe he was so nervous about making this call. Finding a date wasn't a problem for him. But finding a woman who was interested in something more than just having him take them to bed was. It seemed that was all he was good for: fucking.

Taking a deep breath in, he let it out slowly. Just because he'd been treated like an extra dick in his last relationship, which had been a permanent ménage, didn't mean that was all Thea saw when she looked at him. He didn't know her. It wasn't fair to bring his baggage to the table.

The past had to stay there. That's what he'd learned over these last couple of years. That he wasn't going to move forward until he stopped looking back.

It was harder than it sounded, though.

It had been hard not to check in with Thea every day. He found himself wanting to call her, ask her how her day was going and wish her a good night's sleep.

Considering he barely knew her, he figured that would come across more stalkerish than caring. So, other than the voicemail he'd left her that first night, he hadn't called or texted her. However, her piece of junk car was now fixed. It was time for his date.

Settling on his small back porch, he took a sip of beer before picking up his phone. Would she still want to go on a date with him? Maybe once she knew her car was fixed she'd turn away from him. Wouldn't be the first time that had happened.

Shit. Sally had really done a number on his self-esteem. He might not be rich or live in a mansion, but he now owned his own garage and house. Well, the bank owned most of it, but he was slowly paying that debt off.

He was a good guy, had all his own teeth, and kept himself in shape. And he sounded like he was trying to sell himself.

Just make the damn call.

Hitting her name on the screen, he waited nervously as it rang. Would she even answer?

Course she will, she wants her car back, doesn't she?

"Hello?" The breathless note in her voice hit him hard. Immediately, he frowned. Had he interrupted something? She'd said she didn't have a boyfriend but still.

Stop being a suspicious ass.

"Carrick? Is that you? Are you there?"

"Uh, yes, hi. It's me."

Lame, man.

He blew out a breath. "How are you? Am I interrupting something?"

"More like rescuing me from something."

"What? What's wrong?" he barked, tensing up. He was way too protective of this woman. It must have something to do with the way they'd met.

"Oh, nothing except a blocked shower drain and two fighting children."

"You have children?" She seemed too young for kids, but that was stupid. She had to be in her mid-twenties, of course she could have kids.

"Uh, no. They're my brothers. Would that be a problem if I did?" There was a funny note to her voice that warned him to tread carefully.

"No problem at all," he replied smoothly. "I could come help you with that blocked drain if you like."

As soon as he said it, he willed the words back.

Too soon, idiot.

"Oh, uh, thank you. I think you're doing enough by fixing my car."

She doesn't want me to know where she lives. That was just weird to offer to fix her blocked shower drain. Fuck it. When did I get so bad at this?

"Right. Sure. Well, if you change your mind . . . "

"Hopefully, it doesn't take me too long to deal with this drain or I'm going to have some stinky boys on my hands." She laughed and it went straight through his body, warming him, leaving him wanting to hear more.

Damn, man.

That's why he stuck to cars. He knew what to say to cars, or more accurately, he didn't have to talk at all. People were much harder.

"Carrick? Are you still there? Sorry, I wasn't laughing at you," she said quickly, her distress clear to hear.

"I know you weren't."

"Oh, good. I'm sorry, I haven't had much sleep these last few nights and I'm afraid I get paranoid when that happens. Everything seems much scarier and harder when you're overtired, you know?"

Why wasn't she sleeping? Was everything all right?

Easy.

"And it seems I also talk strangers' ears off and tell them far too much about my personal life," she muttered.

He had to grin. "I like when you blurt things out. Gives me some more insight into you."

"Right, 'cause you really want to hear about how I'm dealing with a blocked drain, and two grumpy kids on less than three hours rest."

"Any reason you're not sleeping?"

There was a definite pause. "No, just one of those things."

It was a clear lie. And it was on the tip of his tongue to press her for the truth. But it wasn't his place. That galled him, though. He wanted to have that sort of relationship with her. One where she'd call him without hesitation if she needed a drain unplugged or help getting back to sleep. Now, that sort of help he'd be more than willing to provide.

A relationship where there wouldn't be any lies, where everything would be shared. Where things would be equal. Well, kind of. In the bedroom, he'd be firmly in charge. He'd always liked being the boss when it came to sex. Although with the right person he thought he just might take orders.

Don't think about him. You're talking to a hot woman. The past needs to stay there.

He wondered what Thea enjoyed. If she'd like him to tie her to his bed and eat her out until she came so many times and so hard she couldn't remember her own name.

Shifting around, he adjusted his hard cock.

"Carrick?"

Shit, had she said something and he'd been too busy thinking about sex to pay attention. *Get your head in the game, man.*

"Uh, yeah?"

"Were you calling about my car?"

"Yeah, actually. It's all ready to go."

"Wow, that was quick!"

Yeah, well, he might have spent most of the day working on it for her to get it ready before the weekend. "Got a new head gasket and new disc brakes." Along with four new tires and a complete service. But he was hoping she wouldn't notice the tires since he guessed they were a cost she couldn't afford to bear. He'd driven her car through a few puddles today in order to muddy them up a bit.

"Oh, thank you. How much do I owe you?"

"We can chat about it over dinner. If you'd still like to go out?" He knew he'd kind of coerced her into it. But he'd never force her. If she wasn't interested in him there wasn't any point. He wasn't the type to mess around.

"I'd love to," she replied, sounding almost shy. "If you're sure that's what you want."

"I do." Listen to the two of them. He needed to find that confidence he'd once had. "How about tomorrow night? I can pick you up around seven?"

"Oh, uh, would it be okay if I met you at your garage? Then I could get my car?"

"All right. That would work." Again, he got that she'd rather he didn't know where she lived. She didn't know she was safe with him. Likely safer with him than anyone else since he never intended to allow anyone to harm her.

He rattled off the address for the garage. "Meet you there just before six? I'll make reservations for six-thirty."

"That's perfect. See you then."

The call ended far earlier than he would have liked. But at least he now had something to look forward to.

A date with Thea. He could tell this was going to be the start of something special.

THEA WAS RETHINKING HER SHOES.

She was wearing the same ones she'd worn on Monday when her car had broken down. She was starting to think they were some sort of bad luck.

"They're not bad luck, Thea. Just damn uncomfortable."

Somehow, she'd managed to get off at the wrong bus stop and, instead of having to walk one block in these things, she'd ended up walking six. Her feet hurt. She was running late. She'd had to wear another high-necked, long-sleeved top in order to cover up her fading bruises, so she was also hot.

All she wanted was to sit down and drink a cold beer with a fan blowing on her.

Finally, she limped up to the address she'd been given. She raised her eyebrows as she stared up at the sign above the tidy-looking building.

Jim-Bob's Garage.

Hmm. Carrick hadn't actually told her the name of the garage, just the address. Since his name wasn't Jim-Bob—

The large, retractable door went up and there was Carrick. He was even bigger than she remembered. Today he was wearing black jeans and surprise, surprise, a black shirt with the sleeves rolled up to show off his tats.

Yum.

"Hi, Thea." He gave her a smile, which dropped as she limped toward him. "You've hurt yourself? What's wrong?"

"Nothing that burning these damn shoes wouldn't fix," she told him with a smile. "Sorry I'm late. I got off at the wrong stop and ended up walking a few more blocks than I'd expected. And these shoes were not made for walking. These shoes were made to torture people. It's probably why they only cost a buck fifty."

His eyes widened. "Now, I don't know much about fashion but a dollar fifty seems cheap."

You idiot. Do you really want him knowing you shop from thrift stores?

"Well, now I know why," she joked.

"What do you mean you got off on the wrong stop?" he asked. "Did you take the bus to get here?"

"You kind of have my car so . . ."

He ran his hand over his face, looking exasperated. "Babe, why didn't you call me? I could have picked you up at the bus stop. Hell, if you didn't want me picking you up at your house, I could have met you someplace public so you didn't have to take the bus. Exactly how many blocks did you have to walk anyway?"

"Um, about six."

He gave her a knowing look from those blue eyes. "It didn't even occur to you to call me, did it?"

She shrugged. What could she say? She'd never had someone to call. Someone she could rely on. No, it hadn't occurred to her.

"I'm here now."

Sighing, he walked up next to her, wrapping his arm around her. She stiffened at the feel of him against her, getting a whiff of his cologne. Oh, that was nice. He smelled like the woods. Fresh and masculine.

"Easy, I'm gonna help you into the garage so you can sit down, all right? Unless you'd rather I pick you up?"

"Uh, no, best we save your back," she joked. "I'm not exactly light."

He looked her over. "There's absolutely nothing wrong with the way you look. Unless you were trying to insult me? I have missed a few gym sessions lately. Are you saying I'm looking puny?"

Her mouth dropped open. Insult him? "I wasn't insulting you. You . . . you look perfect. And there's nothing wrong with your muscles."

"So, you were insulting yourself then?" he asked calmly. But something warned her to be careful of her answer.

"Not sure if you noticed, but I'm carrying plenty of junk in my trunk."

"From what I can see, your trunk is perfect. Good for grabbing. And for spanking." He winked down at her, making her wonder if he was just joking.

She let him half-carry her into the garage. And there was definitely nothing puny about him. He walked into her small office that seemed to be overrun with paperwork.

"Sorry," he told her, red filling his cheeks. "Administration is my nemesis."

It kind of surprised her, because from what she'd seen of his garage, it was spick and span.

"This is a disaster," she told him bluntly.

He drew out a chair on wheels for her to sit in and she did, spinning around as she took in the piles of papers everywhere, along with sticky notes pasted onto almost every available surface.

Placing his hand on the back of his neck, he gazed around almost stupefied, as though he couldn't work out why this room was in such a state. "I know. I just can't seem to get on top of everything."

"Maybe I can help," she said. *Wait. What? You don't have time to help.* She had a full-time job and two kids to look after. The only reason she'd been able to come out tonight was because of Juanita. She'd agreed immediately to take Keir and Ace for the night, telling Thea she could pick them up as late tomorrow as she liked. As though she thought Thea would be sleeping in for some reason. She'd had to explain this wasn't that sort of date. Juanita wasn't buying any of it, especially after hearing about how she'd met Carrick. She thought it was romantic.

Thea wasn't even sure she'd know what romantic was unless it bit her in the ass.

"You don't have to do that," he told her, although there was a hopeful look to his face.

"I kind of owe you."

He frowned. "No, you don't. And I don't want you to do anything out of obligation. You owe me nothing. Now, what are we going to do about your feet? Can't take you out if you're limping."

Now she felt terrible. She hadn't meant that the way it sounded.

"Carrick, I'd like to help you. Really. I wish I had more free time. Would you mind if I brought my brothers with me? Maybe I could come on a Saturday morning? Are you open then?"

"You have custody of your brothers?"

"Um, not exactly. My dad isn't around much. So, what do you think?"

"If you don't mind, that would be perfect. I'll pay you, of course."

"No need to pay me." With what she figured she owed him; it would take her a good couple of months to pay him back.

"Thea," he reached out and gently grasped her chin, raising her face, "I'm going to pay you and I'm not hearing any arguments about it."

There was a dominant note in his voice that sent a shiver down her spine. He wasn't dominant in the way Jardin was. Jardin had a natural air of authority. People looked to him to take charge and he did. Easily. Even though Carrick was bigger and rougher looking, he had more of a laidback air.

But it seemed he could be dominant when he wanted. And for some reason, she really liked that.

She had to stop thinking about Jardin. He was her boss. Nothing more.

"Well, how about I work off what I owe you?"

He opened his mouth and she kept going. "For the parts, I mean. I know you won't let me pay you for your labor."

He looked thoughtful. Then he glanced round the office. "All right, I can live with that."

She smiled up at him. This worked out far better for her anyway. It would have wiped her savings clean to pay him back, that was supposing she even had enough.

Suddenly, Carrick crouched in front of her.

"What are you doing?" she asked as he reached for her shoes.

"Taking these off you," he replied calmly. "You can't walk in these."

"Well, I can't go into a restaurant in bare feet," she joked. "And shouldn't we get moving? We're already late."

He gave her a thoughtful look. "What if we skip the restaurant?"

He didn't want to take her out anymore. She guessed that was his prerogative. And really, he was probably doing her a favor. She was tired and in pain.

"Okay, sure. I guess I'll grab my car and head off. I'll see you tomorrow morning. What time should I come in?"

She pushed herself off the chair, but he grabbed hold of her shoulder, pressing her back into the seat.

"Stay there."

She gave him a confused look.

"I didn't mean that we shouldn't do something. My house is a few blocks from here. I was thinking, if you felt comfortable, well, I could grab a couple of steaks on the way and I've got some cold beer."

"Do you have a fan?"

He blinked. "Uh, yeah."

"And a bucket?"

"I guess so. Do I want to know the punchline?"

"What? Oh," she laughed. "I was thinking as I walked those six blocks that I'd kill for a beer, a fan and a cold bucket of water for my feet."

"That so? Well, think I can do you one better than a bucket."

"Then take me to your place."

He hesitated. "Do you want to text someone and tell them where you're going?"

"Why? Do I need to?" she joked.

He shrugged. "I'd never do anything to hurt you, rocket. But it's always a good idea to be safe rather than sorry."

She just stared at him for a long moment. "You're a good man, Carrick Jones."

Red flushed his cheeks. She loved that this big, tough-looking man could blush. Holy hell.

She bet Jardin had never blushed a day in his life.

Argh. Stop thinking about Jardin.

"You're safe while you're with me. I promise you that. But text a friend. It will make both of us feel better."

Giving him a small smile, she wrote down the address he gave her and sent it to Juanita in a text. Her friend texted back immediately that she'd send over some condoms. She groaned.

"Everything okay, rocket?" he asked her.

"Yeah, just my friend being a dork. Why do you call me rocket?"

"Oh, the other day you were like a pocket rocket. Small but feisty."

"Not so sure about the small part, but I can be feisty when I need to be. Especially if someone is trying to hurt someone I care about."

"I like that. Loyalty is something I value."

"Me too." She cleared her throat. "So that went deep quickly. Shall we get those steaks?" She picked up her shoes to force them back onto her feet.

"That's not going to work," he told her. "Your feet are already swollen. Why don't you come with me in my truck? We'll stop at the store for steaks and some salad since I doubt I've got the fixings for one, and I'll see if they've got some flip-flops there for you. I mean, if you're okay with them?"

"Are you kidding? They're what I live in on the weekends."

"Good. How about we trash these then?" He picked up her shoes and walked them over to the garbage can.

"Hey! I still need those for work."

"You seriously want to wear these again?"

"Want to, no. Need to, yes. I only have two pairs of suitable shoes for work."

He gave her a knowing look. Shit. She needed to watch what she said around him. He was perceptive and smart.

Sighing, he walked away from the garbage can, her shoes dangling from his huge hands. There was something about that image that did it for her. Big, rough hands holding her tiny, delicate shoes.

Yep. Sexy as hell.

You're a weirdo, Thea.

He held out his hands to her and she reached up with her injured hand without thinking.

"What did you do to your hand?" he asked, noticing the bandage on her palm.

"Oh, nothing," she squeaked.

Shit. Shit. Shit.

He seemed kind of protective. Sweet and thoughtful. But definitely the type who wouldn't like hearing that she'd injured herself the other day and hadn't told him.

"That's a guilty fucking face if ever I saw one," he said to her roughly. "Thea, what happened to your hand?"

He still had a hold of her, and she was grateful her sleeves hadn't ridden up to show the fading bruises on her wrist. She'd been wearing long-sleeved shirts all week. She just hoped that by Monday they'd be faded enough for her to go back to something lighter.

"I burned it," she admitted.

"On what?"

"I'm guessing a radiator lid?"

He stared down at her in shock. "You did this the other day?"

Biting her lip, she nodded hesitantly.

"God damn it! You touched a hot motor? What were you thinking?"

"Well, obviously I wasn't thinking that if it was smoking it would be hot."

"Thea," he growled.

"I'm not sure I know what you want me to say," she told him. "I touched something I shouldn't have, it burned me. End of story."

"Not end of story. End of story would have been you telling me you burned yourself as soon as I turned up."

"It was nothing."

He gently held up her hand. "This is not nothing, Thea. Let me see it."

"No," she replied stubbornly.

"Thea," he growled. "Let. Me. See. It."

CARRICK HAD NEVER HAD the urge to spank someone more. He enjoyed dispensing discipline in the bedroom, but he'd never spanked someone outside the bedroom or a scene.

Maybe that's where he'd gone wrong.

Perhaps if he'd spanked Sally, his life wouldn't have imploded the way it had.

"Thea, let me see your hand. This is the last time I'm going to ask."

Her gaze narrowed. "What happens if I refuse again? Are you going to force me?"

Yes.

Shit. She barely knew him. He couldn't force her or she might just disappear on him. Taking a deep breath, he let it out slowly searching for patience.

"Please let me see it. I hate knowing you were injured and hid it from me. That you were hurting when I could have done something."

The tension faded from her body. "I'm not your responsibility."

But he wanted her to be.

"Please, Thea. I won't be able to stop thinking about it until I see that you're okay."

She gave him a puzzled look. "Are you even real?"

"What do you mean?"

"It's just . . . most people would have driven past me. They wouldn't have cared that my car had broken down. That I didn't have the money to pay for repairs. They definitely wouldn't have bribed me to go on a date with them. Especially not someone who looks like you. Obviously, you don't have a problem getting a date."

"You'd be surprised."

"I'd be shocked."

He shrugged. "Maybe I could find a date, but I'm getting older. I'm getting less interested in some fling or a one-night stand or someone fickle. I want something real."

"You think I'm that something real?" she asked incredulously.

"Think you could be, if you'd let me through those walls of yours."

She shook her head. "You know nothing about me. I could be a terrible person."

He pushed her hair behind her ears. "I know you're a hard worker because you were so worried about being late to work. I know you care about your brothers; by the sounds of it you're more of a parent to them than your own are. I know you took one look at my mess of an office and immediately offered to help even though you likely don't have the time or energy. I know you don't have much, yet you're not out to take me for a free ride."

"I'd never do that. I hate people who use others."

"And that's why I know you're real, Thea. That's why I want to get to know you. If you'll let me."

She puffed out a breath. "I've got baggage."

"We all do, rocket. You think I got to the ripe old age of thirty-eight without plenty of shit in my past?"

"Oh, God, you're thirty-eight! You're ancient." Her eyes twinkled with laughter.

"Brat," he mock growled. "Never met anyone as much in need of a spanking as you."

"Hmm, is that a promise?"

He raised his eyebrows. Now that surprised him. "You want to be spanked, rocket?"

A flush filled her face. She licked her lips. "Maybe this is, uh, going a bit fast."

Shit. She wasn't wrong. His cock was hard, pressing against his black jeans. He'd meant what he'd said, he wasn't looking for a one-night stand or a meaningless fling. Sex wasn't the endgame here. He had a working hand, after all.

What he wanted was something real. And the last thing he needed to do was scare her off by moving too fast. But he couldn't resist leaning down to kiss her forehead.

"Christ, you're small."

"You're the first person to ever say that."

Fuck, he hated that she put herself down like that. There was a light note in her voice meant to convey she was joking, but he didn't think it was funny. And he was certain she didn't either.

His mouth moved to her ear. "You keep saying things like that about yourself and I'm gonna forget I need to take things slowly. I'm going to put you over my knee, pull up that skirt of yours and smack your ass. Then if you take your punishment like a good girl, I'll play with what I'm certain is the most beautiful pussy in the world until you're screaming my name. Begging for more."

Her breath was coming in harsh pants as he reached around and placed his hand lightly on her ass. She startled but then relaxed as he just massaged the firm cheek. "Got it, Thea?"

Pulling back slightly, she stared up at him. Her eyes were wide, filled with excitement and trepidation. "Are you serious?"

"Yep. Utterly."

He felt sure she'd tell him off. Walk away. Maybe slap him.

Instead, she looked intrigued. Hungry.

"We could just skip to the orgasm part."

Placing his huge hands on her hips, he drew her closer. "Christ, don't tempt me. I'm hanging onto my control by a thread here. But you were right before. We should slow down, get to know each other. I can stand a few cold showers."

She sighed. "I guess so."

"Good. Now show me that hand."

"Anyone ever tell you you're seriously stubborn?"

He grinned. "Not all that often. Maybe it's something you bring out in me."

"Lucky me," she muttered. But she offered up her hand and he carefully tugged at the bandage.

He sucked in a breath at the red, sore-looking burn underneath.

"Oh, rocket, you should have told me."

She shrugged. "It's really not so bad and it wasn't like you could have done anything."

"I could have taken you to the damn urgent care clinic," he countered. "What did the doctor say?"

"What doctor?"

He narrowed his gaze. "You didn't go to the doctor?"

"My boss saw it and put some cream and a bandage on it. It's been healing pretty well. Still can't really write with it but typing is a lot easier as long as I'm careful not to bang it."

"Your boss didn't insist on taking you to see a doctor?" *Who is this fucker?*

"Oh, he tried. But I refused to go." She pressed the bandage back down. He brought her hand to his mouth and kissed the tips of her fingers.

She stared up at him, enthralled.

"From now on, rocket, you're to tell me every time you're injured. Understand? Even if it's a damn papercut."

"You're gonna get sick of hearing from me then, because I'm a klutz."

"I'll never get sick of hearing from you."

'll never get sick of hearing from you.

She shook the words off as she followed him through his house. It was small, with the living areas downstairs and three bedrooms upstairs. There wasn't a lot of furniture. A couple of recliners and a huge TV in the living room and a round table with four chairs in the dining room. That was about it.

But it was a hundred times better than where she lived. Mind you, most places were better than where she lived.

There were a few dirty dishes in the sink of the small kitchen, but, other than that, it was surprisingly tidy.

"Come through here."

He opened a door out to the backyard. She stepped out onto the small porch and her breath caught. "You have a pool?"

"Yep. Bought this place because it was close to the garage, but this was a definite bonus."

"A garage called Jim-Bob's. Something you want to tell me?"

"That my name is secretly Jim-Bob?" he joked. "Afraid not. But I did buy it from a guy called Josh, whose grandfather was Jim-Bob. Apparently, everyone has just kept the name."

So, he had too. That was sweet.

"While I'm grilling these steaks, how about you take a dip?"

"Um, I don't have swimsuit."

"I can find you a T-shirt and shorts. Gonna be a bit big, though."

He could say that again. He was huge.

"I'll just dip my feet in."

"Sure?"

She nodded. Stripping wouldn't be wise anyway. Not with the fading bruises she was still trying to hide.

"Want a drink?"

"Beer if you have it."

"You got it, rocket."

Settling by the edge of the pool, she took off the flip-flops he'd grabbed from the store for her and dipped her bare feet in. She groaned.

"Feel good?" he called out from the porch where he was lighting up the grill. The backyard wasn't huge but it had a good-sized porch and a small grassy area that was well taken care of.

"Amazing. The boys would love this."

"Bring them over anytime."

"You might want to meet them first before you say that. They can be a handful." She leaned her head back, letting the sun bathe her. Summer heat could be a killer, but she loved that time of night, just before darkness fell. When everything felt like it was slowing down. When she could just sit and be, without any stresses or fear.

She really had no business being there. She couldn't afford to get involved with anyone. Not when everything was such a mess. But Carrick was so sweet. So caring. So fucking handsome it made her teeth ache.

"How old are they?"

She started, opening her eyes to realize he'd walked closer and was standing over her. He handed her a cold beer and she took it with a grateful smile.

"Oh, uh, Ace is seven and Keir is nine. They're super smart. But they're also hellions. Full of energy."

"And you look after them a lot?" It was a simple question; one anyone would have asked. But she had a feeling Carrick saw more than most.

"Yeah, my mom died several years ago, when Ace was just a baby. I've been looking after them ever since."

"Your dad?"

"Is useless."

"You must have been just a kid yourself," he guessed.

"I was nineteen."

"Most nineteen-year-olds wouldn't want to look after two kids."

"It wasn't Ace and Keir's fault. They lost their mom too. They had no one but me to look after them."

He nodded. "Bring them over. Anytime. I mean it."

And she knew he did. Carrick was something special. The sort of man she'd always hoped to meet but had never dared to dream of. And yet here he was in flesh and blood. So why was she also thinking of another man with cold, caramel-colored eyes and a sharp tongue?

Because you're screwed up, that's why. You can like two men. But you can't have them both.

Dinner was nice. Conversation flowed easily. She'd laughed, she'd eaten good food, and she wished she could do it every night. But all too soon, it seemed, it was over. He drove her back to the garage to pick up her car, crowding her up against the side as she went to say goodbye.

His hands clasped her cheeks, raising her face up so he could kiss her. And, boy, what a kiss. He devoured her, stole her every breath, her every thought until she was slumped against him, grateful for the support of the car behind her.

"Damn, you're beautiful."

She huffed out a breath, about to tell him how wrong he was but then she noticed the firm glint in his eyes. Okay, so he didn't like it when she spoke the truth about herself. She'd need to learn to keep her mouth shut if she wanted to avoid that spanking.

Then again, she was pretty certain she didn't want to avoid that spanking. She was no innocent, but she hadn't been with a lot of guys; she didn't have much time for that. But there had been a few who'd drifted in and out of her life. While she'd never been spanked by a lover before, she'd been with guys who liked to take control in the bedroom. It was pretty hot.

She'd bet with Carrick it would be even hotter.

"Drive home carefully. I don't like that I'm not taking you home and seeing you safely inside, so make sure you text me when you get there, or you'll earn yourself that spanking I've been promising. I'll see you in the morning?"

She cleared her throat. She'd never had anyone tell her to text when she got home. It had been a long time since anyone had cared she was safe. The boys loved her, but they weren't old enough to worry about her like that. It was her job to worry about them.

She was kind of in a daze, from the epic kiss and his words, as he opened her door and she climbed in. She started the car.

"Wow, it's never started so easily before." It sounded like a whole new car.

"I'm guessing it's been a while since any work was done on it," he commented without judgement. She figured what old Joe had done didn't really count.

"Thank you for dinner and for fixing my car."

"Thank you for letting me bribe you into having a date with me."

"I feel like it should have been me cooking for you."

"Next time," he told her warmly.

So, there was going to be a next time. Thank God.

"Good night, Carrick."

"Aren't you forgetting something?"

"Oh." She thought they'd already had their goodnight kiss. But she leaned up to brush her lips against his, which wouldn't have been possible if he wasn't bent down already.

He cleared his throat. "As nice as that was, rocket. I was talking about your seatbelt."

"Oh right. Yep." She blushed. *Whoops. Messed that up. Idiot.*

She buckled her seatbelt. It wasn't something she usually bothered with. Then he surprised her by swooping down, wrapping his hand around the back of her head and taking her lips with his.

"And that's how you give a goodnight kiss. See you tomorrow."

HER HEART WAS STILL RACING when she got home. She drove up the small, potholed driveway to park outside the dilapidated garage. She hadn't parked inside it in years, she didn't trust it to still be up in the morning.

Climbing out of the car, she moved toward the house still wearing her flip-flops and searching through her handbag for her keys. She should have left a damn light on. She hated coming home in the dark.

Walking inside, she immediately felt a dark blanket of despair slide over her. Without the boys there, the place was cold and lonely. There was no ignoring how awful it was. She sighed and moved into her bedroom, sitting on the side of the bed.

At least she'd had a good night. A great night. And her car was fixed. Things could be worse.

Her phone started to ring and she smiled, grabbing her bag and searching through it. He'd been too impatient to wait for her to text him, huh?

Her smile fell as she saw the name on her phone.

"Danny? What's going on?"

Danny was an old friend from school who worked at a bar down in the Bywater district.

"Hey, Thea, hate to tell you this but your dad's here. I cut him off and he's fallen asleep against the bar. The boss isn't happy, but I've managed to stop him from calling the cops if you'll come get him right away."

Part of her wanted to tell him to call the police. At least then she could be sure he wouldn't be home tonight. Her wrist ached. It was psychological rather than physical. The bruises only hurt if she banged them. But the memory was still raw and hurting.

She'd thought about telling Carrick after he'd said that stuff about letting him know if she had a paper cut. But she knew he didn't want to hear all about her darkest shit. They'd just met. Just had their first date. He didn't want all her baggage. *She* didn't want it.

"Thanks for calling me. I'll come get him."

"Sorry, Thea."

Ending the call, she dragged herself back out the door. Twenty minutes later, she made her way into the dim bar. The smell of body odor, stale beer, and cigarette smoke assaulted her, turning her stomach. It was a smell she was all too familiar with. That stench was something she associated with her father.

There had been so many bars like this where she'd gone to find him and drag him out. Back when she'd actually cared. When she'd figured he might be worth saving.

She no longer thought that.

So, what are you doing here?

That was a good question. One she had no answer to. Maybe she was simply a masochist. After all, the thought of Carrick spanking her turned her on.

Yeah, but Carrick would never harm her. Wouldn't make her feel powerless and small. That she was so certain a man she'd known a week wouldn't harm her and yet a man who was supposed to love and care for her would . . . well, that said everything, didn't it?

Yet, there she was.

There was still a tiny part of her, deep inside, a little girl crying for her daddy to protect her. Soon, that little girl would completely disappear. And she wondered if that time wasn't very, very close.

"Thea!" Danny waved over at her, his face filled with worry. "Shit! I'm glad I caught you. I tried calling you again."

"You did?" She pulled out her phone and saw it was dead. Shit. And she hadn't texted Carrick. Guilt filled her but she couldn't do anything about that right now. "Where is he?"

Danny grasped her wrist and started dragging her through the surprisingly large crowd of people. She flinched and tried to pull her poor, bruised wrist free, but he tightened his hold until they were walking through a door and out into the employees only area.

"Ouch! What are you doing?"

He finally let go of her wrist and she cradled it against her chest. Shock filled his eyes. "Fuck! Did I hurt you? I didn't mean to. I just needed to talk to you before they found you."

"I hurt my hand the other day. It's fine." She showed him the bandage and he didn't say anything about the fact he'd grabbed her wrist not her hand. Even though it throbbed something wicked, she forced herself to lower her hand to her side.

She knew all about not showing weakness.

"What's going on? What do you mean you needed to talk to me before they found me?" she asked.

"About ten minutes ago, some nasty looking guys grabbed your dad. My boss was riding my ass about him, and I was explaining you were on your way when they came in and dragged him out the back."

"What the hell? Where is he now?" Fear thrummed through her. "You just let them take him?"

Who had him? Were they going to hurt him? Shit.

"I tried, but my boss held me back. Thea, he recognized one of them. He's an enforcer for Derrick Silvers."

She froze. Shit. Fuck. Derrick Silvers? There were few people in New Orleans who didn't know who Derrick Silvers was. He was bad news. He was slime. A crime lord who had his fingers in almost every underground deal going. Drugs, gambling, and prostitution. He'd been arrested several times but usually evidence went missing.

Or witnesses did.

"Why . . . why would Silvers' guys grab my dad?" He was a small fry. He couldn't be mixed up with Silvers, right?

"I don't know, Thea. But whatever he wants with him, it can't be good. And you need to stay the hell out of it, understand?"

Danny laid a hand on her shoulder. But unlike when Carrick or Jardin touched her, it felt wrong. She had to work hard not to shove it off. She knew he was trying to help her. He was one of the few people who had attempted to over the years. And she was grateful to him. Just not so grateful she welcomed his touch.

"What if they're hurting him?"

"No offense, Thea. But so what? The guy's a drunk and a bully. How often did you come to school with bruises?"

Fuck. Shit. "I'm clumsy."

"You're not that clumsy. And you might have fooled the teachers, but you didn't fool those of us that cared. Stay away, Thea. You're better off without him in your life. If he's involved with Silvers, you need to keep yourself safe. You need to keep your brothers safe."

Fuck. He was right. She couldn't risk Ace and Keir to save her father. He'd never do the same in return.

"You're right. I know you're right." She raised a shaking hand and wiped it over her face then gave him a tired smile. "Thanks, Danny."

"You know it, babe. Come on, I'll walk you out to your car."

"Danny!" a deep voice barked. She glanced over to find a bald, overweight man glaring at them. "Go check the kegs. The Heineken tap has stopped working."

"I'll do it in a minute," Danny called back.

"You'll do it now. You're on my dime, not your girlfriend's."

Danny gave her an apologetic look. "I'm so sorry—"

"It's okay. I'm not your responsibility, and you've done more than enough for me."

"Just promise you'll stay out of Silvers' way."

"I will. I promise. I'm not going anywhere near that asshole." She moved to the door and turned to wave at Danny before stepping through. She pushed her way through the crowd, suffering some asshole groping her ass, and someone else slapping it. Jesus, why did these dickheads think they had the right to touch her?

She finally reached the door and had just walked outside when someone moved up beside her, grabbing her bicep with a hard grip. Great, now she was going to have more bruises to add to those on her wrist and neck. Something cold and hard pressed to her side and she glanced down in shock.

"Miss Garrison?"

"Are you holding a gun on me? Is that real?"

"Yes. It's real. Thea Garrison?"

"I don't know, shouldn't you make sure you get the right person before you hold them at gunpoint?"

"Stop being a smart-ass. I know you're Thea Garrison."

"Then why did you keep asking me when you already knew?"

All right, her smart mouth was going to get her into trouble. It was a reflex when she was nervous or upset. But it wasn't going to serve her well in this situation.

"Come on, Mr. Silvers wants to talk to you."

Shit. Fuck.

"Well, I'm kind of busy right now. Maybe he'd like to make another time we could meet and talk?"

He dug his gun into her side. The door opened behind them and he stepped aside as a drunk couple appeared. The woman already had her hand down the front of the man's jeans.

"Say a word and I'll shoot and then where will those brothers of yours be?"

Terror flooded her. Stealing her mind. Her breath. Her thoughts.

"What? Nothing smart-ass to say now? Didn't think so." He kept a tight hold on her arm as he steered her to the parking lot where a dark car sat. He opened the back door of the car. She glanced around but other than that couple who were currently fucking against the wall of the bar there was no one else around.

No one was saving her.

Why hadn't she told anyone where she was going? Why hadn't she just taken a minute to send a text to Carrick?

Well, likely because he would have made you wait for him and you didn't want him to see your secret shame.

But that seemed inconsequential now when she was faced with her own demise. What would happen to the boys if she died? They'd be put into foster care. Would they be split up?

Fear flooded her. So sharp and consuming she wondered how she managed to keep moving, breathing.

"Get in the car, bitch and don't give me any more trouble." This guy's breath stank of garlic and onions and it made her stomach roll over. "The boss don't like to be kept waiting. He told me to bring you in alive, but he won't much care what state you're in."

With no other choice, she slid into the back of the car. The man in the front seat didn't bother to turn around. As soon as the goon with the gun slid in, the car took off.

She didn't bother with her seat belt, wasn't much point.

"Hand over your bag."

She wanted to hold onto it. To open the door and throw herself out. Except she was pretty sure that would end badly for her. So, instead she handed over her bag. He started pawing through it. He grabbed her phone, checking it over then pulled out her wallet, opening it up and tipping it upside down. It only had a bank card, her ID and a few coins in it.

"Appreciate it if you left my tampons alone," she told him. "I'm going to need them soon."

"Shut up, bitch."

Yeah, that was probably good advice to follow.

After he'd gone through her bag, he threw it on the floor of the car. She reached for it but he pushed her back.

"You'll get it back if the boss says it's all right. Not before. Now sit the fuck still before I start to lose my patience."

Asshole.

They drove for another ten minutes before pulling up outside a corrugated iron fence. Where were they? The driver lowered his window and waved his hand at someone. Then they were driving slowly forward.

There wasn't much light other than the car's headlights, but it was enough to show the stacked piles of flattened cars.

A junk yard.

Oh, she didn't need to be a genius to know it wasn't good. Not good at all.

"What are we doing here?" she asked as the car came to a stop.

The jerk next to her let out a cackling laugh that raised the hairs on her arms. "Like I told you, bitch. We got a meeting with the boss. Word of advice, he don't like it when you talk back to him."

Oh, God. She was done for.

9

The asshole with a gun dragged her toward the shipping container in front of them. It looked like it had been converted into an office because they stopped in front of a proper door. She didn't know what happened to the driver, he must have stayed with the car. Hopefully, he was hunting down her tampons for her.

Jesus, Thea, you need to stop worrying about tampons. You have bigger concerns here.

Besides, if this got any freaking scarier it wasn't tampons she was going to need but a Depends, because she was close to peeing herself. The door opened and the asshole shoved her forward. She tripped over the threshold in the doorway and fell onto her hands and knees.

With a groan, she rolled onto her bottom, cradling her hand to her chest. Shit. Fuck. That hurt so much. The jerk laughed.

Douchebag.

"Here's the bitch, boss."

She glared up at the thug then around her as she sensed movement. Her breath left her in a whoosh as she saw her father tied to a chair at the other end of the rectangular container. His head was drooped forward, and blood splattered his dirty wife-beater.

She bit back a cry of horror. Of fear. She didn't know if he'd passed out from pain or too much alcohol. She couldn't even tell if he was breathing.

"Now, Marcus, is that any way to treat a lady?"

Two men stood on either side of her father. One was enormous. Even bigger than Carrick with meaty fists and a hard, cold face. Not cold like Jardin; this man was dead inside. On the other side, stood a slimmer built man. He wore a charcoal suit with a white shirt. His hair was slicked back.

Sleazy. Nasty. He stepped forward with an oily smile meant to lure you in. Only she knew better. He held out his hand to her. She wanted to spit at him. She wanted to hurt him.

You have to be smart about this, Thea.

False bravado was going to be her downfall. She could be feisty. She did things without thinking through the consequences.

She stared at his hand. She really didn't want to touch him.

"Maybe you need to hire a higher class of thug," she suggested as she forced herself to reach up, to let his hand clasp hers. A shudder rushed through her she hoped he didn't see. But from the way the smile on his face grew she thought he did.

He helped her up. She had to force herself to stand there when he didn't immediately let go. Instead, his gaze roamed her body, studying every part of her until she felt like she needed to scrub her skin clean.

And even then, she wasn't sure there was enough soap in the world to feel completely clean again.

This man oozed menace, danger, and pain. And not in a sexy way. No, in a completely creepy, downright terrifying way.

"Hello, Thea. I'm Derrick Silvers. It's so nice of you to join us."

"Wasn't aware I had a choice."

His hand tightened on hers. Thank God it was her uninjured

one. Although, if he tightened his hold any further, it wasn't going to stay that way.

"When someone holds a gun on me, I'm kind of inclined to do what they want. I'm weird like that."

No, what was weird was her inability to stop spewing shit.

Shut. Up. Thea.

His gaze narrowed, and she stopped breathing.

Then his hold lightened. And he laughed. "Got a mouth on her, doesn't she?"

"Want me to beat it out of her, boss?" Marcus asked.

The meathead standing by her father hadn't said a word yet. He just watched everything calmly.

Moving so fast it shocked her, Silvers let go of her and stepped in front of her to slap his hand against the side of Marcus's face. "No, I don't want you to beat her, you dickhead. We don't beat women."

"We don't?" he said, dumbfounded. Obviously, it was something he'd done in the past. She shuddered.

"We don't. Thea is here as our guest." He turned back to her, straightening the lapels of his jacket. "So sorry about that."

"I hear it's hard to get good goons nowadays."

The boss stared at her for a long moment then laughed again. It didn't sound natural. Did he practice that creepy sound in the mirror each morning? The nausea in her stomach bubbled. Marcus laughed along, although the sound was more hesitant, as though he didn't understand what was so funny.

"Ah, Thea, you're not at all what I expected."

"You're not what I expected either."

And he wasn't. Even though she'd seen images of him on the news, they hadn't done him justice. He should be as ugly on the outside as he was on the inside. Unfortunately, that wasn't the case. In fact, she could see why women flocked to him. The good looks, the power, the money. She got it. But she wondered how many of those women made it out with their souls and with their lives intact.

"I'm going to hope I'm even better than your expectations."

Don't say it, Thea. Don't even think it.

She had to forcibly hold in her need to tell him exactly what she thought of him.

"Why have you brought me here?" she asked.

He turned from her to her father then looked at her again. "You obviously take after your mother. There's very little of him in you."

"Something to be thankful for."

Silvers grinned. "Indeed. You don't like him."

"What makes you say that?"

"You haven't asked if he's breathing, if he's all right. You haven't tried to go to him. To help him. To call me a monster for having him beaten. Not that we've done much damage, have we, Milo?"

Milo, the big gorilla-like man, just grunted.

"You'll have to excuse him. He'd rather use his fists than words. Would you like a drink?"

He moved over to the small table that held a decanter. It looked so out of place that she had to blink a few times to make sure she wasn't imagining it.

"I always bring my own glassware," he told her. "That way I can be sure of the quality."

Weird.

Focus, Thea.

"No, thanks," she told him, trying to swallow past her dry throat. "Why am I here?"

"Ah, well, I thought that would be obvious, yes? You're here because your father stole from me."

"Stole from you?" What the fuck?

"Yes. See, your dear old dad has a bit of a gambling problem. And a drinking problem."

"Tell me something I don't know," she replied.

"Careful," he whispered in a cold voice. "I won't allow any disrespect."

Holy shit. Her heart raced, making her feel ill.

Calm. Calm.

"How much does he owe you?"

"Fifty thousand dollars."

"Fifty thousand dollars?" she asked with a bark of laughter. "You're joking, right?"

"Do I like to joke about money, Marcus?" Silvers asked.

"No, boss," he said. "You do not."

"How can he owe fifty thousand dollars?" She reached up with her hands to tug at her hair. Fuck! This was worse than she'd thought. "How could you let him get fifty thousand in debt to you?"

Suddenly, she found herself slammed against the wall of the container, Silvers' hand was around her throat, pressing down on her airway.

She raised her hands, trying to tug at the hand that was tight around her throat, but he just pressed down harder.

"I warned you not to push me. You'd do well to heed me; I'm not a man you want to get on the bad side of."

He let her go and she slid to the floor, coughing as she attempted to force air into her lungs.

Shit. Shit.

Her entire body trembled in reaction.

"I didn't let your father do anything. He is the one who made bad bets. And I'm not a bank. My interest rates are rather steep," he said calmly, moving over to grab his glass he'd left on the table while he was strangling her. Wouldn't do to spill a drop of booze, obviously.

And she just bet they were steep.

She forced herself to stand, although she stayed leaning back against the wall. "I don't have fifty thousand dollars."

And even if she did, she wouldn't want to spend it to get her asshole dad out of debt. Why had she come out tonight to get him?

Even if she hadn't, she had no doubt those guys would have found her. Maybe when she had the boys with her. She shuddered at the thought.

Silver looked her over. "That much is obvious. I brought you here tonight to test your suitably to do some work for me."

Work? She could just imagine what sort of work he was talking about. She swallowed back the rising bile.

"I'm not prostituting myself to pay back his debt."

He strode back toward her, and she froze, terrified. Prey waiting for the predator to lash out. He raised his hand and she tensed, waiting for the pain. Instead, he tucked her hair behind her ear. Much like Carrick had earlier.

But with Carrick, she hadn't had to fight the urge to vomit. She hadn't been shaking in terror.

God, had it only been three hours ago she'd been laughing with him on his back porch. That seemed so far removed from the situation she now found herself in it was laughable.

"You know, there's something about you, Thea. It's strange. I've never liked my women mouthy. I like them obedient. I like them quiet. Maybe that's where I'm going wrong. Maybe all along I needed someone strong to stand by my side."

"Stand by your side?"

"Hmm. Like I said, I was going to give you an ultimatum. Work for me or I'd kill your father. But now . . . now I think I want something different. It's time I had something more permanent in my life. I need an heir."

Was he . . . was he saying what she thought he was?

"Are you seriously asking me to carry your child?"

He smiled. It wasn't pretty. Or handsome. Or kind.

"Of course not." He wrapped his hand around her hair and tugged. Hard. She couldn't stop the whimper that crossed her lips. "I'm *telling you* that you're going to carry my child."

She shook her head. No. Not happening. Tears filled her eyes, but she wasn't sure if they were due to the pain he was inflicting or fear. She forced herself not to let them spill. She couldn't show weakness.

"Nobody tells me no, Thea. Is it really such a bad proposition? Instead of becoming a whore, you'll be the mother of my child."

He was seriously delusional. How could he think she would have his child? Why would he even want her? Then again, she was under no illusion her usefulness would eventually run out.

But, wisely, she said nothing. Her breath heaved in and out of her lungs.

"Instead of living a life in poverty, you'd have everything you could desire. Money. Power. Your life. Think of your brothers. Don't you want them to have the best of everything?"

She wanted them to be free. She wanted to be free.

"What if . . . what if I can find the money?" She couldn't. There was no way.

His face grew cold and he stepped away from her. "Be very careful you don't insult me, Thea. I've just given you an offer thousands of women would take up in a heartbeat."

Shit. Fuck. She'd just made a stupid move; she could see that. She waited for him to explode. To turn to his goons and order one of them to shoot her. Instead he took another sip of his drink.

A knock on the door interrupted the tension and she turned to watch as Marcus opened it. Someone spoke on the other side, too quietly for her to hear.

"Boss, best you hear this."

Silvers left the container along with Marcus, leaving her alone with her father and Milo. She guessed she should probably use this chance to escape. Except there wasn't anywhere she could go that Silvers wouldn't find her. Plus, Milo looked like he could crush her with his pinky. She didn't think he was going to let her just waltz out that door.

"Is he alive? Can I check on him?"

Milo just stared at her. He didn't say no, so she stepped forward and raised a shaking hand to her father's neck. His pulse was a bit slow, but it was still there. She reached out and raised his head, her stomach revolting as she took in his swollen, bloody face.

He didn't wake up and she figured that was a blessing. She carefully let his head drop back and then took a step away. And another one. Until suddenly, she was on the other side of the container, staring at Milo and her father with horror.

The door banged open and Silvers stepped in, a frown on his face. "Milo, get him out of here. Put him in the trunk and take him to storage."

Maybe she should protest. He was her dad, she should try to defend him, but she found herself at a loss. Plus, she was angry at him. Furious. More furious than she could ever remember being.

This was all his fucking fault. He'd put her and the boys at risk.

Silvers turned to her. "Come here, my dear."

She didn't want to move, but she made herself shuffle forward. He wrapped a hand around her sore wrist, and she winced. She didn't miss his smile at her show of pain.

Fuck.

He cupped her face between his hands. They were cold and clammy. She had to work hard not to vomit up her dinner.

"Yes, such an unexpected surprise." Abruptly he stepped back. "I have business to attend to. Thea, I can be a reasonable man."

He could?

"I can see all this has shocked you. You're obviously an innocent. I'll give you a chance. You have one week."

"One week?"

"Come up with fifty thousand dollars by next Saturday, and I'll never bother you again. But fail, and you're mine."

Jesus. There was no way she could do that. But what choice did she have? She could run, but how did you hide from a man like him? She'd be forever looking over her shoulder, worried he'd be coming for her. And it wasn't like she had the money to run with.

But what was the alternative? Find the money? No chance.

Give herself to this man? Sacrifice herself to save her father?

"I don't care about him," she whispered harshly.

"Your father? Hmm, now, I would understand if that were true, however I don't think it is." He shrugged. "It doesn't matter. The debt is no longer just his. He mentioned you several times. Told me how beautiful you were. I'm afraid I didn't believe him. You understand I can't afford to let him get away with this or everyone would be trying to take me for a ride. I'm a businessman first and foremost. Now, I don't have time for this. I have to go. One week, Thea. And don't bother trying to run or hide. I will find you. And it won't end well for you." He strode toward the door then turned back. "Oh, and I don't need to tell you what will happen if you tell someone about tonight, do I? It would be a shame if something happened to those brothers of yours, wouldn't it?"

Oh, God. Oh, God. She shuddered at the threat. She was still standing there, trying to catch her breath, to force herself to move when she realized the place was fully dark and quiet.

Shit! Fuck! Had they left her there?

Gathering up her nonexistent courage, she opened the door and stepped out. There was no one there. No cars. No men. Nothing.

She didn't even know where she was. She heaved in a breath. How was she supposed to get home? Had he really just propositioned her and left? She turned to walk back inside hoping there was something in there she'd missed. A phone, something to help her.

But she didn't see anything. She was stuck there. A sob broke free from her lips. She dropped to her knees on the ground, wincing as her already bruised joints protested.

What the fuck just happened? And how am I going to fix it?

She didn't know how long she knelt there, but eventually she realized she had to get up and moving. She didn't even know what time it was. Or how she was going to make her way home. Struggling to stand she moved into the back of the container and looked around. There wasn't much in there other than a table, the chair where her father had sat, and some blood stains on the floor. She swallowed heavily at that.

Lights suddenly shone through the door, making her cry out. She looked for somewhere to hide as a dark car pulled up. But she was too late to leave the building without them seeing her and there was nowhere for her to hide in there.

So, she stood in the doorway, frozen, watching as a short, squat man climbed out.

"You Thea?" he asked.

Oh, Christ. There was only one reason he'd know her name.

"Yes."

"Boss said you'd be here. I'm here to take you home."

Home? Okay, so at least she wasn't stuck there. But she didn't want Silvers knowing where she lived.

"Can you take me to the bar where I left my car?" she asked, hating that she had to ask this guy to do anything.

"Sure."

Thank fuck. She walked down, shutting the door behind her. It all felt surreal. "They took my handbag."

He reached into the car and pulled it out. She took it with a nod. She knew she had to be in shock. She slid into the back of the car and let him close the door behind her, then he drove them out of the lot.

What was she going to do?

10

Why the fuck hadn't she texted him?

He'd made it very clear she was to text when she got home safely. That was hours ago. And nothing. Had she been in an accident? Should he start calling hospitals?

Why hadn't he found out where she lived?

Because you didn't want to push too hard, too fast. That's why.

Carrick ran his fingers through his hair and blew out a breath. He needed to get some sleep. It wasn't long until he'd have to get up and open the garage. He'd left Thea several texts and one voice message. But he couldn't sleep until he found out she was all right.

Suddenly, his phone buzzed in his hand. Relief flooded him as he saw her name. Then his gut tightened in anger.

What the fuck?

Sorry I didn't text. My phone died. Something came up. Can't come in to help you.

He didn't want sorry. He wanted a damn explanation. And saying her phone died wasn't it. Where had she been for the last few hours? He hit the call button. It went to voicemail.

Fuck!

He resisted the urge to throw his phone against the wall. Was she sending his calls to voicemail? Had she somehow decided on the drive home he wasn't for her? Had she been using him to get her car fixed and now that she had what she wanted, she was going to push him aside?

Well, good luck with that. Because Carrick Jones wasn't a man to be pushed to the background.

Never. Again.

"Thea? Thea?" Jardin frowned as his assistant didn't even move or acknowledge him. What was she doing?

These last two days there had been something off about her. She'd been jittery. On edge. And her work had suffered. Irritation filled him.

But, surprisingly, not because her preoccupation was affecting her work.

It was because something was wrong. And he had no clue what it was.

And he wanted to know.

These feelings he had toward his assistant really had to stop. He listed all the reasons it was a bad idea: she worked for him, if things didn't work out, he'd be down an assistant, she was way too young, she'd likely run a mile if she knew how truly dominant and controlling he could be—both in and out of the bedroom.

He'd made a complete mess of a relationship once; he couldn't do that again.

And yet he couldn't stop thinking about her. Dreaming of her. Wanting her.

Striding over to where she sat at her desk, he cleared his throat. Still nothing. He placed a hand on her shoulder, and she jumped out of her seat, turning toward him with her arms up over her face.

As though defending herself. From him?

What the fuck was going on?

"Thea," he said in a low, calming voice. "It's all right. It's just me."

She heaved in a breath, looking around the room. "Sorry. Um, sorry. You just startled me."

Startled her? Terrified her was more like.

"I called your name several times," he pointed out as she composed herself. She was pale and drawn with dark smudges under her eyes that even makeup couldn't hide. Wasn't she sleeping? Why not?

"I'm really sorry. What did you need?"

Oh, no. She's not getting away with that.

"What's the matter?"

"Nothing."

Lie.

"Nothing, huh? Then why do you look like you haven't slept in days? Why did you jump when I touched you? Why have you been walking around here like a ghost?"

She stiffened, her face becoming a mask, free of emotion. "I'm sorry if my work has been suffering. It won't happen anymore."

He deserved that. He'd focused on work and only work with her in order to keep some distance between them. Until the day he'd gone to her brothers' school. He'd stepped into her private life. Something he tried not to do with employees.

"Is it your brothers? Is something wrong with them? Is it the school?" He'd have thought James would have brought the principal to heel. But maybe he needed to place another call.

Perhaps the school needed a new principal.

Thea gave him a surprised look. "No, the boys are fine. Thanks for asking."

"I'm not an ogre, Thea."

Her mouth dropped open slightly. "I never thought you were."

"I'm not all about work either."

"You . . . you're not?" she asked.

"You can tell me if something's wrong."

"I can?"

She looked so befuddled. As though everything he said was a complete shock to her. *Well, why wouldn't it be? You've been only about work with her.*

"Come on. We're going to lunch."

"Lunch?"

"Yes, lunch."

"You never go out for lunch unless it's for business," she pointed out.

He sighed. "Thea, do you have to argue with everything I say?"

"I . . . I'm sorry."

"Don't say sorry. Say, yes, sir."

Shit, man. Why did you say that?

"Yes, sir."

Fuck. Those words went straight to his dick. *Stupid move.*

HAD SHE FALLEN ASLEEP? That was the only explanation for what was happening, right?

Because there was no other reason why she'd be walking along the street with Jardin Malone, on their way to lunch.

He stopped outside a small, quaint restaurant she couldn't imagine him patronizing in a million years. She'd figured he'd head for one of the flashier restaurants where all she'd be able to afford was water.

She shouldn't be going out for lunch. She couldn't afford

lunch. She had to find fifty freaking thousand dollars or shack up with a crime boss.

It was all so surreal.

It was not real life.

Right?

A female server rushed over. "Mr. Malone! How are you today? Usual table?"

"Thanks Rae," Jardin replied warmly, surprising her even more. Had she ever heard him sound so friendly?

Nope. She wasn't sure she had. She was in a bit of a daze as the server led them to their table and told them the specials of the day.

What the hell was she going to do? Should she even be coming to work? Maybe she should be working on an escape plan. But what if Silvers caught her? She had no doubt things would not go well for her.

"Thea? Thea?"

Oh, shit. She'd spaced out again.

"I'm sorry. What was that?"

She braced herself for him to give her an irritated look. Instead, he just looked thoughtful. Then he turned to Rae with a smile. "She'll take an unsweetened iced tea. I'll have my usual. And sparkling water for the table."

"Sure thing."

"You know what I drink?"

Really, Thea. That's what you wanted to say? But it was such a shock. She'd felt sure he'd never noticed anything about her that didn't pertain to work.

He tapped a finger against the table as he leaned back. They were in a round booth. It was a big table for the two of them, and this was his usual place to sit?

"What's going on, Thea? And before you say nothing again you should know that lying to me is just going to annoy me."

"And what happens when you're annoyed?"

He smiled. It wasn't a reassuring smile. "Are you sure you want to find out?"

She stiffened. "You'll fire me?"

He sighed. "No, of course not. Why would I fire you for that?"

"You fired me twice last week," she pointed out. "You've fired at least ten assistants in the last two years."

"Their work performance was sub-par. Yours hasn't been."

Big praise indeed. "Is that what's going on my work performance review? Her work isn't sub-par."

Ah, crap, Thea. Why did you go and say that? He's your boss.

But to her shock, his lips twitched. Before he could say anything though, the server returned with their drinks. "Ready to order?"

Crap. She hadn't even looked yet. She glanced over the menu for the cheapest, healthiest option. "I'll have a Cobb salad, thanks." Even though shrimp and grits were very, very tempting.

"I'll have my usual," Jardin told Rae.

She left and Thea shifted around uneasily on the seat.

"Are you going to tell me what's going on?" he asked.

No. Nope. Uh-uh. She wasn't even sure she should be there with him. Maybe she was putting him in danger. Over the past few days, it had felt like she'd had eyes on her, but she wasn't sure if she was just being paranoid. Would Silvers send someone to watch her?

Would Jardin be at risk if he had? Damned if she knew. She'd forced herself to cut things off with Carrick. Tonight, after work she was going to drop some money in his mailbox, hopefully she could do it without him seeing her. She felt bad for ignoring his texts and voicemails. Although, they'd stopped now. She guessed he'd gotten the message.

Her stomach dropped. She hoped he wasn't too pissed off with her. It seemed to be something going around if the way her boss was clenching his jaw was any indication.

"I take it your silence means you're not."

"It's better if you don't know."

"You're in trouble," he stated.

She shook her head. "My life . . . it's complicated."

"Whose life isn't?"

Yeah, well, there was complicated and then there was having some raging psycho fixated on you.

"Over the past two years, my ability to be patient and understanding has almost eroded. So has my tolerance for bullshit."

Had he just said bullshit?

"You don't need to tell me about your private life, Thea. However, I would appreciate you not bringing it to work with you."

She felt like she'd been slapped. Gone was the man who'd helped her with the boys with school. This wasn't Jardin the man. It was Mr. Malone, the lawyer and her boss.

"Fuck," he muttered.

Rae brought out their food, and she looked down at the salad, trying desperately not to cry.

"Thea, look at me. Look at me." The command in his voice was unmistakable and impossible to ignore. She glanced up and he winced.

"I can be an asshole."

He wasn't going to get any objections from her.

Leaning toward her, he placed his hand just a few inches from hers. She wished he'd touch her. It would be nice to have someone touch her who wasn't out to hurt her.

Carrick touched you. She couldn't think about him right now. Had to forget him.

"A few years ago, a relationship I was in ended with a lot of bitterness and regret. Since then, I've kept myself from getting involved with anyone else on anything but a superficial level. I've been told more than once I've turned into an uptight prick."

Her eyes widened. "Someone actually said that to you?" *To his face?*

"My cousins pretty much tell me that every time I see them."

"Maddox?" She could see him saying that. He didn't seem to care much what anyone thought of him.

"Yep. And Maddox has six brothers. He's not even the worst of them. Wait until you meet Tanner. He has a penchant for taking pot-shots at people's cars."

Yikes. She kind of hoped she didn't meet him. Not that she was ever likely to.

"Thing is, I don't want you to think you can't come to me about things. I know I've been acting like a cold asshole, but if you're in trouble, Thea. I can help."

It was tempting. God, it was tempting. To lay all of it on someone else's shoulders would be amazing. But she knew she couldn't do that. And, anyway, he didn't know what the problem was. And if he did . . . he'd probably run a mile.

She licked her dry lips as she stared into those caramel-colored eyes. They were hypnotic. Jardin Malone was a potent man. One who would too easily pull her under his spell. He was the type of man who seemed capable of anything.

But he wasn't prepared to deal with Derrick Silvers. And even if he wanted to help, he wouldn't get involved in this. He had a family, a career, a life. He wouldn't risk any of that for her. Someone who worked for him, who he'd only known a few months.

And then there was the threat to her brothers. No, she couldn't tell him.

She didn't want to reject the offer outright, though. Maybe she could tell him just enough so that . . . so if she disappeared, he might understand why. Even if she couldn't risk him coming after her.

Reaching over, she took a sip of her iced tea. "It's about my—"

"Well, now, isn't this cozy? My ex-best friend with the woman who just conveniently fell into my lap, used me, then ghosted me? Something tells me this isn't just a coincidence."

11

Fury rode Carrick like a bull let out of the pen. It was a red haze covering his eyes. His heart beat so loudly it was all he could hear.

He glared down at Thea and Jardin. At first, he hadn't believed his eyes when he'd walked into the restaurant that his accountant insisted had the best gumbo in the city. He'd been seated before he'd spotted them.

This couldn't be a coincidence. He didn't know their angle. Why Jardin would send her to him. To hurt him? It didn't make sense.

But right then, he didn't care about what made sense. He wasn't thinking sensibly. He was acting on emotion.

And his emotion was pure anger. Hurt-fueled anger.

"Didn't think you'd go this low, J," he told his former best friend. The man he'd loved more than anyone. And not just platonically, although he'd never told Jardin that part. He wasn't bi-sexual like Carrick. He hadn't been interested in anything more. And Carrick had loved him enough to just be happy to be around him.

What an idiot he'd been. A naïve fool.

"Carrick? What are you doing here?" Jardin stared up at him in shock.

"Wait," Thea said. "The two of you know each other?"

She looked genuinely surprised, but there was no way this could be a coincidence.

"Don't pretend you didn't know that, babe," he said harshly. "What did he do? Recruit you to get friendly with me? To make me think you wanted me? Then dump me? Use me? That's low, even for you, J."

"What are you saying?" Jardin snapped, looking around the restaurant.

"Like you don't fucking know," he replied. "Or was I never meant to find out you were behind our meetup?" He nodded over at Thea, who'd gone pasty white.

"I have no idea what you're insinuating," Jardin said stiffly. "But perhaps we should go somewhere quiet and discuss this."

"Oh, I'm sorry, am I embarrassing you?" he asked, raising his voice. "Am I making a scene? How inappropriate of me. I'll just go back to my little box, suitably chastised for acting out. My lack of breeding is showing, huh?"

"For fucks sake, Carrick, what the fuck are you talking about?"

"Oh, about to lose that great Jardin Malone temper? Heads up, babe, it happens rarely but when it does, you'll usually want to duck and cover."

"Carrick, I'm not sure what you think's going on here, but—" Thea reached up to place her hand on his arm and he grabbed her wrist, shoving her away. He didn't grab her harshly, but she sucked in a breath, paling even further, and bringing her arm to her chest.

Shock filled him. Fuck! He'd hurt her. He was furious, but that didn't mean he wanted to harm her. He'd never harm a woman.

"What the fuck?" Jardin snapped, standing and glaring at him. "What do you think you're doing?"

"I didn't mean to hurt her," he said, his fury draining as he took Thea in. "Rocket, I didn't—"

"It's okay," she said hastily. "It wasn't you. I . . . I hurt it the other day. I need to go to the bathroom. I just— "

"Thea, let me see your wrist," Jardin demanded.

She shook her head. "It's fine."

Oh, she was going to learn that no one said no to Jardin when he used that voice. That usually ended up with someone getting their ass reddened. Not him. He'd never played with the other man. Even if he'd secretly dreamed about it.

Thea attempted to slide to the end of the booth and Carrick moved, blocking her path. The look she gave him was filled with betrayal. He felt bad for a moment. So bad he almost shifted.

But then he remembered that she had no right to look at him like that. That he was the one who had been deceived and betrayed.

"Show me your wrist," he ordered. Jardin wasn't the only one who could be commanding when needed.

Although, with Jardin, it was part of his personality.

"Please," she whispered. "Please get of the way."

"Not until you show me your wrist." He was starting to wonder if it was a ploy. A way of getting his sympathy. Of getting him to leave. "Unless it's not actually hurt and it's just another lie."

She sucked in a breath, her eyes wide and filled with tears as she stared up at him. He had to harden his heart against softening toward her.

She'd used him. She was somehow involved with his ex-best friend. The man who'd hurt him. Who'd thrown him away.

So, yeah, he wasn't giving her anything.

"What do you mean? Another lie?" she whispered. "I never lied to you."

He snorted. "Right, sure you didn't. Which is why you're sitting here all cozy with the man who hates me."

. . .

HER HEART STUTTERED in her chest. She had no idea what was going on. Carrick knew Jardin? And seemingly had some unpleasant past with him? And he seemed to be mad at her. She got that part. She'd totally reneged on her promise to help him. She'd been ignoring him.

If only she could tell him she wished she didn't have to. That she was doing it for his protection. But there was more to Carrick's anger than that.

Thea didn't think she could take the pure anger in his eyes for much longer. She needed to get out of here. It was becoming hard to breathe, to think with the two of them so close.

She'd never been as interested in another man as she was in the both of them. Jardin, stern, imposing, and demanding. Carrick, kind, caring and protective.

They both stirred her.

"Hates you?" Jardin stated. "I never hated you."

"You sure acted that way. You went all cold on me. Could barely speak to me."

Jardin looked pained. "Carrick, I'm sorry. I was feeling guilty and took it out on you. I tried to call you, but you wouldn't listen—"

"And I still don't want to listen. Because it seemed you weren't done fucking with my life, huh? What happened? You found out I was back in your precious city and decided to mess with me by sending her?"

The way he said that her made her wince. Like she was shit on his shoe. The lowest of the low. She couldn't take any more. Her wrist was throbbing. Even though Carrick hadn't touched her harshly, it had still hurt like hell. She needed out of there. She didn't know why Carrick thought Jardin had anything to do with them meeting and she didn't care. She just needed to leave.

"Get out of my way, Carrick. Now," she demanded.

"No."

"Please."

Both men stared down at her.

"Thea," Carrick said, looking conflicted.

"Mr. Malone? Is there a problem here?" A man in a suit approached. He looked like the manager or owner.

Jardin gave him a charming smile. "Sorry, Emmanuel, we'll take our conversation somewhere else."

Carrick turned his body and she took the opportunity to ease past.

"Thea!" Jardin called out.

She knew she should stop. But if she stuck around any longer, she was going to cave. She was going to give in to the emotions riding her and she couldn't do that. Because if that happened, she might just let go completely. And she wasn't certain she'd be able to put all the pieces back together.

"Rocket!" Carrick yelled.

Nope. Not happening. She didn't know what was going on between the two of them, but they weren't using her as a pawn in their feud. Her life was enough of a mess.

As she reached the door, a hand slipped gently around her upper arm, turning her. She looked up into Jardin's face. Carrick stood over by the table, watching them. There was such pain on his face it made her heart ache.

"I need to get back to work."

"You can't leave when you're upset," Jardin said gruffly.

"I'm fine. Really. I just . . . I need a minute alone. And the two of you clearly need to talk. Please, just give me that time."

Jardin scowled but then looked back to Carrick then to her. He nodded. "Fine. But I'll have someone check in on you to make sure you made it safely back to the office. No arguments."

He drew out his phone and tapped out a message to someone. She knew it was pointless to argue. Jardin was going to do whatever he thought best. And she just wanted out of here.

Without looking at Carrick again, she slipped from the restaurant.

12

J ardin turned and walked back to Carrick. He was torn. Part of him wanted to race after her. But another part wanted to deal with the issue right in front of him.

Carrick.

God, he'd missed him. He hadn't handled Sally's death well. He knew that. He'd felt guilty and withdrawn from the one person who'd always been there for him. The one person who'd been hurting as much as he had.

"Aren't you going to go after your girlfriend?" Carrick asked bitterly.

"She's not my girlfriend," he growled.

"Sorry . . . fuck-buddy."

Jardin ground his teeth together, holding back the need to lash out. Carrick was doing enough of that. He turned to the owner who was still hovering worriedly. "Emmanuel, can we borrow your private room for a moment?"

"Of course, Mr. Malone."

"What if I don't want to talk to you," Carrick bit out, glaring down at him.

Once, he'd been closer to this man than anyone. Now? Now, he was looking at him with hatred. And the worst thing was, Jardin knew he deserved every bit of that hate.

But Thea didn't and he couldn't understand why Carrick had acted the way he had. It had been obvious by the end that Carrick's relationship with Sally was messed up. Or maybe it had been like that for a while and Jardin hadn't noticed.

"I get it," Jardin told him. "I wouldn't want to speak to me either."

Carrick gave him a shocked look.

"But you seem to have some misconceptions about Thea and her role in whatever you think is going on."

Carrick frowned.

"I've never known you to hurt a woman, no matter how angry you were," Jardin added.

"I didn't mean to hurt her. I barely touched her." Shame crept into Carrick's face then it was chased away by bitterness.

Since when had he become so angry?

Maybe since you kicked him out of your life without listening to his side of things?

"I don't deserve your time, but I'm asking for it."

"Fine. Fuck. What have I got to lose, right? Just need to go tell my accountant I'll have to postpone our chat." Carrick walked over to a middle-aged, balding man who was watching their interaction with unabashed interest.

The man nodded at whatever he said, then Carrick and Jardin followed Emmanuel to the back room.

Carrick started pacing. As usual, he was dressed all in black. Tight T-shirt, jeans, and boots. Jardin looked him over with admiration, taking in the way his T-shirt molded to his arms and chest.

Jardin had never been interested in men. Except for Carrick.

"You've got five minutes," Carrick said sharply. "You gonna

spend the whole time staring at me or you want to explain what the fuck is going on?"

Jardin narrowed his gaze, working hard to keep his need to snap back under control. He wasn't used to riding the edge of his temper. He made cool and calm decisions. He didn't let emotions filter through. The last time he'd done that he'd lost the man standing in front of him.

"I made a mistake."

"Excuse me?" Carrick asked.

"After Sally died, I blamed myself. You know emotions and I don't do well together. I know I drove you away and I've regretted it ever since. Regretted that it cost me you."

Carrick let out a breath as he looked up at the ceiling. Jardin wasn't sure what he was doing, but when he dropped his head to stare at Jardin, his face was emotionless.

"This wasn't why I came back here. I'm not interested in rehashing the past."

"No? Then why are you still angry at me?" Jardin asked.

"I didn't say I forgave you."

"You weren't blameless in what happened, you know."

Carrick raised his eyebrows. "So, I don't roll over and accept your apology like a good boy, you're going to turn things back on me?"

Shit. He had a point. But Jardin needed to get through the barrier he'd erected to protect himself. Carrick had always been an open book. Or Jardin thought he had been. But he'd hidden shit. And he wasn't blameless.

"Hmm, have you ever been a good boy, Carrick?" He strode forward, not touching the bigger man but crowding in close. Physically, Carrick had him beat. But he wasn't as dominant as Jardin was. And Jardin had an inkling that Carrick might bottom for him.

"I'm no boy."

"But you could be, couldn't you?"

"Cut it with the bullshit, Jardin. I'm not your sub."

"But did you want to be?"

Carrick swallowed heavily.

"I've always wondered if I misinterpreted things. I'd see the heat in your eyes, I'd start to say something, but I'd always hold back. That was my first mistake. My second was believing in what Sally told me."

Carrick scowled. "What did that bitch tell you?"

"That you were unhappy with us. That she wasn't enough for you. That you wanted out, wanted other people."

Carrick looked away.

"Her death was my fault," Jardin told him.

The other man gaped at him. "What? No, it wasn't. She drank so much she . . ."

Slipped into the pool and couldn't get out. He'd managed to keep that part out of the media, the bit about how intoxicated she'd been.

"I should have gotten her help. Professional help."

"Still doesn't make it your fault," Carrick told him.

"I'm not a perfect man."

Carrick gave him a derisive look. "Oh, really?"

"I was feeling guilty for her death and I took that out on you. It wasn't fair or right. And I apologize. I know you might never forgive me, but I owe you that apology. I've owed it to you for a long time. Earlier that day I confronted her about the way she'd been treating you. I told her she had until the morning to get out, then I got that call about Lottie."

"I remember," Carrick said softly. Lottie had been kidnapped several years before. While she'd been doing a lot better, she'd refused to leave the house and had episodes where she'd hurt herself. That day she'd cut her thigh badly.

"I should have made time to tell you what was going on, but I thought I'd have time to figure it out when I got home. Then when she died . . . I was messed up, Carrick. I never should have said those things. I don't know how else to tell you I'm sorry."

Carrick looked away for a long moment.

This was it. The moment of truth. But he owed it to him. "I didn't like the way she treated you. And if I thought there was a chance of me being with you, I wanted to pursue it."

"But you're not gay."

"No, I'm not. I'm not into men."

Carrick flinched.

"I'm into you. It's always been you. I liked the idea of the three of us more than the execution of it. I thought I could have it all. A sweet sub to protect and cherish and discipline and the man I fucking loved."

Carrick breathed out harshly. "Sally never wanted me. I came with you and she tolerated me. But her end game was always to get rid of me and have you to herself. After all, why would she want to be involved with a dirty, broke mechanic when she could have a Malone?"

"Except all I wanted was you."

It's always been fucking you.

This couldn't be real.

All I wanted was you.

"I was your best friend—"

"Yeah, my best friend. And I didn't want to lose that. So, I held back. I hoped something might build between us."

He shook his head. *What?* "What the fuck, man? This isn't possible."

Amusement filled Jardin's face. "It's not possible that I find you attractive? Seriously? Since when did your self-esteem take a total nosedive?"

"Since my best friend told me to get the fuck out, that he didn't want to see me."

"I fucked up. I didn't mean it. Like I said, I was angry at myself, not you."

"Why didn't you ever tell me how you felt?"

"Guess I was scared."

Carrick let out a laugh. "The great Jardin Malone doesn't get scared."

"He does when someone means something to him. When he doesn't want to lose them. When he doesn't know what move to make. And then he makes the wrong one and messes up not just his life but the person who means everything to him."

Carrick paced back and forth. "So, wait . . . let's get this all straight. You and me. We were best friends. We shared a sub. One who was only with me because she thought she had to be to get you but secretly wanted you to herself."

"Which I didn't realize."

"She told you lies about me, about how I wanted out? Wanted other people?"

"How she saw you talking to other men. How you'd come home smelling of cologne. How you stopped having sex with her."

"Fuck," Carrick swore. "She knew what buttons to push."

"Being stupid wasn't Sally's issue. But she knew where to hit at me. I thought I was going to lose you. I didn't know how to tell you what I felt without risking you leaving or rejecting me. And it took me a while to work through my feelings for you. Plus, you seemed to be pulling away from me."

"Fuck." Carrick shook his head.

"I still don't know if you'd ever be attracted to me. I know I'm not an easy man to love. That I'm controlling and pushy and domineering."

Carrick slumped into a chair. Jardin pulled out another and sat across from him. "I'm a flawed man, Carrick. I make mistakes. Big ones. But I hope I learn from them. And if there's any chance you could ever forgive me . . ."

He knew Jardin's faults. He liked to control everything around him because there was less chance he could be hurt that way. He also blamed himself when things went wrong. He also knew Jardin found it hard to believe that anyone could love him. Not after growing up in the household he had. There had been little love between his parents or for their children.

But could he forgive him for everything? He'd ripped out Carrick's heart and stomped on it.

Except he never knew he had your heart. Because you're guilty of not telling him shit. About your feelings.

"Sally used to tell me how I'd never fit into your life. About how I couldn't be seen with you. About how lucky I was to be allowed to live in your house, to have you pay for me. Shit like that."

"That fucking bitch," Jardin growled. "Why didn't you say anything?"

Carrick shrugged. "Guess we've both got too much pride for our own good."

"And she knew how to play to our weaknesses like a pro."

They were both silent for a long moment.

"So now you're back."

"You knew I left?" Carrick asked.

"I did."

He should have known he would have. Carrick had moved to Alabama after their breakup. He nearly snorted at the use of that word. They hadn't had that sort of relationship.

Not then anyway.

"I own my garage. Got a house." He didn't know exactly why he'd come back. Only that he'd never felt at home in Alabama. Never fit in.

Maybe you came back for Jardin.

"You really wanted me? You think you could be into me . . . like that? Fuck, I sound like a teenager with my first crush." He could feel his cheeks growing red.

"Always loved how you could blush. Carrick, I've wanted you for a long time. I was a prick. A selfish asshole. And I get it if you can't forgive me. But I hope like hell you'll give me another chance. That you'll let me show you my feelings for you, how much you mean to me."

"We haven't seen each other in two years. I might have changed."

Jardin watched him guardedly. "I'm sure we both have. That's not a bad thing."

Might not be a good thing either. "We've both got a lot of baggage."

Jardin nodded. "But we know what that baggage is. And I never make the same mistake twice. All I need is a chance. A chance to earn your forgiveness. To be with you. I'll show you how much I still need you. I never stopped thinking of you. Wanting you."

"You never came for me."

Jardin grimaced. "Not true."

Shock filled Carrick and he straightened. "What are you talking about?"

"I tracked you down, about three months after you left. Got a PI to find you— "

"I wasn't hiding."

"No. I know."

"What happened? You changed your mind?"

Jardin cleared his throat. "When I got there, you were shutting up the garage. This woman came up to you. Big, blonde hair, short, red skirt."

"Gemma," he said. He rubbed his eyes. "Jesus."

"You looked happy. You hugged her. You smiled. And I realized

I couldn't remember the last time you'd smiled. It was then I wondered if you weren't better off without me in your life. You were miserable with us, weren't you?"

"With her, yeah. Not with you."

"I wish you would have told me."

"Yeah, well, as worried as you were about losing me? I was just as worried. Especially since I knew you weren't into guys. As far as I knew there was nothing tying us together but Sally and friendship."

"And if there could be more? That woman is she— "

"She was just a fling. I don't . . . there's no one. Well, I thought that maybe Thea— "

"Thea?" Jardin straightened, a strange look coming over his face.

"Yeah, Thea. When I first saw you with her, looking all cozy, guess I just lost it. I thought you'd sent her to torture me. I know how stupid that sounds. It's not like you could have set our meeting up. I was being an idiot."

"It's okay. I get it." Jardin looked thoughtful. "Can we talk about Thea later? Right now, what I want to know is if there is a chance you could forgive me? That you could give me a chance?"

CHRIST, it was hard to ask.

He was a man more used to demanding and getting his way, but he'd had to eat his share of humble pie. He'd fucked up. And whatever way Carrick chose to punish him would only be fair.

Jardin hardly dared breathe as he watched Carrick. As he waited for his reply.

"I don't know, J. Don't you think there's too much water under the bridge? I mean, maybe we could just be friends again."

He'd take that, but it wasn't what he wanted.

"I think life's too short not to go for what you want. For what you need. I regret too many things in life, Carrick. I don't want to add to those regrets."

"You've never been with another man before?"

"No, like I said. It's just you."

"And women? You're willing to give up being with a woman?"

Jardin leaned back in his seat. "If the right one came along, I wouldn't be opposed to having a third. Provided you agree. We'd have to both want her and for her to want both of us. Equally. And she would have to be okay with our relationship."

Someone like Thea would be perfect. Nope. Not mentioning that.

"You've never been with a man, Jardin. What if we did get together and then you figured out, you're not actually into guys at all. What then?"

Jardin thought that over. It was one thing to say that wouldn't happen, but it would just be words. They were all too easy to say but harder to mean.

He stood up. Carrick looked at him in surprise but before the other man could move, he leaned down, placing one hand behind Carrick's head, the other under his chin.

And he kissed him.

At first Carrick just sat there. Frozen. Unresponsive. And he wondered if he'd made a horrible mistake. It was all one-sided. He didn't have the same feelings toward him. His hard-on started to shrivel. He drew away.

"I'm so—"

Carrick grabbed him, dragging him back. Jardin moved onto his knees between the bigger man's open legs. Not a position he was used to. He was a man who liked to control everything. But whatever Carrick needed in order to forgive him, to take another gamble on him, he would give to him.

Carrick's mouth moved against his, taking charge of the kiss.

His tongue dipped between Jardin's lips; sipping from him. Owning him.

His cock pressed against his pants. Aching and hard. Jardin ran his hands up Carrick's thighs, feeling how muscular he was. Then he pressed his hand to the other man's cock

Fuck. Yes.

Carrick groaned into his mouth. "Jardin . . ."

"Let me show you how much I want you. Let me prove it to you."

Carrick shook his head.

It was like a bucket of cold water over his head. He'd misread him. Sure, he was rocking one hell of a hard-on, but it didn't mean he wanted this.

"Fuck. Jardin. I just . . . I need a minute to think. Christ, that was everything . . . it was everything I ever wanted and yet . . ."

"You're worried it might all disappear." Jardin got it.

"Can you . . . can you get up? Seeing you on your knees like this, well, it doesn't seem quite right. I don't want you begging me. I thought I did. But fuck, it's not like I didn't make mistakes. We both know that. And you aren't a man who gets on his knees."

"I do for the people I love when they need me to. I do when I've been an idiot and it's no less than I deserve."

"I don't want to punish you, J."

"You don't?"

Carrick's lips twitched. "Okay, maybe I'd like to punish you a bit. But I messed up too. I just don't know if we can come back from that."

"And you don't know if you want to try."

"My life is in a good place right now. Not sure I can risk messing it up."

"You're not sure I'm worth messing things up for." Jardin got it. "You're likely right." He started to get to his feet when Carrick grabbed his shoulders.

The other man groaned. "You're fucking with everything I thought I wanted. That I needed."

"I could say sorry, except that I'm not."

"Bastard." But it wasn't said with ire. "Fuck." Carrick leaned in and kissed him. Hard. Hot. He had to resist the urge not to take charge. Whatever Carrick needed to let him in, he'd give to him. No matter the cost.

Carrick finished the kiss, placing his forehead against his. "You're holding back."

Jardin stiffened.

"Because I'm a guy? Because I'm me? Or something else?" Carrick asked.

"Because you're you. And I want to give you what you need."

"Don't do that, J."

"Don't do what?"

"Change your needs for me. Just don't . . . things won't work if you do that. We both know you've got to be the dominant one in any relationship."

"You're a Dom too. Have you ever thought about submitting?"

Carrick shrugged. "I enjoy being dominant in the bedroom. But there were times I watched you with Sally and thought about what it would be like to submit to you."

"Yeah?" Jardin said huskily.

"Not always. And fuck, if we ever did add a third, she'd need to be a sub because I'm not bottoming for anyone else. But, yeah, I could do it. For you."

Arousal flooded Jardin but he never wanted Carrick to feel pressured. "I would never expect you to—"

"I know."

"Does this mean we're giving this a try? Us?"

.   .   .

THE HOPE in Jardin's voice floored him. It showed him how much he wanted this.

Could he do it?

It was everything he'd ever dreamed of. And the truth was, holding onto resentment took too much out of him. It was making him bitter, and he didn't want that. In the end, he knew he'd regret it if he walked away and his life was already filled with too many regrets.

"We're doing this."

"Fuck. Thank God." Jardin's gaze ate him up. From the inside out. They just stared at each other for a long moment before Jardin pulled him in for another kiss.

Christ. He was going to self-combust soon.

"What now?" Carrick asked as Jardin drew back.

"Well, maybe we could have lunch before I have to get back to the office. Shit. Thea!" He pulled out his phone. "Stein said she made it safely back."

"Thank God. I owe her an apology. Wait, the office? How do you know her?"

"She's my personal assistant."

Okay, that surprised him. "Your personal assistant? That wasn't what I expected you to say."

The way he'd looked at her . . . it was likely similar to the way Carrick looked at her. Like she was sunshine while he lived in perpetual darkness.

His heart feeling lighter, he stood and moved toward Jardin, shocked when the other man entwined his fingers with his, slipping his phone away. "You know what? I'm not real sure I want to go back to work."

Carrick gave him a shocked look. "You? Not want to work?"

Jardin shook his head. "I think I've earned some time off. Wanna play hooky with me?"

Carrick just smiled. "Fuck, yes."

13

J ardin looked completely out of place in his house with his designer suit.

"So, this is your place? I like it."

He couldn't stop the snort from escaping.

Jardin turned to give him a look. "What does that mean?"

"You don't like it."

"I just said I did." There was a note to the other man's voice that should have warned him to tread carefully. But he didn't heed it.

"You can't possibly like it. My whole house would probably fit into the master suite at your place." The master suite he'd given to Sally.

He wondered how Thea would fit in there.

Nope. Don't think about her.

Besides, he couldn't imagine Thea in that space. It would overwhelm her.

Not with you there to take care of her.

Shut. Up.

"I don't live there anymore."

"You don't?"

"No, I moved back to the family estate."

Now that did surprise him. He wouldn't have thought Jardin wanted to live with his family again. Not that he didn't love them, but they weren't an overly demonstrative lot. Then again, neither was Jardin.

"And what does the size matter? Does a place have to be huge for me to like it?"

"Come off it, Jardin. This place is a shit hole in comparison."

"This is not a shit hole."

"Well, no. But it's not a palace, either."

"You think I could only be happy in a palace?"

Carrick shrugged. He didn't want to say it, but, yeah.

"Fine. Then I'll move in here."

Carrick had just taken a swig of beer that he'd pulled from his fridge when he heard those words. He choked on the mouthful.

"What?"

"Well, obviously, not right now. Not unless you want me to. But when we're ready for that step. I'll move in here."

"Jardin, you're not moving in here."

"Like I said, when we're ready."

Christ, he was no less of a bulldozer than he had been two years ago. In fact, he might be more of one.

"No. Never."

A flash of hurt filled Jardin's face and Carrick cursed. "I didn't mean . . . when the time is right, I want to live with you, I just meant . . . fuck. I'm bad at this shit."

"Talking?"

"Yeah. Talking. I'll move in with you. You can't live here. This place isn't right for you."

"I don't give a fuck where I live, so long as I'm with you."

They were nice words, but he didn't truly believe them.

"Maybe we should table that for now. Want a beer?" he asked.

Jardin nodded, taking the beer Carrick offered him. Since they'd gotten there, there was a kind of awkwardness between them. As though neither knew what to say.

"I need to make a call to Thea, let her know I'm not going to be in and to move my appointments."

Carrick nodded, watching as Jardin walked away. Was he doing the right thing? Letting him back into his life? Then again, had it been much of a life without Jardin in it? The other man had hurt him. But would he have walked away if he hadn't let Sally gouge a huge hole in his self-esteem? If he'd just opened up to Jardin, maybe they could have avoided the mess that came later.

Maybe it wouldn't end well again. But, this time, there was honesty between them at least. Jardin's revelation had been a shock, and he still wasn't entirely sure he knew what he was getting himself into. But he'd suffered through his family trying to tell him how to feel when he'd first come out. He still didn't talk to them because of it. No way was he telling Jardin how to feel.

That wasn't the only thing niggling away at him, though. This was new, yes. And he got that they should focus on the two of them. But then there was Thea.

Thea, who he couldn't stop thinking about.

Thea, who had looked confused and worried. And scared.

Thea, who'd run out of the restaurant as though the hounds of hell were on her heels.

None of that sat right with him. But was Jardin interested in her? And would it be fair to bring her in to a relationship that was just starting off? Even though they'd known each other for years, and though they'd shared a woman, they'd never been in a relationship together.

No, they needed a solid foundation first, then they could think about Thea.

Except he couldn't get her out of mind. He needed to talk to her, explain things. Find out why she'd never answered his messages.

"Everything okay?"

He glanced up as Jardin walked in and moved over to where he was leaning against the kitchen counter.

Carrick took him in. Fuck, he was hot. The man oozed power and authority. Yet, Carrick knew he had a softer side too. He just didn't let many people see it.

"Changed your mind?" Vulnerability entered Jardin's gaze.

"Fuck. No." Carrick reached out and drew him close, holding him against his chest. His cock hardened, thickened at the feel of Jardin's body against his. "I want this. Want it so much it's fucking scary."

"I know what you mean," Jardin admitted. "I'm scared as well."

"Didn't think much ever scared the great Jardin Malone."

"Yeah, well, the great Jardin Malone isn't so great. He's just a man who wants his best friend to love him again."

Carrick groaned. "Fuck that's hot."

"What is?"

"You. Letting down your guard. Letting me the fuck in. I want you."

"Me too."

"Is it moving too fast?"

Jardin shrugged. "Not like we haven't known each other for years."

That didn't mean they should immediately jump into bed with each other. Still, he couldn't resist leaning down to kiss the other man. Reaching around, he squeezed his firm ass.

"Fuck, Carrick," Jardin muttered. "You're killing me."

"You sure you're ready for this?"

"Fuck, yes. What the hell do you think I've been jerking off to for the past two years?"

"You dreamed about me?" Carrick asked.

"Course I fucking did. All the ways I would take you. All the ways I would make you mine."

Jardin reached down and rubbed Carrick's dick through his jeans. Fuck. He needed more. Jardin must have sensed that as he undid the button and pulled the zipper down then dragged his jeans over his ass to grab his cock through his boxers.

He ran his thumb over the tip, and Carrick jolted. Fuck. Him. That felt so damn good.

Carrick's breath came in fast pants as Jardin released his dick from his boxers and started to pump the hard shaft.

"Keep your hands on the counter behind you," Jardin commanded.

He moved his hands to do as he was told.

"Fuck. I like that you just obeyed me. Not gonna lie. Never thought I'd have this. Any of this."

"Me either. Christ, can't believe I didn't know you wanted me like this."

Jardin squeezed Carrick's cock. Fuck. Fuck.

To his shock, Jardin grabbed hold of his hips then bent down, running his tongue over the top of Carrick's dick.

"Fuck!"

"Always wondered what you'd taste like." He took Carrick's cock deep into his mouth. Carrick had to count backward from a hundred not to come then and there.

"Jardin," he moaned as the other man drew back.

Jardin cupped his face between his hands. "You know I like to be in control. Of everything. I know you won't always want to submit, but right now I don't think I can hold back my need to take charge. If I go too far, you tell me. But, Carrick, I want to take you. I want to feel your mouth wrapped around my cock. I want to take your ass. And I want you in mine."

Carrick's breath came faster. Harder.

"Tell me you want that too."

Jardin stepped back, giving him time to think. Or he thought that's what he was doing. But he didn't want to overthink it anymore. He quickly tugged his jeans and boxers off his legs. Jardin's gaze heated as he watched him. Then he reached over and grabbed Jardin's hand.

"Come with me."

14

J ardin watched Carrick's tight ass as he led him toward the bedroom. He had to fight the urge to be the one in the lead. Although he did admit the view was good.

He wondered what that ass would look like red. How well Carrick would take his whip. His belt. His paddle. His pulse raced.

He'd expected more of a push back to his dominance. But then, Carrick wasn't a typical Dom. Or a typical sub. Jardin knew he wouldn't submit for anyone else. And that fucking pleased the hell out of him.

Sometimes he'd take his commands perfectly, other times he wouldn't. Maybe sometimes he'd want the pain Jardin enjoyed giving. Maybe other times he'd tell him to fuck off.

He grinned at the thought. Jardin hadn't felt so alive in years.

He wasn't losing Carrick. Not ever again.

Thoughts of Thea flitted through his head. With her, they'd have balance. They could both command her. Both watch over her. Both keep her safe. He'd damn well enjoy taking her over his knee and spanking her. Then fucking her. Then watching Carrick fuck her.

Or taking her together.

That's what he'd dreamed of. Thea sucking on Carrick's cock while Jardin took him from behind. Jardin inside Thea's pussy while Carrick took him.

All in good time.

Right now, he needed to show Carrick how much he meant to him. How much he needed him. How seriously he took this.

"Shirt off," he commanded as soon as they entered Carrick's bedroom.

The other man just raised an eyebrow, but he quickly stripped off his black shirt. Sally used to complain about Carrick's limited wardrobe and lack of style.

Jardin didn't give a fuck. The other man was hot. Gorgeous. Sexy as hell. Sally had never seen that. And it had been her loss.

But enough about that bitch. There was only one woman he'd allow to come between them. And he meant that in a physical way, not an emotional one, because that shit wasn't happening again.

When Carrick was finally naked, Jardin ran his gaze over his firm chest. The man was sculpted from his wide shoulders down his rippling six-pack to his Adonis belt.

His gaze snagged on the thick cock sticking up. Hell. Yes.

"You planning on just staring at me all night?" There was a note of challenge in Carrick's voice.

Jardin's darker side started to rise. *Go easy.* "Get on the bed. Hands above your head."

Carrick raised his eyebrows. "Always the bossy bastard."

"Would you want me any other way?"

Carrick let out a bark of laughter. "Shockingly, no." He climbed on the slightly messy bed. Unsurprisingly, the sheets were dark gray and the duvet was black.

Most people might look at Carrick and think he was uncomplicated. That he liked things simple. And he did. But there was more to him than the surface. Jardin slowly stripped as Carrick put his hands behind his head and watched, his gaze filled with admiration.

He wasn't as cut as Carrick, but he didn't slack on time in the gym. He'd never needed much sleep and it wasn't as though his nights were occupied with anything else. The occasional visit to the club when it all got to be too much. When he needed to release some tension.

"Like what you see?" he asked, wrapping his hand around his shaft.

"Fuck, yes," Carrick said gruffly.

"Good."

He crawled onto the side of the bed then knelt down by Carrick's head. "Do you want to know what I taste like?"

Carrick licked his lips. "Fuck. Yes."

"Take me into your mouth then."

The other man rolled over, positioning himself on his hands and knees, leaning in to take Jardin's dick into his mouth, he sucked him down.

Holy. Fuck.

That felt so good. Jardin's eyes rolled back in his head as he struggled for control as Carrick took him deeply. He swirled his tongue around the head, his hand reaching for Jardin's balls. He widened his legs to give him more room to play with. And play he did. He ran his tongue up and down Jardin's shaft. Then he sucked him slowly into his mouth. In slow, out fast. Fuck, the man knew what he was doing.

It wasn't long until the rush of orgasm neared.

"Fuck. Carrick. I'm close."

Carrick hummed. Then he moved his hand around to Jardin's asshole. Just the tip of a finger entered his puckered hole, but it was enough. Jardin shouted as he came in the other man's mouth while Carrick continued to suck on him. His breath came in fast pants, his skin was coated with a fine sheen of sweat. He felt like he'd done a hard session of cardio when all he'd done was sit there while Carrick had sucked him off.

When Carrick drew back from his dick, he reached down for him, pulling him onto his knees so he could kiss him. He didn't give a fuck that he could taste himself. It was hot.

"Christ, you're good at that." Jardin reached down and ran his hand up and down Carrick's cock where they faced each other on their knees. "Lube?"

"Top drawer of the bedside table."

He moved away and opened the drawer, pulling out a tube of lube and a butt plug. Excellent.

Carrick's eyes grew heavy-lidded as he watched Jardin place the lube and plug on the bed.

"On your back again. Legs bent, feet flat on the mattress. Time for me to play."

Carrick didn't argue, he just laid back and bent his knees. His cock wept pre-cum. His hands went behind his head.

Jardin knelt between his bent legs and just took him in for a moment. "As much as I want you inside me, I think I'm going to need some prep first."

Carrick made a low, grumbling noise in his throat. "Fucking love that I'm going to be your first."

"First and only."

"Fuck. Yes. First and only. Jesus, man, hurry up, I'm dying here."

Jardin grinned. He liked the pain in Carrick's voice. "Patience is a virtue."

"Fucking sadist, you're enjoying this."

Oh, hell, yes. He certainly was.

But there was only so long he could resist the lure of the man in front of him. Leaning over, he rested his hands on the mattress on either side of him and licked one nipple. Then he moved to his other nipple and tugged on it lightly with his teeth.

"Fuck. Yes. Christ, Jardin."

He licked down Carrick's firm abs. Damn, the man was in even better shape than before.

"You're so fucking hot."

Jardin had never felt attracted to another man. Didn't think he ever would be. Carrick was it for him. And he made no apologies for it. He reached the other man's cock and swirled his tongue around the tip before taking him deep into his mouth and sucking. He didn't mess around. He kept his movements firm. Taking him in deeply before rising to let his cock slide from his mouth.

"Fuck! Fuck! I'm so close."

He let him go with a plop. "No coming until I give permission."

"Christ. Fuck. How did I know you were going to be like this?"

Jardin chuckled. "You've known me a long time. You knew exactly what you were getting into when you said yes."

"Bastard." But there was no heat in the words.

Jardin reached over for the lube and coated two of his fingers in it. Then he took his time spreading the lube on Carrick's asshole. Jardin raised his gaze to the other man's face. But his eyes were shut, a look of unguarded pleasure on his face as Jardin slowly slid one finger deep into his ass.

"Christ. Christ. Christ."

Carrick moved his hands away from his head and twisted them into the comforter beneath him. They probably should have pulled that back. They were gonna make a mess of it.

Not that Jardin really gave a fuck. He pumped his finger in and out of Carrick's ass while he moved his mouth back to the other man's shaft. Another finger joined the first, preparing him for the plug although Jardin figured he was well used to taking the plug since it was sitting in his nightstand drawer.

He drew his mouth back then slid his fingers free.

Carrick opened his eyes to glare up at him. "No. Fuck. Don't stop."

"Sh, not stopping," Jardin told him. "Just ramping things up." He grabbed the plug and coated it slowly in lube while Carrick watched. Then he sat back on his heels, holding it. "Legs to your chest."

Carrick groaned as he got into position. "Damn it."

This position gave him a good view. He ran a finger between Carrick's cheeks and over his hole, dipping the tip in.

"Fuck, Jardin. Don't tease."

Oh, but he liked to tease. And more. But he pressed the plug against Carrick's ass and slowly started pushing it inside him. Fuck. Him. His cock grew hard at the sight. When the plug was deep inside, he tugged at it, pulling it out a few inches and slamming it back in. He stared down at Carrick as he fucked him with the plug. The other man's eyes drifted closed and he slapped his ass cheek.

Carrick opened his eyes to glare at him. "What the fuck?"

"Eyes on me," Jardin demanded.

They stared at each other for a moment, neither giving in.

Carrick rolled his eyes. "Fine. Fuck. Shit. Keep going. But don't think you'll always get to be in charge like this."

Oh, he knew he would always be in charge. Maybe not always like this with Carrick. If they had a third, they could dominate her together. But at the end of the day, Jardin was always going to be the boss.

Jardin grinned as he moved the plug out again then thrust it back. "Lower your legs again."

As soon as Carrick's feet hit the mattress, he took his shaft back into his mouth. With one hand, he circled the base of Carrick's cock, with his other hand he started pumping his own dick. Fuck. Yes.

He swirled his mouth around Carrick's shaft. Fuck. Why had he waited so long? What had he been so afraid of?

Losing your best friend. Yeah, well, fuck, that happened anyway, didn't it?

"Jardin. Shit. Jardin!"

Jardin swiped his tongue over the head of Carrick's cock then pulled back. "Come for me. Come in my mouth. Let me taste you."

He took him deeply, his eyes never leaving Carrick's blue ones. And he saw the moment he let go, tasted him as he came in his mouth. By now his own dick was rock hard. He drank down all that Carrick gave him then withdrew from him.

"You trust me to take you?" he asked the other man.

"Fuck. Yes."

"Condoms?"

"Got some in the bedside drawer. But I'm clean."

"Me too," Jardin told him. "Tested two months ago and there's been no one since."

"I got tested four months ago."

"Then I'll take you bare," Jardin said with satisfaction as he slowly drew the plug free. He threw it on the floor to take care of later. Carrick shoved a pillow under his hips to raise himself up, as Jardin coated his cock in lube.

"Unless you wanted a different position?" he asked.

"Nope," Jardin replied. "I want to look at you when I take you. And I want you to know exactly who's claiming your ass. Because I'm the only one who is going to be taking you there from now on."

Carrick's face softened and Jardin leaned in to kiss him. A light kiss. To tease. Then he drew back and grabbed hold of his dick, guiding it to the other man's hole.

"Oh, fuck yes. Harder. Faster."

"I'm trying to go easy," Jardin gritted out as Carrick rose up to meet him.

"Why? I can take it."

Fuck. Christ. He didn't want to end up blowing his load too quickly. He had to push to get past the tight ring of muscle but once he did, he was surrounded in heat.

"Feels so good, Jardin. Please. Move."

He didn't need any more prompting. He pulled out then drove in deeply. Christ. So good. Carrick wrapped his big legs around his waist as he moved, thrusting hard.

"Carrick!"

"I know, man. I know. Feels fucking good to me too. Just come."

He stared into his best friend's face. The man he loved more than anyone. The he drove deeply one final time, coming hard.

Fucking bliss.

THEA GOT off the phone with Jardin and placing her elbows on the desk, rested her head in her upturned hands.

She was still shaking. After asking her if she was okay, he'd only talked about work. Which had been a relief. She was still processing everything that had happened. That had been . . . it had been a complete mess. She wasn't even sure what the hell was going on. Obviously, Carrick and Jardin knew each other.

But why would Carrick think their meeting had been a setup? How would that have even been possible?

She wasn't sure. But she'd seen his anger and his hurt. And that made her feel ill. Her entire life was a mess and she had no idea what to do. Where to turn next.

At least she didn't have to face Jardin this afternoon. That gave her some time to think. Not always a good thing in her situation.

Mr. Stein had popped his head in before to check on her. She couldn't believe that Jardin had sent one of the law firm's partners to check in on her.

She hurriedly got to work, moving Jardin's appointments

around. He'd only had two this afternoon. And none in the morning. She managed to shift them both to Friday then she did a few other jobs. The afternoon seemed to tick by, and she was ashamed to say she counted down the last ten minutes before she thought she could safely leave.

Without looking around, she hurried to where she'd parked her car. She didn't get a parking spot in the same building as where they worked like Jardin did. But she'd managed to find a cheap parking lot not too far away. It was outside and looked more like an abandoned lot. And it was poorly lit at night, which was going to be a problem when the days grew shorter. But, right now, it was a godsend.

It wasn't until she got close to her car that she spotted it. A single red rose sat under her windshield wiper.

Her hands shook as she pulled it out. There was a note attached.

Three days until you're mine.

Her stomach revolted and she leaned over to vomit. When she'd rid her stomach of what little food it contained, she moved around to the driver's door and opened it. She sat inside, tears streaming down her face. He knew what her car looked like. She was under no illusions he didn't know where she lived. And worked.

She had until Saturday. What the hell was she going to do?

15

Carrick groaned as he came.

Jardin had woken him with his mouth around his dick. Fuck, what a way to wake up. Jardin hummed and swallowed him down, licking his cock clean before he slid up his body, pressing kisses to his skin.

Smiling, Carrick leaned in and kissed him. "Fuck, man, you suck cock like you've been doing it all your life."

Jardin threw his head back and laughed. Joy filled Carrick. Most people only saw Jardin's serious side. And he *was* an intense guy, but he had a softer side. Usually, it only came out around women and children. And Carrick.

"I'm going to take that as a compliment," Jardin said with a grin that turned into a groan as Carrick grasped his firm cock with his hand.

"Oh, it certainly is."

"I can't believe how much we fucked all night. I'm not twenty anymore."

Carrick snorted as he continued to jack him off. "Neither of us are. But we've got lost time to make up for."

"Fuck. Yes. God, we do." Jardin leaned in to kiss him. "Nothing I want more than to spend the day here with you."

"But you have to work. I get it."

"I . . . holy fuck, Carrick, that feels good . . . don't have appointments this morning. I can sleep in for a bit. If you can."

"Hmm, I think we can do better than sleep in." Carrick scooted down the bed until he came face-to-face with Jardin's hard-on.

Well, good morning.

THEA WALKED into the office the next morning in a daze. She hadn't slept all night and, truth be told, it was starting to catch up with her. She was feeling woozy and out of sorts.

She hadn't wanted to come in today. She hadn't wanted to see Jardin. To talk about yesterday. She didn't want to do anything except hide from her problems. As she reached her desk, her heart started to go into overdrive.

Fear flooded her system, with an overload of adrenaline that made her feel ill.

There, sitting on the desk in a vase was a single red rose. Her hand shook as she reached out to grab hold of the card. She didn't need to read what it said. Yet, at the same time there was no way she couldn't not read it.

Two days until you're mine.

Bile rose in her mouth, and she barely made it to the garbage can. Shaking, tears flooded her eyes, and she sat for a moment trying to pull herself together.

It was messed up.

It wasn't real.

Get up, Thea. Sitting on the ground isn't going to do anything. Jardin will be here soon.

Big girl panties on.

❦

"THERE'S something I need to talk to you about," Carrick said. They were both lying on the bed, facing each other. Both sated from their morning lovemaking.

He really needed to get up and open the garage. And Jardin would need to go home and get changed before heading into work.

But there was still something niggling away at him and he couldn't let it go.

Jardin opened his eyes, watching him with sharp intelligence. "Yeah? What's that?"

"Thea."

Did the other man flinch or did he imagine it?

"What about Thea?" Jardin asked. "You never did say how you met."

"That's part of what I have to tell you. In the interest of honesty and communication. Thea and I . . . well, we . . ."

Jardin's eyes widened. "You slept with her?"

"No. No, I didn't sleep with her. But we did go on a date. And we kissed." He explained how he'd met her, bribing her into a date with him. How that date had ended up here at his house.

"When she left that night, I told her to text me when she got home but she never did. My messages went unanswered. When she finally did text, it was to say she couldn't come help me the next day in the office like she'd promised."

Jardin frowned and sat up, resting against the headboard. Carrick stared at his cut chest. Damn, the man was hot.

"That doesn't sound like Thea. She's only worked for me for two months, but she's a hard worker and she does what she says she will."

"I didn't think it seemed like her either. But she ghosted me.

She didn't reply to any of my messages or texts. And when I saw you with her yesterday—"

"You came to the conclusion I sent her to mess with you?" Jardin asked incredulously.

Carrick winced. "Far-fetched, I know. But I was angry. There was the woman I thought liked me, whom I liked, sitting with the man I loved, who'd hurt me."

"I get it," Jardin said quietly. "But I didn't know the two of you had met." He reached over and ran his finger over Carrick's nipple. "You like her?"

He stiffened. "Well, yeah, I did. But like I said, haven't heard a thing from her so, obviously, she doesn't feel the same."

Jardin shook his head. "No. I don't think that's the case. She was hurt when you were mad at her yesterday. And she's been off her game these past few days. Staring off into space, jumpy. I took her out for lunch yesterday to pry answers from her. I touched her yesterday and she acted like she thought I was going to hit her."

"I barely touched her wrist, J," he said with a frown. "I couldn't have hurt her, not unless . . ."

"She was already hurt," Jardin said. He looked thoughtful. "She's worn long-sleeved, high-necked shirts all week."

Carrick sucked in a sharp breath. "I don't like this. You think someone's abusing her?"

"I don't know. But there's something going on with her." Jardin stared at Carrick. "If she'd replied to your messages, come to the garage that day, you'd still be seeing her? Want to be with her?"

Carrick swallowed. How the fuck did he answer that? "Well, yeah, but I'm with you now."

"One doesn't have to preclude the other," Jardin mused.

"You mean you . . . you like her too?"

"I'm having a lot of trouble keeping her out of my head. I keep having to recite all the reasons I shouldn't want her, yet none of them seem to stick."

"So, what are you saying?"

"I'm saying that we need to figure out exactly what's going on in my PA's life. We need to fix it. And then we need to convince her that having two men dote on her, protect her, dominate her, is better than one."

"She might not go for it," Carrick warned. "And I . . . I can't be just another dick again, J."

Jardin reached over and grabbed him behind the back of the neck, his face fierce. "You were never just another dick. I don't ever want to hear you say that about yourself. But if for some reason you ever feel it, you'll tell me."

Carrick nodded. "Yeah. I will."

"Besides, Thea isn't Sally. And I do believe it might just take both of us to take care of her."

~

"I've got to go," Jardin told Carrick at this front door.

Carrick sighed. "I know. So do I. You'll text me if you find out anything about Thea?"

Jardin frowned. "Yeah. I've got a meeting with a client and then I'll go into the office and try to have a talk with her."

"Should we take things slowly with her? I mean you and I have just started . . ." Carrick trailed off.

Jardin reached up and cupped the side of his face. "You and me? Always meant to be. We've known each other for years."

"Not like this." Carrick's eyes ran over him and Jardin felt his blood heat.

"No, not like this. But I suppose you could be right."

Carrick raised his eyebrows in shock. "I am? Never thought I'd hear you say those words."

Jardin mock-scowled at him. "I can admit when I'm wrong."

"Uh-huh." Carrick leaned against the doorway, his arms

crossed over his wide, naked chest. Fuck, it was hard to remember he had to work and couldn't take him back to bed.

"Jardin? You okay?" Carrick teased. "You've kind of spaced out. Did I keep you up too late last night, old man?"

"I'm only a year older than you. Watch yourself."

Carrick's eyes flared in challenge.

Shit. He didn't have time for this.

"We likely have to take things slower with Thea. The idea of being with two men is probably foreign to her. And, well, when one of those men is—"

"Domineering? Demanding? Sometimes a complete prick?"

"Hey, don't talk about yourself like that," Jardin warned, holding back a grin.

Carrick rolled his eyes. Then a hint of vulnerability entered his face. "You really think Thea could want both of us?"

Fuck. He hated that he doubted his self-worth. Jardin knew it was his fault that he felt insecure.

"I think Thea has shown she's attracted to us both. She wants you. I want you. We just might need to convince her that two are better than one."

"Hmm, I can think of a few ways to do that." Carrick's face grew serious. "What about what's happening to her?"

"That's another problem we need to figure out."

"But if we push too hard, she might run like she did with me."

"This would be much easier if she were already ours. She'd either tell us or I'd take her over my knee and redden her ass. Something she desperately needs."

"What if she's not a sub?"

He shrugged. "She doesn't have to be a sub for me to discipline her. In Haven, all women are protected. And disciplined if they disobey the rules set by their guardian."

"But we're not in Haven."

"Maybe that's the problem," he mused. "I might have to visit

Haven. Maddox is riding my ass about it. Think you could take some time off from the garage?"

"The previous owner would likely come in and cover for me. You're finally going to take me to Haven?"

"You and our girl. And if I get the urge to tie someone up and whip their ass, there's always you." Jardin grinned at Carrick's shocked look. Was that a hint of heat? He thought maybe it was.

Jardin pulled him in for another kiss. "I'm so fucking glad you're back in my life. I love you, Carrick. And I missed you like crazy."

Carrick stared down at him then closed his eyes and swallowed heavily. When he opened them again, tears swam in them.

"I love you too."

Shit. He was glad his meeting was a twenty-minute drive away. He was going to need that time to calm his raging hard-on.

16

This was hopeless.

She couldn't work. Couldn't eat. Couldn't think.

What was she going to do? There was only one way she could think of getting out of this, but she didn't know how she was going to pull it off.

She had this constant feeling of being watched. Could be paranoia, but she also wouldn't put it past Silvers to have a goon on her. They'd found her car in the parking lot. They'd left a rose where she worked.

He was telling her loud and clear there was no where she could run to. Except it was run or become his. And she knew she wouldn't live long if the latter happened. And what about the boys?

Thea's head spun with all the thoughts, and she leaned her elbow on the desk, propping her head up with her hand.

"Hello there, darlin'," a low voice drawled.

She let out a screech, jumping up out of her seat, heart racing.

Maddox. It's Maddox. Not Silvers or his thugs. It's only Maddox.

"Hmm, not the normal reaction I get from females," he said, studying her closely. "Something the matter, darlin'?"

She forced herself to smile as she tried to get her racing heart under control. "No, nothing's wrong. Sorry, my mind was a million miles away and you gave me a fright."

He gave her a look that screamed disbelief. "That so? Must have been thinking about something mighty hard."

Yeah. He could say that.

"Boss in?"

She frowned. "Aren't you staying with him?"

"Yep. In that giant mausoleum my cousins refer to as home. Do you know how hard it is to find someone in that place? It's like a hotel. There's even an intercom so if I need Jeeves, I can call him up in the middle of the night for a burger."

"Jeeves?"

"Their butler."

"They have a butler? And he's called Jeeves?"

"Course he's not, darlin'. That would be strange, wouldn't it? His name is Gerald."

Okay, she was completely losing track of the conversation.

"I just call him Jeeves because it pisses him off." Maddox grinned at her and she found herself smiling back.

"And you enjoy pissing him off." she guessed.

"He's extremely stuck-up and fussy. Apparently, I traipsed mud across his precious marble floors and now he keeps getting the chef to make shit for dinner like foie gras and pork terrine."

"And that burger you ordered?"

He sighed sadly. "Haven't gotten one yet. Can't wait to get back to Haven and Mia's cooking. That woman knows how to prepare a good steak."

"Are you headed back soon?"

"Still trying to convince my cousin to come back with me. He's not here?"

No. Thank God. She wasn't really prepared to face him yet. Then again, what happened yesterday was really the least of her worries. It wasn't like she had any long-term prospects at this job.

"He's at a meeting. He'll be back in about an hour or so."

"Guess I'll just have to wait, you don't mind, do you, darlin'?"

She didn't think it would matter much to him if she did mind. But she shook her head anyway. He'd be a good distraction.

LAUGHTER HIT him as soon as he walked into her office. Perhaps whatever was bothering her wasn't as big of an issue as he'd first thought. He scowled as he looked from her smiling face over to his cousin.

"Maddox, what are you doing here?"

"You didn't come home last night. I need to speak to you again before I leave for home."

Jardin sighed. "I don't have time right now."

Maddox straightened. "Well, when will you have time?" A stubborn look crossed his cousin's face.

"We can talk tonight at dinner."

Maddox grimaced. "Can we eat out? Cause the food they serve at the mausoleum I wouldn't even feed to the pigs back home."

"Fine. Yes. But Carrick will be coming too."

Maddox stiffened. "Carrick?"

"Yes." He braced himself for his cousin's teasing. He flicked a glance over at Thea to find her standing still as a statue.

"Carrick? Your ex-best friend Carrick?"

"I don't know any other Carricks."

"So, you and he are talking again?" Maddox asked.

"Yep."

"Was that where you were last night?" Maddox asked slyly.

"It was."

"You old dog. Kept that quiet, didn't you? You and Carrick planning on adding a third?"

"Not immediately, perhaps we could talk about this tonight?" Or not at all. He could see how uncomfortable Thea was growing.

Over the idea of him and Carrick being together? Because she liked them? He wished he knew.

"Thea, I'd like to see you in my office please," Jardin demanded.

Walking into his office, he sat behind his desk. She walked in slowly, tablet in hand. She took a seat across from him. She looked paler than yesterday with dark circles under her eyes.

"How was the meeting?"

"Fine. Did you sleep at all last night?" he snapped out. Then he winced. That hadn't been what he'd intended to ask her. But, fuck it, she looked like death warmed over.

"I'm fine."

That wasn't a yes.

"I know there's something wrong, Thea."

She straightened, her face shutting down. "I apologize if I let my personal life affect my work yesterday, it won't happen again."

He tapped his fingers against his desk. To push her or not? He didn't want her running from him, shutting him out completely like she had Carrick.

"Thea, you know you can come to me if something's wrong." He made his voice warmer, cajoling.

Shock filled her face. As though she'd never heard him speak that way. Fuck, she was never going to open up to him. She saw him as a cold, emotionless bastard. That wasn't really him at all. It was just a façade to keep people at bay. To stop himself from getting hurt.

"Thank you. I really am fine."

"If you're more comfortable speaking to Carrick about it—"

"Nothing is wrong."

He narrowed his gaze. She was still his employee; threatening her with a spanking was going to land him in the middle of a lawsuit. But Carrick certainly could.

"About what happened yesterday—"

"You don't have to explain anything to me," she told him. "I could tell you knew each other."

"That's twice you've interrupted me, Miss Garrison."

She bit her lip. "Sorry."

Hmm, it was getting harder to remember she was his employee and not his sub. Maybe he should fire her again. Would make his life easier in some ways because he had a feeling it wouldn't be long until he gave in and put her over his knee. But harder in others because having her close by settled the protective beast inside him.

Sort of.

"Carrick and I were once best friends. We also shared a lover."

He waited for her reaction then saw the way her mouth popped open. He was taking a gamble here, guessing she'd be more intrigued than horrified. That she wouldn't spread his business around the water cooler. But from what he'd seen, Thea had more integrity in her little toe than most of the other people in this building. He was betting even if she were uncomfortable, she'd never say anything.

But mostly what he saw in her face was longing and arousal.

"Does it shock you? That we lived in a permanent ménage?" he asked silkily.

He knew talking about this while they were in his office was pushing the boundaries. But those boundaries had been pushed yesterday while they'd been out to lunch. And when else was he going to get the chance to speak to her?

Right now, she was a captive audience. One he intended to take advantage of.

She licked her lips. "Um, it might have before I had a chat with

Maddox. He told me about Haven. About how polyamorous relationships were normal there."

Okay, that shocked him enough to have him sitting forward in his chair and resting his arms on the desk. Why had his cousin been talking to her about relationships?

"You know Maddox is a player, right? He's never been serious about a girl. He won't settle down."

She blinked. Opened her mouth. Closed it again. "Are you warning me off your cousin?"

"Has he made a move on you?"

He was going to kill the asshole.

"No." She frowned. "I mean, he flirts a lot but I'm thinking that's just his personality."

"It is. He won't ever give you anything more than a good roll in the sheets."

"Because there's no way a man could want anything more than that with me?" she spat out.

Christ.

Warning signals rang in his head. He should have left this to Carrick. He was smoother with these things. Jardin was feeling a bit possessive of Thea, and it was coming out in ways he didn't intend.

A *bit* possessive? Right.

He cleared his throat. "That's not what I meant."

She stood.

"Sit back down," he barked. Then winced. Fuck. Yes, he should have left this up to Carrick.

"Unless this is about work, then I don't think I need to be in here."

He deserved that. "I'm sorry I spoke like that. I just don't want my cousin to hurt you."

"Well, he hasn't. I've met him twice. He's only been friendly. He's not interested in me like that. Let's face it, he's way out of my league anyway. And I can't just believe I said that to my boss," she muttered.

He frowned. So, she would be interested if Maddox showed some interest?

And what did she mean he was out of her league?

"Can we just get back to talking about work?" she asked.

Perhaps that was best. Before he found himself without a personal assistant. After they'd discussed a few things and she'd left, he pulled out his phone and called Carrick.

"Hey," his deep voice answered the phone.

Jardin's entire body relaxed at that sound. How long since he'd felt such ease? So happy?

Since Carrick was last in your life? But then, Sally had been around. Ruining things.

"Hey yourself."

"Miss me?" Carrick teased.

"Like you wouldn't believe," he said fiercely, not meaning just these past few hours they'd been apart.

There was silence on the other end then Carrick cleared his throat. "Me too."

"But that's not why I'm calling. We're having dinner with Maddox tonight."

"Oh. And do you want him to know about our relationship?"

Jardin scowled at that. "You think we should keep it a secret?"

"I don't . . . but I thought you might want to."

"Like fuck. I don't care who knows. Well, I'd rather no one at work knew but that's because they're gossipy assholes. But otherwise, I don't give a shit. You're mine. I've claimed you. There's no way I'm hiding you like a dirty secret."

"Say what you really mean, I'm finding it hard to read between the lines," Carrick teased but there was a hitch in his voice that betrayed his real feelings.

"Ass," Jardin growled at him.

"I guess I can do dinner with your cousin. It's been a long time since I saw him. How's Thea?"

"Jumpy. Secretive. Came close several times to putting her over my knee."

"Jardin," Carrick warned.

"I know. I know. I thought Maddox might have been coming on to her. She's under the mistaken impression that he's way out of her league."

"She made a few comments to me about her weight," Carrick admitted. "Think she's got a skewed view of herself.

"We'll add that to the list of things to teach her. Anyway, I fucked up a bit when I was trying to tell her about our relationship. I got to the bit about how we used to be in a ménage relationship and the conversation unraveled."

"You want me to come in before dinner to speak to her, don't you?"

Even after two years apart, Carrick could still read his mind.

"She leaves here at five."

"I'll be in by four-thirty. Not sure she'll talk to me, though."

"You've got more of a chance than I have. And if she won't talk, you actually can spank her ass."

"And land myself with an assault charge?" Carrick asked.

"I know a good lawyer."

"Right, and all it will cost me is a few BJs huh?"

"More than a few. He's very expensive. And particular. Although you give very good head."

"Asshole. Now I've got a hard-on."

"Be a good boy and I'll take care of that later on for you," Jardin purred.

"Fuck. Later."

The call ended and Jardin grinned. Finally, things were coming together. He had Carrick back. They'd work on bringing Thea into their relationship.

Yep, things would work out perfectly.

17

"Hello, Thea."

She squealed, turning away from the storage cupboard to find Carrick standing in front of her desk, watching her from too-knowing eyes.

"Shit. You gave me a fright."

He raised his eyebrows. "You're very pale, rocket. Why don't you sit down?"

He was concerned, for her? Shouldn't he hate her? Yesterday, he'd been so angry at her. And he'd had every right to be. She'd completely messed up. Treated him badly.

With a hand that shook, she reached up and tucked a stray piece of hair behind her ear.

"Thea?"

"What? Sorry. Did you say something?"

"Thea, sit down," he said more firmly. "Before you fall down."

Not bad advice, really. She grabbed the chair and sort of slumped into it. She managed to give him a small smile. "Sorry."

"What's going on? Aren't you feeling well?" His gaze roamed

over her. She guessed she looked like shit. Why shouldn't her outside reflect her inside?

"Are you here to see Jardin?" she deflected. "He's on a call but he'll be free soon."

"I'm meeting him but I'm early," he said, not pointing out that she'd avoided answering him.

"Please take a seat. Can I get you tea? Coffee?"

There. She sounded almost normal. Then she noticed how his gaze was on her hands. Her shaking hands. She tucked them down under the desk.

"When's the last time you ate, rocket?"

Please stop calling me that. Please stop being nice to me. She didn't deserve it.

"I'm so sorry, Carrick."

He sat in the chair across from her. Today he was dressed in another black shirt and black jeans. God, he was gorgeous.

She wished the circumstances were different. That she didn't have that threat hanging over her.

Right. Because things would have worked out for you both. He's with Jardin now.

She wasn't quite sure how their relationship worked. Were they together-together? Did that mean they were both bi? Because she knew Jardin had dated plenty of women; she'd seen them in the society pages. The Malones were wealthy and respected. Powerful. And people lapped up information about them. That's why there was so much gossip around the office about Jardin.

More than one of the other PA's had tried to throw herself at him.

Pathetic.

Oh, like you haven't thought about what it might be like to be his?

Scary. Intriguing. Safe.

She'd bet anyone he cared about was kept under close watch. Jardin was an intense guy. Having all his focus on her might be almost too much. She wasn't sure she was strong enough to take it. Not without someone else to even him out.

What? Like Carrick?

Okay, ever since he'd mentioned the fact they'd been in a relationship before with someone else, she hadn't been able to think of anything else.

What would it be like to be theirs?

"What exactly are you sorry for?" he asked in that low drawl of his.

She wished she could get up and leave. Escape. But she owed this to him. An explanation. Of sorts. Because she couldn't exactly tell him everything.

"I'm sorry I didn't help you after promising to. And for ignoring your calls and text messages."

He nodded. "You're forgiven on one condition."

"What's that?

"You tell me why."

Fuck a duck. She couldn't tell him the truth. She licked her dry lips. "I have a lot going on in my life. This job and my brothers take up all my time. I didn't think it was fair to you to continue things when I couldn't give you much."

There. That sounded plausible.

"I understand."

She nearly heaved out a sigh of relief.

"Too bad I don't believe a word of it."

Fuck. Shit.

She gaped at him. "What do you mean? It's the truth."

"Oh, I'm sure your job and brothers take a lot of your time. Can't be easy to be a sole parent to two young boys because your father is a useless prick. However, if that were the reason you ghosted me, you would have just told me. Likely you wouldn't have come on that date with me in the first place. Or offered to help me with my mess of an office. Now, I thought maybe I'd done something to scare you off. But, again, you would have given me a reason. No, I think something else entirely happened to you. What aren't you telling me, Thea?"

"There's nothing else. You're imagining things. I simply don't want a relationship with you. I'm not interested."

He snorted out a laugh. "Now you are getting desperate for excuses. I know it's definitely not that by the way you reacted to me." He leaned forward. "And just so you know, once we're in a relationship together, you're getting your butt spanked for all the lying. If you're lucky, I'll do it. If you're unlucky, he will."

Carrick nodded over to Jardin's office.

Her pulse raced. She should have been outraged at his words. Definitely should have gotten up and told him the conversation was over. Instead she sat there, stunned, her clit throbbing at the thought of being spanked by them both.

You've got problems, Thea.

This is all Maddox's fault. He started her thinking about ménages and spanking and . . . shit. She'd gone too long without saying something and the look on Carrick's face could only be described as smug.

"You can't threaten to spank me!"

"Not the first time I have."

"No . . . but . . ." Back then she'd thought there was a chance for them.

"You know much about BDSM, Thea?" Carrick asked, studying her closely. As though he could read all her secrets.

Holy. Shit.

"A bit," she rasped. "Are you saying that you're a . . ."

"Dom? Yeah, I am. Although there are times I enjoy a bit of pain too. So maybe I'm more of a switch. Although, I don't think I could bottom for anyone except the man in there. Just like I'm the only man for him."

"You and he are . . ."

"Together. Yep. It's still new but we know each other well. It fits. You just know when it works, right?"

She nodded. She wouldn't know.

"You ever played?"

"I'm not a-a submissive or a Domme."

"Rocket, I know you're not a Domme. But you could enjoy submitting. To the right person. You certainly enjoy the idea of being spanked."

Earth swallow me up now.

"We shouldn't be talking about this," she whispered. Her nipples had hardened to points and her panties were getting wet with how turned on she was. "He's my boss and you're—"

"A friend. A friend who's attracted to you and who wants to get to know you better. Who's worried about you." The sincerity in his face struck her hard.

"You don't need to worry about me. You shouldn't. Yesterday—"

"Yesterday, I overreacted. Felt like I'd gotten the dirty end of the stick. But I have to say, I've never been more grateful for having to meet with my accountant."

"Because of Jardin?"

"And you."

"You seemed to think that I'd . . . that he and I . . . I didn't know who you were!"

"I know, rocket. Jardin and I have a past. One where we both made mistakes and got hurt. I'm sorry for scaring you yesterday. I'm sorrier for hurting you. How's your wrist?"

She looked down at her wrist, trying to figure out what he was talking about. Oh, right, when he'd grabbed her.

"Can I have a look at it, please?"

"It's fine," she dismissed. "It had a bruise from the other day. Banged it while I was doing some stuff around the house. That's all."

"Then there's no reason I can't check it. It would make me feel better."

"Maybe you should go wait in Jardin's office."

"And disturb the bear while he's working? I don't think so."

"I have a lot of work to do."

"And I'm interrupting."

She gave an abrupt nod and expected him to move away. Instead he leaned back in his chair to study her. "Jardin told you we used to share a woman?"

"I'm not sure how this is any of my business." Hadn't he shared enough personal information? She was already reeling over the fact that both he and Jardin were into BDSM, that they were Doms. Well, Carrick might be a switch. Holy. Shit.

If things were different, she might be all over that. She'd always been curious. One of her past sexual partners had been willing to get a bit kinky in the bedroom. She'd loved being restrained. She wasn't so sure about all the protocol stuff though.

"You're not? Huh, he really did make a mess of things this morning."

"What?" she asked.

"Jardin and I used to be best friends," he continued on as though she hadn't spoken. "We shared a partner, Sally. I thought she wanted us both. I also thought that sharing her was the only way I could be close to Jardin."

"You mean the two of you weren't—" she broke off with a blush. "Sorry, that's none of my business."

"You can ask as many questions as you like, rocket. I brought this up. Nothing's off-limits to you."

Was he serious? Why would he want to talk to her about it? She was nothing to either of them. It was so confusing.

"We weren't together like that back then. I came out as bisexual years ago. I would have told you that, had our relationship gone beyond one date."

Shame flooded her.

"Does that worry you?" he asked, his face shutting down.

She frowned slightly. "Should it?"

He shrugged. "Lots of people don't get it. I've had partners who were intimidated by it for some reason. Had a fallout with my family over it. They wanted me to pick a side."

"Seriously?"

"Yeah, and they wanted me to pick the female side. I refused. Haven't spoken to them in close to eighteen years."

That was so sad.

"I'm so sorry."

"Truth is, rocket, I'm better off without them. I met Jardin about seven years later. I was attracted to him, but he was my closest friend and he wasn't bi or gay. Or at least I didn't think he was. We were best friends for years before we met Sally, and she got involved with both of us. I thought she wanted both of us. Turns out, she just wanted to be the next Mrs. Jardin Malone. In the beginning I think she got off on having two dicks to lead around. Course, nobody leads Jardin around. He's a workaholic, and I'm sure I don't need to tell you how, uh, abrupt and arrogant he can be."

She actually smiled at that description.

"Sally wanted us both to worship her. Things started to unravel. I felt like a third wheel. I never told Jardin though and that's on me. Thought I'd lose him to her. Turns out, he was starting to see her true colors. He confronted her, told her it was over. That night she drank too much and drowned."

"Oh, God."

"I was at home. I had the music up loud. I was avoiding her. Was just sitting there while she drowned."

"Oh, Carrick, you couldn't have known." She got up and walked around to his chair, kneeling on the floor in front of him.

She reached up and took his hand in hers. "It wasn't anyone's fault."

"I was an idiot, though," a deep voice said from the doorway. She started, her eyes rising to Jardin, who had his hands in his pockets as he leaned against the frame. His gaze was intense as he looked down at her. "I felt guilty and I withdrew from him. He thought I didn't want him around and I lost him for two years."

"And now you've found each other again." That was so romantic.

"Finally got the chance to tell Carrick how I feel about him. How I've always felt about him."

"You left it so long . . ." she trailed off, hoping Jardin didn't see that as a criticism.

"I was a fool. When I tracked him down, I saw him with someone and thought he was happy."

"Short story is, I wasn't happy," Carrick told her. "And now I know that Jardin has the same feelings for me as I do for him."

The way they stared at each other made her heart hurt. She wished she had that. Desperately.

"So now you have a happy ever after."

"Not yet. But we're planning on getting there," Jardin told her. "Just need to find the perfect third."

"You want a ménage again?"

Shit. Should she really ask something so personal? But why were they telling her?

"This is probably not a conversation we should be having." She quickly stood and Carrick stood as well.

"Not here, no," Jardin agreed. "Would you like to come to dinner with us, Thea?"

He wanted her to go to dinner with them? Why? Not that she could, but they didn't mean they wanted her to be their third?

She shook off the thought as ridiculous.

Yeah? Then why was Carrick talking to you about BDSM? About being a sub? Why did he watch you with hungry eyes?

But what about Jardin? He was harder to read.

"I can't. I have to pick up the boys," she said quickly.

"Can you arrange a babysitter for this weekend? Maybe we could take you out to dinner on Friday night?" Carrick asked. "Then we could be on our own."

"And you can tell us what's going on with you," Jardin told her.

Oh. So that's why they wanted to get her alone. They wanted to know what was going on with her.

Disappointment flooded her.

You're an idiot, Thea.

Well, that wasn't happening.

"I don't . . . I'm not sure why you're asking me out to dinner. But I'm really sorry . . . I can't . . . I have to go," she said abruptly.

She walked around her desk to grab her handbag.

"Thea, wait," Carrick said.

"I'm really sorry for the way I treated you," she said hastily. "I hope you two will be happy."

Jardin scowled. "Thea, what—"

She raced out of the room before either of them could detain her. And although Jardin's voice was filled with clear command when he told her to stop, she paid him no heed.

It was better this way. She could have agreed to dinner, knowing she wouldn't turn up but that didn't feel right. And she couldn't tell them what was going on without endangering them as well.

No, getting away was the right option.

CARRICK RAN his hand down his face. "Shit."

"I should have stayed in my office."

He looked over at Jardin and shook his head. "Not your fault. She wasn't gonna open up to me."

"I pushed too hard with the dinner suggestion." Jardin looked unsure. It wasn't a usual look for him.

"Not sure how we're going to get her to open up to us when she won't even give us a few hours of time," Carrick said with frustration.

"We'll get to her," Jardin said. "Even if we have to kidnap her."

"Finally some decent food." Maddox stared at the burger on his plate like it was a gold nugget.

Carrick had to grin. Maddox Malone was just as he remembered him. Outspoken, outrageous and funny as hell.

Maddox picked up the burger and took a huge bite. "Yeah, this is the shit." He didn't bother to swallow before he spoke.

Jardin sighed, grimacing.

They'd ended up at a steak house for dinner. Not somewhere Jardin would usually eat and he looked out of place in his suit. Not that he seemed to care.

"Could you swallow before you speak?" Jardin said coolly, cutting up his steak.

"Hmm, nope. I'm starving. Jeeves hates me."

"His name is Gerald not Jeeves."

Maddox took a few gulps of beer then flagged down the waitress. "Another beer thanks, darlin'."

The waitress smiled at him, leaning over him to grab the extra glass. "Sure thing, sweetie."

Carrick shook his head as Maddox watched her walk away. "You haven't changed."

Maddox grinned. "Sure as shit hope not."

"So what did you want to talk to me about?" Jardin asked after the waitress brought back a new beer for Maddox.

"Oh, now he wants to talk."

"Maddox," Jardin said warningly.

"How is that cute PA of yours?" Maddox asked slyly.

Jardin tapped his fingers on the table, clearly losing his patience. "We're not here to discuss Thea."

"Sore spot, is she?"

"Maddox, you came to me for help. This is not the way to get it. You guys have never wanted me to visit before so why are you in an all-fire hurry to get me there nos?"

Maddox placed his hand over his chest dramatically. "Jardin, you wound me. You're family. Our house is your house."

"Right, that's why Tanner takes great joy in using my car as target practice."

"Well, now, that's just our way of saying we care."

Jardin let out a breath. "What do you want?"

A serious look crossed Maddox's face, surprising Carrick. "There's this big corporate company. They've been trying to buy up some land in Haven. They're putting pressure on a number of locals. They want to build a big ugly strip mall. We need to stop them. And we need your help."

Jardin pinched the top of his nose. "You do realize I'm a family lawyer. This isn't my area of expertise."

"So you won't help."

Jardin shared a look with Carrick. "I didn't say that. I'll look into it. I can probably come to Haven in about a week's time."

"Awesome. Make sure you bring Thea with you. She might like the place so much that she'll stay."

Jardin shot him a quelling look.

"What? She'd fit in well in Haven. Somebody would snatch her up real quick."

Both Carrick and Jardin glared at Maddox. He just grinned. "Like that, is it?"

"Thea is ours," Jardin told him.

Maddox hit his cousin on the back. "Congratulations on pulling your head out of your ass, cousin. Isn't the air fresher out here?"

Jardin just groaned.

Yep, Maddox hadn't changed one bit.

18

Thea wasn't really listening to her brothers as she drove up into the driveway. She'd picked them up after soccer practice.

Maybe she shouldn't have run away from Carrick and Jardin like she had.

Had she made a mistake? Perhaps she should have told them what was going on. But, no, she couldn't risk something happening to Keir and Ace if she said something. This was her problem to solve.

Fuck. Shit. She was so scared.

"Why's the door open?" Ace asked, interrupting her thoughts.

"Did you forget to lock it, Thea?" Keir glared at her. God, he was nine going on fifty.

"No, I didn't forget to lock it." She frowned as she viewed the open door. It looked fine. No signs of forced entry.

"Do you think Dad's here?" Ace whispered.

"Why don't the two of you leave your bags and go see Diego?" she suggested.

Ace gave a happy grin. Always so carefree and innocent. She wanted him to stay that way for as long as possible.

Keir scowled again. "We should stay with you."

"I'll be fine." Her pulse pounded. Was it her father? Wasn't he with Silvers? But if not him then who? "Go on, leave your bags."

Keir hesitated again.

"Keir. Go." She gave him a firm look.

"Fine," he muttered. "But he better not hurt you again."

Ace's smile faltered.

"Keir," she warned.

"Come on, Ace, let's go." Keir tugged his brother away and Thea took a deep breath. She opened the door cautiously. The inside was as dark and dingy as usual.

But there was an air of evil that was new.

Jesus, Thea. Your imagination is working overtime.

Then she saw him, standing in the middle of the room.

Unfortunately, not her imagination then.

"Mr. Silvers."

"Now, now, my dear. I rather think we're on a first-name basis now, don't you?" he said in that oily voice. "Call me Derrick, I insist."

"Derrick," she whispered. "How can I help you?"

"Hmm, how can you help me? Such an open-ended question." He stepped toward her. "You can help me in lots of ways, Thea."

Her breath came faster, panic making the room spin. Or maybe that was just because she hadn't eaten in days. She saw movement in the doorway leading to the bedrooms and couldn't believe she'd missed the hulking man standing there. Milo.

Shit. Shit.

"Did you like my roses, my dear?" He reached out and brushed a lock of hair from her face.

She forced herself to stay still. Not to shudder in disgust or push him away.

It was hard. Very hard.

"They were lovely. You needn't have."

He grasped hold of her chin. Oh, crap. Was he going to kiss her? Please don't let him kiss her. She wasn't sure she could fake that.

"Of course I had to. I'm courting you, after all. Doesn't matter that by Saturday you'll be mine." He looked around with a sneer of disgust. "Of course, if you'd rather not wait you can come with me now. By tonight, you can be drinking champagne in my mansion. You'll find being mine has a lot of perks, my dear. You won't have to work, you'll have all new clothes, plenty of good food, a mansion, staff at your beck and call."

And all she had to do was sell her soul. Yep, sounded like a great bargain to her.

"W-what about my brothers?" she asked.

"Ah, yes, Ace and Keir."

He knew their names. It sent goosebumps over her skin.

Of course he does, idiot. He knows where you work. He knows where you live.

"Yes," she whispered.

"They're important to you."

"Yes." She didn't know if that was the right answer to give.

"We'll look into boarding schools," he said dismissively. "I will admit to being a greedy man and wanting you all to myself."

Maybe some women found him charming. Jardin could be forceful. He could be arrogant. But he didn't make her stomach roil in fear and horror.

"O-okay," she managed to get out.

Then he leaned in and brushed his cold lips across hers.

Don't gag. Don't gag.

"You won't come now?"

Her mind raced for a good excuse. "I . . . I need to talk to the boys. Get stuff packed up."

Irritation filled his face. "You don't need any of this shit. I told you I'd buy you all new stuff."

"Yes, but the boys have things they will want to keep. Tomorrow. I can't just spring this on them. It's not fair."

She waited for his anger, braced herself for it. Instead he just smiled and ran a thumb over her cheek. "I knew you'd make an excellent mother to my children. Until tomorrow then."

He quickly left, Milo following him. The big guard didn't even spare her a glance. She stared out the window as a black car pulled up to the curb and Silvers and Milo climbed in.

As soon as he was gone, her legs gave in. She collapsed to the floor and pulled her legs up against her chest, curling into a ball.

Fuck. Fuck. Fuck.

19

It was the only plan she could come up with. It wasn't exactly a good plan and she wasn't sure it would work. But she had to try.

Ace and Keir needed her. They weren't going to be sent away to boarding school. And she wasn't going to become some criminal asshole's wife. She had no doubt that if she stuck around, by tomorrow night, she'd be a prisoner. Kept by a predator. Her free will gone.

But she needed to be smart about it. She dug up her stash of cash that she had hidden under one of the floorboards in her closet. It wasn't nearly enough. And there was only one way she could come up with more cash to fund their escape. She drew out the necklace that was hidden in with the cash. It was gold filigree interspersed with diamonds and sapphires. She didn't know where her mother had gotten it. Certainly not from her husband.

When she was fifteen, her mother had shown her the hidey-hole in her closet and the necklace. She'd told her if she ever needed the money, it was there. It was the only thing she had left of her. Wiping the tears from her eyes, she stashed the necklace and the cash in a pocket in her handbag.

She looked at the time on her watch. The boys would be up soon. She'd spent all night awake and planning. She knew just what she had to do. While they were sleeping, she'd packed one school bag with clothes, their tablets and headphones and some spare clothes for her. The other school bag held as much food as it could hold without the bag looking suspiciously large. She was under no illusions they weren't being watched.

Now the tricky part. Explaining this to the boys.

"So, some bad guy wants to marry you and move you into his house?" Keir asked. They were up and dressed in their school uniforms. She was wearing a work outfit. They were just finishing up breakfast while she gulped down a cup of coffee. She was going to need the caffeine to get through today.

"Yes." In a nutshell. She hadn't told them about their father's role in all this. But Keir gave her a knowing look. Yeah, he knew way too much for his age. She wished she could give him a more carefree childhood.

"But that's so cool! Does he have a gun? Are we gonna live in some flash house?" Ace bounced around on his chair.

"Idiot!" Keir told him. "He's not gonna want us. Besides, that flash house is all paid for from him breaking the law and stuff."

"Keir, speak nicer to your brother," she admonished then she turned to Ace. "But he's right, honey. Crime isn't cool. And this man, he isn't a good man."

Ace chewed his lip. "He doesn't want me and Keir?"

"Baby, I don't want him anywhere near the two of you. You're my priority. Always."

"I'm not a baby," Ace muttered.

"No, you're not." Shit. She already had a headache.

"What are we gonna do?" Keir asked. "Do we need to tell the cops?"

"This man . . . the police won't be able to do much." She didn't want to dispel their belief in the police. But they couldn't go to the cops.

"Then what're we gonna do?" Ace asked.

"We're going to have to leave," she said as gently as she could. Both boys stiffened then looked at each other.

"Where are we gonna go?" Keir asked.

She licked her dry lips. "I'm not exactly sure yet. First thing we need to do is get away safely."

"What do you mean?" Ace asked.

"She means we're being watched, right?"

"I think so," she said.

"So how do we do it then?" Keir asked.

"I've packed some stuff in your backpacks. Keir, you've got our clothes and the tablets. Ace, I'll carry yours since it's got our food. We're gonna drive to school like normal. I'm going to walk you in and then we'll go out the back entrance. I'll have an Uber waiting. We'll take it to the mall. Go in one entrance. Out the other to the bus stop. Take a bus to a station. Get us tickets out of here."

Both boys watched her with wide eyes. She waited tensely for their reaction.

"That. Is. So. Cool." Ace grinned wide.

"We should change our clothes," Keir said.

"What?"

"In the mall. We should change our clothes. Our uniform is too noticeable. We can change in a bathroom. You too. It will help."

Why hadn't she thought of that?

Then again, the two of them were far smarter than her.

"Good thinking. Thing is, I need the two of you to act like this is any other day, okay?" She wasn't worried about Keir, but Ace was another story.

"We can do that!" Ace said cheerfully.

"We got this, Thea. Don't worry about us."

Thing was, she did little else, except when she was thinking about Jardin and Carrick. She winced as she thought of how angry Jardin was going to be with her.

But he'd get over it. He'd find a new assistant. They'd find someone to love together. They'd live happily ever after.

Right now, she just had to focus on keeping herself and her brothers alive.

CARRICK ANSWERED HIS PHONE, smiling as he saw Jardin's name. He'd only left him an hour ago. But he wasn't complaining. After two years of being on his own, he wanted to spend every second he could with the other man.

"Forget something?" he answered.

"She's gone!" Jardin's frantic voice came through the phone.

"What? What do you mean she's gone?"

There was only one *she* he could be talking about. Carrick's heart started to race.

"She wasn't here when I came in and when I checked my email there was one from her, tendering her resignation."

"Fuck. Shit. Do you think we scared her off yesterday?"

"I don't know. But we need to find her. What's she going to do for money? What's she thinking? Fuck."

"All right. Let's not panic." It was a sign of how much Jardin truly did care about her. Because he was usually the calm one. "Have you tried calling her?"

"Yeah. It goes straight to voicemail."

"Fuck. Okay. What about her address?"

"HR should have it on file. Let me check."

"Pick me up on the way there. I'm going with you."

JARDIN WAS ABOUT to lose it. And it was going to be epic. He stared out at the dilapidated shack in front of him in horror.

"This is where she fucking lives? Here! How the fuck did I not know this!"

Goddamn him. He should have checked. He'd never have allowed her to continue living here if he'd known.

"You couldn't have known, I didn't," Carrick replied calmly.

"But I knew things had to be hard for her. I knew the boys were on scholarships to that school." He'd checked up on that. "I just didn't realize things were this bad."

"We know now. We'll help her."

If they could find her. They approached the house and Jardin knocked.

"Thea! Thea, are you in there?" He tried the door. Locked. He looked over at Carrick, who sighed and started peering in windows.

"Fuck it," Jardin said. "It's not like we're gonna let her live here any longer." He used his foot to kick the door open. Piece of shit crumpled in.

It didn't take them long to see that no one was home. And that the inside was possibly worse than the outside.

"There're still clothes here," Carrick said, walking through the rooms.

Jardin was in the kitchen. "Hardly any fucking food, though. Christ."

"Do you think we should wait here for her?"

He frowned, thinking it through. "I'm going to ring the school. Just make sure the boys are there."

"Why? You don't think she's actually run off? Why would she leave town? Besides, her clothes are still here."

"There's barely anything in her closet."

"Probably because she didn't own much," Carrick said gently.

"Fuck. Fuck. I'm checking anyway." He had a bad fucking feeling about all of it.

"Will they tell you? You're not their guardian."

Oh, they'd tell him.

A few minutes later, he got off the phone. Carrick eyed him, face pale. "They're not there, are they?"

"No. And the secretary very gleefully told me that they just had her car towed from out front. Fuck it. She's gone and we have no idea where she is!"

THEA PULLED the old car over to the side of the road. They'd gotten off the bus in Lafayette and stayed the night in a cheap motel so she could pawn their mother's necklace. She'd used some of the money to buy a crappy car. Although, it was actually better than their last car.

She'd been driving for hours, only stopping to pee and so the boys could stretch their legs. Right now, they were asleep in the back seat. The sun was rising over the horizon as she stared out at the sign.

Welcome to Haven, Texas.

Hopefully, Maddox was right, and this place really did look out for women. She hoped it was big enough for her to blend in. Maddox said he lived on a ranch out of town, so maybe she wouldn't see him. Or at least not for a while.

Even if she did see him, what did it matter? What would he do? Tell Jardin? He wouldn't care.

And if Jardin comes to visit?

Well, she'd cross that bridge when she got to it. Right now, she had to find a job and somewhere for them to stay.

One thing at a time. And if this place didn't work out, they'd just have to go somewhere else.

20

Haven was an interesting place.

They'd only been there a few days and she'd just enrolled the boys in school today. The teachers were welcoming. It was small, less than two hundred students. Unfortunately, there wasn't an advanced class they could go into, and she worried they wouldn't be pushed enough. But for the moment it would have to do.

She'd even found a job. She couldn't use any of her former references, so it was just a job cleaning some houses and businesses. Her boss, Marcy, was getting on in years and needed some help. The pay wasn't a lot, but the owner of the motel was giving her a cheap, weekly rate and she was on the lookout for a small rental.

The people there were unusual. And Maddox was right, polyamorous relationships were very normal. And there was even a BDSM club, Saxon's. Which most of the population of Haven seemed to be members of. It was crazy how open everyone was. And friendly. But it wasn't home.

As she hurried down the street towards the diner, a strange

feeling came over her. She paused and looked around. It felt like someone was watching her.

She shook it off. There was no way Silvers could have found her. They'd taken every precaution.

Don't bother trying to run or hide. I will find you. And it won't end well for you.

Panic flooded her and she fought hard to take a breath. Maybe she should grab the boys and run again. But she didn't know that Silvers had found her. And she couldn't help but feel safe here. Maddox had been telling the truth when he'd told her the men of Haven were protective of women. She'd seen signs of it all over the place.

She was just being paranoid. She had a new burner phone, she'd left her old one at the mall where she and the boys had changed clothes. She hadn't used any of her cards. And Marcy was paying her under the table.

She'd been worried about enrolling the boys in school, but after talking to the school they'd promised that no one would be able to track the boys down. They'd also told her to go speak to the sheriff if she was in trouble.

It was inevitable that she'd need a chat with the sheriff. Especially from what Maddox had told her about Haven. But she'd avoid it for as long as possible.

She pushed the door of the diner with a yawn. She was so tired. She was trying to keep her spending down so she could afford a down payment on a rental, so she'd just been eating breakfast and dinner. And she was feeling more than a bit light-headed.

Coffee. She needed coffee. Which she could have gotten at the motel, however Marcy suggested she ask the diner owner about her apartment upstairs.

She slid onto a stool at the counter, next to two women who were chatting away with each other.

"Flick, I don't think you should ask West to marry you," the woman closest to her said. She had long strawberry-blonde hair and a fairly large baby bump.

"Why not? It's the twenty-first century. Women can ask men to marry them," the other woman replied. Her dark hair lay in loose waves down her back.

"Yes, but not Malone men," the first woman hissed back. "They're cavemen. They haven't come out of the dark ages. You ask West to marry you and he'll likely spank your ass."

She stiffened? These women knew the Malones? And it sounded like at least one of them was involved with one of Maddox's brothers.

Holy. Shit.

Maybe she should just slip off the stool and slink away. But there was no use hiding if she was going to live here. And it wasn't like they knew who she was.

"What can I get ya?" the waitress stepped up to her, chewing gum. Her name tag said Doris.

"Coffee, please," she said quietly.

Both women had stopped talking beside her.

Doris grunted and poured her a cup of coffee. "You'll also have pie."

"Oh, no, thank you."

"You want pie. You need pie. I'll get you pie."

She gaped after the weird waitress in shock. What the hell?

"You get used to her," the dark-haired woman leaned around the other one to say to her with a smile. "Doris is . . . well . . ."

"Different," the strawberry-blonde haired woman supplied. She smiled at Thea. "Hi, I'm Mia."

Holy. Shit. Maddox had talked about Mia. She was married to his brother, Alec, who spanked her when she broke the rules.

Thea really wished she didn't know that. She could feel her cheeks getting red.

"And I'm Flick," the other woman said cheerfully while Mia studied her closely.

"Hi, I'm Thea."

A plate filled with a slice of cherry pie landed in front of her. Her mouth watered. But she shook her head at Doris. "I don't need any pie. Thank you."

Doris scowled.

"I'll take the pie, Doris darlin'," a deep voice said on her left.

She whirled around. How hadn't she heard him come up on her? Shit. Her heart raced.

"Hello there, darlin'," Maddox said to her, taking a seat on her left. "Just what are you doing in Haven?"

"You two know each other?" Mia asked in surprise.

"Met Thea in New Orleans. She works for Jardin."

"Oh, you know Jardin?" Mia smiled at her. "He's great, isn't he? He helped me when I needed it. If it weren't for him, I'd be dead."

Jesus. Really?

Thea gaped at her.

"And I'd never have met Alec, my husband."

"Now, Mia, you can't be blaming Jardin for the fact that you chose the wrong Malone brother to marry. You know you'll always have my heart."

Mia rolled her eyes at Maddox. "All the younger Malone brothers are terrible flirts, but I'm sure I don't have to tell you that."

"Hey, I resent that. I'm an excellent flirt." Maddox dug into the slice of pie. "So, darlin' you gonna tell me why you're here and not back in New Orleans tied to my cousin's bed while he and Carrick do terrible, unmentionable things to you."

"Maddox!" Mia scolded.

Thea glared at him. "I was his personal assistant."

"Saw the way he looked at you, darlin'. He wanted to be far more *personal* with you."

Flick groaned. "That was horrible. I apologize for him, Thea."

Maddox finished up his pie and wiped his face. "Does Jardin know you're here, Thea?"

She shook her head. There was no point lying when he could easily find out.

"Didn't think so. Way he and Carrick talked about you when we went out for dinner, I couldn't imagine either of them letting you come here on your own."

A blush filled her cheeks, and she gazed down at her coffee.

"Will you tell him I'm here?"

"That depends," he said.

"On what?"

"On why you're here. What happened? Did those two scare you away? Couldn't stand the idea of a ménage? Or was it the fact that Jardin's a sadist?"

"A . . . a sadist?"

Maddox grimaced while Mia hissed a warning at him. "Sorry. Figured you knew. You know they're both Doms?"

"Yes, Carrick told me. But he never said anything about . . . what does that mean? That he likes to inflict pain?"

Holy. Shit.

"Only with partners who are consenting and want to receive pain," Mia said quickly.

"I don't think that I could ever . . . not that it matters. We're not together."

All three of them gave her varying looks of disbelief.

"Are you in trouble, Thea?" Mia asked. "We can help you. Jardin can help you. He's a good guy."

She shook her head. "I'm fine. I don't need any help. If you'll excuse me, I have to pick my brothers up from their friends house."

It wasn't until after she'd fled that she realized she hadn't asked the diner owner about her apartment.

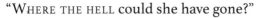

"Where the hell could she have gone?"

Carrick watched as Jardin paced back and forth across the office. They were at the Malone family home. If you could call it a home. The place was enormous. And old. It was gorgeous, but it wasn't exactly homey. Mostly, Carrick was scared to touch anything in case he broke it.

Then Gerald, the butler, would have his ass.

Jardin's oldest brother, Regent, watched him with cool, dark eyes. Regent was scary as shit. If Jardin could be arrogant and cold, then Regent was ice. Pure, chilling ice. The only time he ever saw him warm up was around their sister, Lottie.

"She hasn't used her accounts. We found her phone in the mall. We know she took an Uber from the school to the mall, but we lost her after that," Maxim, the youngest Malone brother said.

Regent was the oldest then it was Jardin, Victor then Maxim. Lottie was the baby. And the only girl. Protected and coddled, especially after all that she'd been through.

"What are we going to do?" Jardin said.

"We'll find her," Maxim reassured him. "She'll make a mistake and we'll get her."

"Course, once you find her you actually have to keep her," Regent drawled. "Shall I have Gerald prepare the safe room?"

Both Jardin and Carrick glared at him.

"We're not locking her up," Carrick protested.

"No? Hmm. Letting her roam around on her own hasn't worked out so well."

"This isn't the eighteenth century, Regent. We can't just kidnap her and lock her up until she's pregnant with our child," Jardin said with frustration.

Regent sighed, looking disappointed in them both.

"There was just a misunderstanding," Carrick said.

"What?" Victor mocked. He'd been silent up until then, sitting in a chair in the corner, sipping his scotch. "She didn't realize she was yours?"

Jardin and Carrick shared a glance.

"We were easing her into it," Carrick explained.

Regent shook his head. "Easing her into it," he repeated. "Ridiculous."

Jardin made a noise of frustration. "Debating what we should have done isn't helping to find her any quicker.

"She'd have to enroll her brothers in school, right? Maybe I can use that to find her," Maxim mused.

"Why did she run in the first place?" Victor asked. "I assume it wasn't just because the two of you wanted to tag team her."

"Victor!" Jardin barked as Carrick scowled.

"We didn't want to tag team her. Thea is special," Jardin insisted.

"I'm sure you thought the same about Sally," Victor said coldly.

"Sally was a mistake. And she never cared about either of us. All she wanted was my money."

"And my cock," Carrick added dryly. "Thea isn't like that. She's sweet. She's loyal and smart. She's the one for us."

"And yet she ran away rather than tell you both what was going on," Regent mused.

Jardin ran his hand over his face looking as exhausted as Carrick felt.

"She was protecting us," Carrick said slowly.

Jardin froze, gaped at him. "Protecting us? Why would we need protecting? We're two grown-ass men. She's tiny. What could she possibly protect us from?"

"I don't know, but think about it. There was obviously something wrong. She wouldn't tell us what it was. Maybe it was because she didn't trust us, but I don't think that's it. I think she was trying to protect us."

Jardin groaned. "When I find her, I'm putting her over my knee. She's not going to sit comfortably for a week."

"There's the brother I know and love," Regent said. "Thought you'd disappeared for a moment there, you were being so reasonable and rational."

"Shut. Up."

"So verbose. Glad to see all that money we spent sending you to Harvard was well spent," Regent replied.

"Regent, you're being a dick," Maxim told him.

"When isn't he?" Victor asked.

"Like you can talk," Regent replied.

Okay, if this kept going, it would turn into a schoolyard brawl. Nobody could be as cutting as these guys. They were harsh. They were controlling.

Yet, they had each other's backs no matter what. And Carrick knew they didn't give a shit that he and Jardin were in a relationship. Or that they wanted Thea in that relationship. They just had pasts that had turned them into the men they were.

Still, none of this was helping find Thea and her brothers. Where were they?

"I've been trying to find the father," Maxim said. "Seems like he's disappeared. Not a good guy. From what we've found, he's an alcoholic and a gambler. Owes money to bookies, including one owned by Derrick Silvers."

"Silvers," Regent spat out. "About time we took him out, don't you think, Victor?"

That was the first time he'd seen Victor smile since they'd gotten here.

"Taking out the trash was always my favorite chore."

Maxim snorted. "Don't think you've ever done a chore in your life."

Jardin's phone rang in the midst of their bickering. He frowned and answered it. "Maddox, I don't have time right now. I'm going to have to delay coming to Haven. What? You're fucking . . . how? Shit . . . yes, I want you to keep an eye on her! Can you take her to the ranch? Since when do you give a shit what the sheriff thinks? Yes, Maddox, kidnap her . . . Fine! Carrick and I will be there by morning. Yes, I'm aware there are speed limits, you shit head. Hey, Mad? Thanks, man."

Jardin ended the call and turned to Carrick. "She's in Haven."

Relief flooded him. Of all the places she could have gone, Haven was the best possible choice.

"He's watching her?" he asked.

Jardin nodded. "Told him to take her to the ranch, but he reckons the sheriff would have his balls. He said he won't take his eyes off her until we get there, though."

"Since when do our cousins care about the police?" Regent asked. "Or any sort of authority."

"They don't," Jardin muttered. "Either he's being obstinate or—"

"He doesn't want to scare her," Carrick said softly.

"Doesn't matter. We know where she is now. Let's go get our girl."

21

Thea headed back to the diner. She'd just dropped the boys off at school and it was her day off. She was determined to talk to the owner today.

Sitting at the counter again, she endured Doris's glare. "You here for pie?"

Thea shook her head. "Just coffee please."

Doris grumbled under her breath. "What about breakfast? You need breakfast. You're just skin and bones."

Uh, she'd have to disagree. But she didn't want to argue with the scary waitress. "I'm fine, could I please speak to Peggy if she's not busy?"

"And what you want with her?" Doris snapped.

"That's for her and me to talk about," Thea said firmly.

"She won't come out for just nothin'," Doris replied.

"Fine. I want to ask her about renting the apartment upstairs."

Doris grunted. "It's just a one-bedroom."

Thea forced a polite smile. "That's fine."

"You got two boys, don't you? They need their own space. Where they gonna sleep?"

"We'll be fine." *Not that it's any of your business.* "Can I please speak to Peggy?"

"Don't worry about bothering Peggy, Doris," a deep voice said from behind her. A voice she'd heard in her dreams hundreds of times. That deep note of command that didn't fail to make her shiver.

Fuck. How did people keep sneaking up on her?

"I do need to speak to Peggy, please, Doris," she said firmly. She would not turn to look at him. She would not.

What was he doing here anyway?

It had to be that rat, Maddox. He'd called him. But would he really have raced here to see her? Why?

"Doris, do not get Peggy. Thea is not moving into that apartment."

She turned on the stool to glare at him, shocked to see Carrick standing beside him. They'd both come? Jardin was dressed in slacks, a dress shirt and a jacket while Carrick had on a black T-shirt and black jeans. Jardin's clothes were rumpled. He clearly hadn't shaved for a few days and the dark hair on his face only made him look more dangerous. Both of them looked like they hadn't slept, and Carrick's hair was almost standing on end, as though he'd been running his fingers through it.

"You know what?" Doris said. "I got other things to do. When you people make up your mind, let me know."

"What are the two of you doing here? And why did you just tell Doris I don't need the apartment. I have to have somewhere to live with the boys. We can't stay at the motel indefinitely."

"We came here for you," Carrick told her darkly.

Jardin crossed his arms over his chest. "You like it here? In Haven?"

"Um, yes." Why was he asking? What did it matter to him? And why were they here for her? So they could yell at her for leaving?

"It's a good place to live. People are kind of quirky, but our relationship would be more accepted here. But Carrick and I have careers in New Orleans. Take us a while to arrange to move out here."

She blinked in shock. "You're not moving here. I am."

"Where you go, we go, rocket," Carrick told her.

"But that's preposterous. You . . . you can't move here because of me." That's what they were saying, right?

Jardin moved into her space and cupped her face between his big hands. "When it comes to you, Thea, we will do whatever is necessary to keep you safe and happy. Living here will make that easier," he mused. "The downfall is we're close to my cousins. Interfering bastards."

Her mouth opened then closed then opened again. "Why?"

She was aware they were in a public place, but she didn't care that there were people watching. She had to know why.

Jardin moved her and Carrick slid in behind her, pressing his hard, hot body against her back. "Seems we didn't do a very good job of telling you that you're ours, Thea." Carrick moved her hair to one side so he could kiss down her neck.

Holy. Shit.

Shivers of pleasure raced through her. Fuck a duck. That felt so good.

"Let's remedy that now, shall we?" Jardin said darkly. "Thea, you're ours."

"We're not letting you go."

"So, you need to deal with the fact that we're going to share you."

"We're also gonna share each other," Carrick added.

Jardin's lips twitched, no doubt reading the heat in her gaze. "Oh, I don't think that's a problem. I think Thea likes the idea of watching us together, don't you?"

She started to shake her head. Then she remembered what

Carrick had said about his family rejecting him for his sexual choices.

"I do. I think it's fucking hot."

Carrick relaxed behind her and she knew she'd made the right choice.

Jardin cupped her face in his hand. "And what about being with the two of us? How does that make you feel?"

She cleared her throat. "Should we really be talking about this here?"

Jardin didn't look around, he kept his gaze on her. "Don't worry, this probably won't be the craziest thing they see today."

"Damn straight it won't," a man called out.

"Mr. Mac, please keep your comments to yourself," Jardin called back without missing a beat. "We wait to talk, we risk you running on us again."

"I didn't run from the two of you," she whispered.

Something like relief filled Jardin's face, before it went back to arrogant. "Good."

Carrick was still kissing his way up and down her neck.

"Carrick can you please . . . can you please stop?"

"Nope," Carrick told her. "I'm determined to show you that you want to be with us."

"That's . . . that's not the problem! Although I'm still unsure why the two of you would want me!"

Both men stiffened.

"Told you," Carrick said mysteriously.

Jardin nodded. "We'll work on it. For now, all we need to hear is that you want us as much as we want you. That you want to be in a relationship with us."

"I . . . of course I want to!" Who wouldn't want to be with the two of them? They were gorgeous, loyal, and smart. Charismatic. Powerful.

"Good. It's settled then. You'll come back with us to New

Orleans, then we can make a decision on where we want to live. Here or there. We'll figure it out. Now, did I hear you say you're staying at the motel? Let's get your stuff and your brothers from school. I assume that's where they are?"

"Wait!" she said, grabbing hold of Jardin's wrist as he stepped back.

Coldness filled his gaze. "You better not be telling me no, Thea."

It would take a stronger woman than her to tell him no except . . .

"I can't go back to New Orleans."

Carrick shifted around to stand next to Jardin. "And why's that, rocket?"

"Because if I go back there, I'm dead."

22

C arrick watched Jardin pace up and down the small motel room. It had two double beds, a tiny kitchen area with a microwave sitting on a counter and a mini fridge, and a bathroom off to the side.

It was a sign of how agitated Jardin was that he wasn't griping about where she'd been staying. He'd likely get to that later. Carrick took the chair that was under the desk. He sat and looked over at Thea, who was fiddling with the coffee maker.

"Thea, come here," Carrick said gently.

"I'll get some coffee on. Coffee makes everything better. Right?"

"Nothing is going to make this better," Jardin growled.

"Thea. Come here." He made his voice firmer this time and she turned away from the kitchen area and walked over to him. When she was about a foot away, he reached out and lifted her onto his lap.

"Eek! Carrick!"

"Hush," he murmured to her, wrapping his arms around her, holding her tightly. "I need to hold you. It's my happy place."

She made a scoffing noise, but she settled onto his lap without another word of protest. He wrapped his big arms around her. He wasn't lying. He needed to feel her against him. To know she was safe.

"When do you think he'll stop pacing?" she asked.

"When he's calmed down enough."

She sighed. "At least one of you isn't angry at me."

"Don't mistake my calm for meaning I'm not upset, Thea. I'm fucking livid. That we didn't make it clear what our intentions were, that we held back for fear of scaring you, that you kept something from us. Something that was threatening you. I'm damn furious, rocket. It's just that I show it in different ways. But to make it very clear," he turned her on his lap and cupped her chin in his hand, "you're in big trouble. And once Jardin is back in his head and we've learned what's going on, you're going to find yourself unable to sit for a week."

Heat entered her gaze before she narrowed her eyes at him. "You can't spank me."

"We damn well can," Jardin replied, coming to stand in front of them. "Something or someone threatened you and instead of telling us so we could take care of it, you ran. From us! You put yourself in more danger. There's more than one spanking owed."

She gulped. "But we're not in a relationship—"

Both men growled at her.

"We weren't in a relationship when I left," she said in a quiet voice.

"You knew we wanted you," Carrick pointed out.

"I knew that you were attracted to me." She looked up at Carrick then turned to Jardin. "But I . . ."

"You weren't sure about me?" Jardin snapped.

She shrugged. "You were my boss. You never seemed like . . . you were always so standoffish."

"We talked to you about our relationship. About getting a third, that wasn't a clue?" Jardin asked.

"I didn't realize that meant me."

Jardin knelt in front of her. "Then let's clear that up now, okay?" He reached out and cupped her face between his hands.

Then he kissed her.

FIRE. Heat. He dipped his tongue between her lips, and she swore he had a direct line to her clit. She squirmed on Carrick's lap, trapped between them both.

Carrick held her tightly while Jardin ravaged her mouth. It was a wonder she didn't come then and there.

When Jardin pulled back, she was panting and her heart raced as she stared at his smug grin. "You're ours. Got it? We want you. And we're having you. No arguments."

She pressed her fingers to her swollen lips.

"Rendered you speechless, has he, rocket?" Carrick asked with amusement.

She nodded. Then she buried her face in Carrick's chest.

"Right. I'm calmed down enough now," Jardin said, sitting on the end of the bed, facing them. "Tell me."

"You're sure you want to know?" she asked.

"Thea, we can start with your punishment if that's what you require," Jardin warned.

A shiver moved through her. All right, was it wrong that it turned her on? That she wanted to find out what it was like to be punished at his hands? To be taken by them both?

"You could still leave. Stay out of this mess."

Jardin's face grew colder while Carrick tightened his hold as though he expected her to bolt at any moment. Like she'd get far this time.

"We're going nowhere, Thea," Jardin warned her. "The sooner you understand that the easier your life will become. Tell us."

She cleared her throat. The threat in Jardin's voice was clear. He'd reached the limits of his patience.

"My dad, he's not a great guy. In fact, he's an abusive alcoholic with a gambling addiction. Before Mom died, he wasn't so bad. He held down a job. But after her death, he turned to drink and well . . . he's never been the same."

"He ever hit you?" Jardin asked.

She nodded and touched her wrist. "One day, I came home, and he broke my arm with a baseball bat. That was before I came to work for you. Another day, he grabbed my wrist hard then choked me.

"He was gone a lot, and I managed to stop him from hurting the boys. That was the main thing, keeping them safe. I don't have legal custody of them, so we had to stay in his house. But I paid all the bills. And kept as much money as I could out of his hands. The boys got scholarships to Elite Boys Academy. They're both really smart. And my neighbor, Juanita, she helped me juggle looking after the two of them and working full-time."

She took in a deep breath, calming herself then turned to look up at Carrick. "The night I had dinner with you, when I got home, I got a call from a guy I know who works at a bar."

"A guy?" Jardin asked dangerously.

"Just a friend from school," she said hastily.

He grunted.

Possessive bastard.

"Dad had fallen asleep. By the time I got there, I remembered I'd forgotten to text you, Carrick, but my phone was dead. Unfortunately, Dad wasn't there when I arrived. A couple of assholes had gone into the bar and dragged him out."

"Who?" Jardin asked.

"Derrick Silvers' guys," she admitted.

Carrick sucked in a breath. "Fuck. Then what happened?"

"My friend convinced me not to get involved. And I decided to go home, charge my phone and text you. But when I left the bar, this guy grabbed me. He had a gun and forced me into the back of this car. They drove me to a wrecking yard and forced me into a shipping container. My dad was in there; he'd been beaten unconscious." She paused to calm her racing heart. "Derrick Silvers was there too."

"What the fuck? He threatened you?" Jardin asked.

"Told me my dad owed him fifty thousand dollars and that I was liable for his debt. Then he said he'd . . . he'd take me as payment."

"Fuck!" Jardin got up to pace again. "Why didn't you tell me?"

"Because he said he would hurt the boys if I told anyone. I believed him. He gave me a week to come up with the money. He started leaving me roses and notes. One was under my car's window wiper. Another appeared on my desk at work. Thursday night I came home to find him in my house. I knew I had to leave. The boys weren't safe. I wasn't safe. So, we pretended to go to school, got an Uber to pick us up at the back entrance and take us to the mall. I left my phone there, and we changed clothes then caught a bus into the main terminal, then got on one headed to Lafayette. There, I . . . I pawned my mom's gold and diamond necklace to buy a car, and we came here."

"Why here?" Carrick asked.

"Maddox told me a bit about Haven. About how women here were protected. It sounded like an amazing place. And I guess, I think it made me feel closer to you," she said to Jardin.

"We're going to take care of this, rocket," Carrick told her.

"How?" she asked. "He's been arrested several times, nothing sticks. He likely has cops and judges in his pocket. How will you stop him?"

Jardin stopped in front of her with a smile. "We won't. We'll set Regent on him."

"Regent? Your brother? How will he get him to leave me alone? I don't want him paying the fifty grand for me."

"Oh, he won't give Silvers a dime. And don't worry about Regent. He and Victor have been dying to take Silvers down. No excuse as good as him making a move against our family."

"But I'm not family."

"You are now."

Her heart fluttered. God, did he know how much she longed to have a family? A place to belong? Someone to share her burdens?

"There are bigger monsters in the world than Derrick Silvers," Jardin told her, pulling out his phone. "My brother is one of them. Stay here."

He stepped out of the room, his phone already to his ear.

"Is he . . . does he really mean that?" she asked.

"Nobody goes up against Regent and wins," Carrick told her seriously. "Jardin's oldest brother can be terrifying. But he's all about family. Derrick Silvers is toast. He's no longer on your list of worries."

She couldn't dare to believe it.

Jardin walked back in, an intense look on his face as he stared at her. "Regent said to consider it done."

"Really?" How could it possibly be that easy?

"Really. But he also suggested we stay here until it is." Jardin looked around the motel with disgust.

Carrick turned her so she was straddling his lap. He grabbed her chin, raising it. "You sure you want to live here? We'll do it if you want to. If you can't go back to New Orleans. But you need to be sure."

"I don't . . . I mean . . . it would be easier here in some ways. But at the same time, New Orleans is home. And even though I dislike a lot of the people at the boys' school in New Orleans, it's a good school. It pushes them. Can I . . . can I talk to the boys about it?"

"Of course, rocket," he told her.

"How long until we have to pick them up from school?" Jardin asked, looking at his watch.

"Uh, about three hours."

"Excellent that should be just enough time to take care of your punishment."

23

Was it bad that he liked the way her eyes flared? That hint of trepidation and excitement that filled her gaze. If it was bad, Jardin didn't care.

He stalked his way over to her. This fleabag motel wouldn't have been his choice of location for their first time together, however, he wasn't waiting. So, this dingy room would have to do.

Okay, it wasn't that dingy. Still, she deserved far better. Especially after hearing about how her father had treated her. After seeing where she'd lived. She deserved everything.

Thea gasped as he pulled her from Carrick's lap to stand in front of him and held her. Reaching down, he gently took hold of her chin, raising her face. Staring down at her, he couldn't believe he finally had her where she belonged.

He watched as she swallowed. "Nervous?"

She nodded.

"Don't be. We're gonna take care of you now, aren't we, Carrick?"

"Oh, yes." Carrick moved up behind her, sandwiching her between them.

"You're our priority now, sweetness," Jardin told her, running a finger down her cheek. "Your health, your happiness, your safety. We'll do whatever is necessary to take care of you."

"It's . . . I still can't believe you both want me."

Jardin narrowed his gaze. "Why wouldn't we want you? Why wouldn't we consider ourselves fucking lucky to have you? You're smart."

"Beautiful," Carrick added, running his hands up her sides. "Loyal."

"Kind." Carrick kissed the side of her neck and she tilted it to allow him better access.

"Courageous. Although, I would wish you had a little less courage and a bit more caution." Jardin leaned down to kiss her, nipping at her lip until she opened up and allowed him in. To taste. To torture. To conquer.

When he drew back, her face was flushed, her breath coming in sharp pants. He placed both hands on her hips, holding her against him. Fuck, he needed her.

"If this is too soon, if it's too much, tell us now, Thea," Carrick said to her. "We can stop, back off a bit, give you time."

Jardin scowled at Carrick. He didn't want to do any of those things. He wanted to claim her. Now.

Carrick just stared back at him calmly. Fine. Fuck. He'd give her time if she needed it. What were they talking about here? A day?

To his shock, she shook her head. "I don't want to wait. If the two of you are sure . . . I mean, I don't think I could handle this if either of you changed your mind." Her head dropped down. "I don't want to disappoint you."

Carrick turned her to face him. This time he was the one to grab hold of her chin and raise her face. "Not happening. Understand me? The only way you'd disappoint us is by not trusting us with the truth. We want you, Thea. You think we just randomly picked you? We feel you, right in here." He patted his chest. "We could be happy without you, but we'd never be complete. Understand me?"

"What he said," Jardin added, making her look over her shoulder at him with a smile.

"Then I'm all in," she whispered.

"You remember what I said about us both being Doms?" Carrick asked.

"Yes, but you're sometimes a bottom?"

"Sometimes. But not for you. I'm always your Top. For sex anyway."

"I'm always in charge," Jardin growled. "Of both of you. But especially you, sweetness. And you'll have rules to follow and consequences if you don't."

She looked back at him pleadingly. "You're not really going to punish me for leaving?"

"Oh, yes. I certainly am. For not telling us what was going on. For running away. For risking yourself. For not telling me you were living in a dive. That you were unsafe. The list goes on."

Her bottom lip dropped in a pout. Oh, hell, no. She did not just do that.

"Put that away," Jardin ordered. "That shit doesn't work on me."

"Besides," Carrick whispered. "You might just like your punishment."

She turned sideways so she could see them both. "Maddox said you're a sadist."

Jardin swore. "That asshole."

"Are you? Because while a spanking seems, um, doable, I don't think I could go for any real pain."

"And you won't have to. Because I don't get pleasure from inflicting pain on people who don't want it. Punishments are different, of course. You break the rules, you get punished to deter you from breaking the rules again. Then, I won't hesitate. But I'm not going to strap you down and take my whip to you because I'm some deviant sadist."

"But then . . . won't you miss it?"

Jardin grinned. "We'll work it out. It's not something I need all the time. Carrick has yet to decide if he wants to feel the bite of my whip. Maybe I'll take you to Saxon's while we're here. There's always someone there who enjoys or needs the pain."

She frowned. "You'd touch them? Be with them?"

He wrapped his hand around the back of her neck then reached for Carrick, bringing him closer. "I'll be with no one but the two of you. You always come first. Helping with a scene doesn't have to be sexual, but if you don't want me to do that, I won't."

"Okay," She whispered. "Maybe we can see."

"Good girl," he crooned. "You're going to be our very good girl from now on, aren't you?"

She looked from him to Carrick. "Yes."

"Yes, Sir," Jardin told her.

"Yes, Sir."

"Now, I'm going to go sit on the end of the bed and go through your rules while Carrick strips you." He met Carrick's gaze, saw the heat and, unable to resist, drew him close to kiss him.

Carrick was a bit hesitant at first, then he threw himself into the kiss, pulling Jardin closer. They drew apart slowly, both of them breathing heavily.

"Oh, God, that was so hot. I think I just came a little. More? Please?"

Both of them looked to Thea. Then Carrick let out a laugh, his shoulders shaking. "More? You have to earn more. Come here."

CARRICK DREW Thea closer as Jardin pulled the curtains closed. He admitted, he'd still held some reservations about how she would take him and Jardin together. Wondering if he'd be left out again. When Jardin was in a room, he tended to dominate it.

But Carrick knew he would have a role to play. Jardin could sometimes be too much, too overwhelming. He brought balance to the possessive beast. Not that he wasn't just as possessive. He simply hid that side better.

As Jardin took off his jacket and shirt, Carrick turned her to face the other man and stepped in behind her. He reached around to cup her full breasts.

"Like what you see, rocket? He's ripped, isn't he? So fucking hot."

Jardin grinned over at them as he stripped off his pants. Each item of clothing was neatly folded and placed on the other bed.

"Well?" Carrick demanded, pinching her nipples lightly and smiling at her gasp of pain. "Answer me."

"Y-yes, he's gorgeous."

"Sometimes I think I could just spend all day watching him move," Carrick admitted, letting his gaze roam over Jardin possessively.

"Easy now, I haven't even got my dick out yet," Jardin joked as he stripped off his boxers and wrapped his hand around the monster in question.

"Holy. Shit."

"Big, isn't he? And gorgeous." Carrick reached for the bottom of her shirt, pulling it swiftly over her head. "But don't worry, if I can take him you certainly can."

"Wow, I'd like to see that." She wrapped her arms around her middle.

"Maybe we should do this later. When it's dark."

"And why would we do that?" Jardin asked in a deceptively soft voice as he laid back on the bed, dick in hand, watching them both.

"Because, in case you haven't noticed, I'm not exactly skinny. I have rolls and cellulite and I really need to shave, like, everything."

"Carrick," Jardin said in a firm voice. "Take care of Thea's punishment."

"With pleasure. Thea, bend over."

"W-what?"

"Bend over," Carrick firmed his voice. He didn't want her thinking he was a pushover just because he was easier going than Jardin. It was never acceptable for her to talk about herself like that.

"But why?"

"Because you just insulted something precious to us," Jardin told her. "And talking badly about yourself is never acceptable."

"I didn't know!"

"You didn't know that you shouldn't put yourself down?" Jardin asked skeptically. "Besides, it's all lies. You are beautiful. Every inch of you. Carrick."

"Bend over, Thea. Every minute you procrastinate is another ten smacks."

She let out a small gasp but bent over. Her skirt molded over her ass. Fucking perfect. He squeezed one cheek. He slid it up over her ass, revealing some very safe, granny panties.

"She needs new lingerie," he told Jardin.

"Excellent, I'll get on that."

"Are the two of you going to take over my life?" she asked.

"Pretty much," Jardin said.

"Objections?" Carrick asked.

"I'll let you know when I have them."

Carrick grinned. He just bet she'd let them know; it was going to make life interesting when Jardin realized he couldn't have his way all the time.

"Good for you, rocket."

Jardin just snorted. "Spank her already."

"All right, that's ten—"

"Ten? It's at least twenty," Jardin interrupted.

Carrick sent him a quelling look. "She's new. Let's cut the difference at fifteen."

"Fine. Fifteen."

Carrick grabbed hold of her panties and stripped them off. She stiffened, but when he tapped each of her feet, she lifted them so he could pull them off. He turned and walked to the garbage can, chucking them in.

Jardin grinned. "I approve."

"Knew you would. Spread your legs, rocket."

"Oh, God," she muttered. But she parted her legs. He took in the sight of her ass, round and firm.

"This is one fucking beautiful ass," Carrick told her.

"It's big," she muttered.

He gave her two firm slaps. "What are you getting a spanking for?"

"Putting myself down."

"And do you think it's wise to talk badly about yourself while getting a spanking for talking badly about yourself?"

"That does sound rather foolish," she admitted.

"Right. It's a count of fifteen."

"Fifteen? But you just gave me two!"

"They didn't count," Carrick told her.

"Be thankful it's not me, I'd have doubled the amount," Jardin told her grimly.

Carrick rolled his eyes at him. But then he moved his attention back to Thea. "Your safe word is red, rocket. Say it if you need to and everything stops immediately, okay?"

"Okay, Sir."

"Call me Carrick. Jardin is the one who likes protocols and sticking to rules. He'll have you collared and kneeling. Me, I want to see you restrained, with his dick in your mouth while I'm buried deep in your pussy."

"Oh, God," she moaned.

He started smacking her ass, keeping a silent count. Her skin quickly turned pink, then deepened to red. Her breath grew faster, a small cry escaped her around number ten, and he stopped to run his hand over her bottom and assess her. "How you doing, Thea?"

"I'm okay."

"Good girl."

He gave the last five quickly. But with firm smacks that would ensure she'd feel it tomorrow. When he was finished, he helped her straighten then immediately pulled her into his arms, holding her tightly. He rubbed his hand up and down her back and looked over at Jardin, who gave him a satisfied smirk. Bastard was happy with himself. He knew Carrick worried about being left out and he'd made sure he got first crack at Thea's ass.

Pulling back, he leaned down to capture all her tears with his mouth, then he tilted her chin up to study her. "Okay?"

She nodded, smiling. "Yes, Carrick."

"Now how about we get you stripped. Then you can go suck off the lord and master."

He nodded over at Jardin, noting the way her eyes flared. Oh, she liked the sound of that.

This girl was perfect for them.

Jardin watched as Carrick stripped her bare. He cupped her full breasts, twisting her nipples lightly between fingers and thumbs.

That was so damn hot. He wasn't going to last long.

He had no clue why she didn't think her body was perfection. Her breasts were lush, her waist tiny, and her hips flared out. He couldn't wait to see that pink ass. His gaze dropped to her pussy. Fuck. He needed a taste.

Climbing off the bed, he stalked toward them. "Lift her for me. I need to taste her."

Carrick got what he meant immediately. He grabbed her under the thighs and pulled her up against his chest, spreading her legs so her pussy was on display.

"Carrick, you can't!"

Jardin stared at her sternly. "And why can't he?"

He saw her hesitate. She knew her answer was going to get her in trouble.

"He'll hurt his back."

"Oh, that was naughty," Jardin told her then he gave her a heavy smack right on her pussy.

"Ow!" she cried out.

"Seems someone has already forgotten the spanking she just got for putting herself down."

He landed another spanking on her pussy. She arched with a cry.

"Sorry! I'm sorry!"

"You will learn not to speak badly about something that belongs to us. That we both adore."

"Thea, you're not heavy," Carrick told her. "I could hold you for hours and not even feel strained. In fact, I think you've lost weight."

Jardin narrowed his gaze, studying her. "Have you not been eating properly, Thea? Have you not been taking care of what's ours?"

He reached out and tugged on her nipple, enjoying her cry. Pain and pleasure filled her face. Maybe she didn't like much pain, but a bite of it seemed to turn her on. "Don't worry, now that we're here, we'll make sure you're taken care of."

He leaned down and took her nipple into his mouth, sucking

on it strongly. She groaned and he moved over to the other one, sucking on it. Then he kissed down her stomach, bending until he could tongue her clit.

Hmm, this angle wasn't giving him what he wanted.

He pulled back and looked over at Carrick. "I want you naked and sitting on the bed with her on your lap. Her pussy spread wide for me."

Carrick didn't argue, just gave him a heated look as he set her down. Jardin had to steady her as she swayed while Carrick quickly stripped. Then he climbed onto the bed, leaning back against the headboard.

"Come here, rocket."

Jardin turned her, slapping her pink ass. Yep, that was perfection. Her yelp just sent pleasure flooding through his veins.

He was fucked.

Carrick settled her between his legs, placing her legs over his then spreading his thighs wide.

Yes. Perfect.

Then he reached around and drew the lips of her pussy apart.

"Fuck. Yes." Jardin crawled forward and laid on his stomach between their legs. "Play with her tits while I make her come. I may not come up for air for a while. A long fucking while."

24

Christ. She was certain they were trying to kill her.

Death by orgasm. It had to be a thing, right? Because Jardin's mouth was utter sin. The things he was doing with his tongue . . . fuck. Combined with how expertly Carrick was playing with her nipples, she hadn't ever felt anything like it.

She was dead. Totally and utterly dead.

They teased her, drove her up to the brink then drew back, leaving her panting and wanting more. She writhed between them. She needed to come. She was desperate.

"Please, please," she begged.

Jardin removed his mouth from her pussy, and she cried out in protest. His lips were wet with her dew as he stared up at Carrick. "What do you think, should we let our girl come?"

"Hmm, I think she's been good enough."

"Me too."

Oh, yes. Thank fucking Christ. Jardin lowered his mouth to her pussy again, his tongue flicking her clit with firm strokes and he pressed two fingers inside. She clenched down around him as she came, screaming her pleasure. No doubt everyone within a mile radius could hear her, but right at that moment she didn't care.

Jardin brought her down with soft laps of his tongue while Carrick caressed the skin of her neck with his mouth.

Shit. Shit.

Then Jardin sat up. "Want a taste?" he asked Carrick.

"Fuck. Yes."

Jardin moved in, placing his hand around the back of Carrick's neck and they kissed. And she swore she came again. It was the hottest thing she'd ever seen. Nope. Wait. Watching Carrick wrap his hand around Jardin's dick was the hottest thing she'd ever seen.

Jardin pulled back with a groan. "Hands and knees, Thea. Carrick is going to fuck you while you suck me off."

Her eyes flared open. "Yes, Sir."

The smile he gave her was everything. Carrick moved off the bed and grabbed his pants, pulling a condom out of the pocket and slipping it on his massive dick. Seriously, how were they both so big?

Jardin sat back against the headboard and spread his legs. She knelt on her hands and knees and stared down at his huge dick. Then leaning in, she licked the top of it.

"Fuck, yes, baby," Jardin groaned. "Take me into your mouth like a good girl. That's it. Suck me. So fucking good."

She felt Carrick move behind her. One hand grabbed her hip to hold her steady as he penetrated her. Slow and steady. She clenched down around his cock.

Shit. Shit.

"She's so fucking tight," Carrick groaned.

"You should feel her mouth. Fuck me, I'm not going to last."

Pleasure flooded her at their words. Their praise. She wasn't going to lie. Feeling wanted and attractive was heady. It wasn't something she'd often felt. She continued to suck Jardin off as Carrick pulled out then thrust deeply. God, he was hitting her G-spot perfectly. Every surge sent her spiraling higher and higher.

"You're coming again with us, baby," Jardin commanded.

She made a murmuring noise of protest.

"Yes, you are. Carrick?"

"On it," Carrick groaned. "I'm close." He reached one hand around and played with her clit.

Jardin chose that moment to thrust deeply, coming in her mouth. She was swallowing him down just as Carrick drove her up and over that edge. He followed her soon after, his own roar mingling with her cries of pleasure.

Together, the three of them collapsed on the bed, and the men tucked her tightly in between them.

"Shit," Jardin said.

"What is it?" she asked, stiffening.

"I forgot to go over your rules."

She let out a deep breath. "I think those can wait."

"Oh, no. These are very important."

"Let me take care of this condom first," Carrick said. He got up and walked to the bathroom. She watched that tight ass move. Hey, she was only human.

Jardin pulled her so she was lying with her head on his chest. She relaxed into his body heat, letting the scent of him surround her. A yawn overtook her as Carrick moved in behind her, spooning her. He stretched his arm over them both.

"Tired, rocket?" Carrick asked with concern.

"Little bit."

"So, you haven't been sleeping or eating?" Jardin asked in a deep voice. "Not winning any prizes for self-care."

She sighed. "I haven't been able to sleep properly since meeting Derrick Silvers. And eating . . . well, it didn't seem like a priority. I've been trying to watch my money. Keir and Ace need to eat more than me."

"You all need to fucking eat," Jardin growled.

"Easy," Carrick soothed. "We're here now. We'll take care of all of them."

"I'm not sure how Keir and Ace will handle this. Us. They don't know you. And Keir, especially is jumpy from our quick departure."

"Don't worry, everything will be fine," Jardin told her. "They'll be fine with us."

"They're just settling into school here."

"Easy, rocket," Carrick told her, running his hand down her arm. "We'll sort it all out. There's a school break coming up, isn't there?"

"In another week."

"All right, let's do this," Jardin said decisively. "We'll stay a few days with my cousins. Talk with Maddox over what he wants from me while Regent sorts out Silvers. We'll get your brothers used to us and the idea of moving back to New Orleans . . . if that's what you want."

"I like it here. But New Orleans is home. And if it's safe . . . I mean, I do have a job there, right?"

"Oh, hell no," Jardin told her. "You're fired."

She sat up, gaping down at him. "What?"

"You didn't give any notice when you left. You quit."

"But . . . I . . . but . . ."

"You thought being in a relationship with the boss was going to get you leniency, you can think again."

"And just who are you going to get to replace me?"

He shrugged. "I'll find someone."

"Jardin! I need that job."

"No, you don't." He sat and pulled her into his lap. "You're ours now. You don't have to worry about money or putting a roof over your head or food in your belly. You worry about nothing from now on."

"Keir and Ace—"

"Are our responsibility as well," Carrick told her.

"This isn't the way it works. Besides, I want to be able to support myself."

"If you could choose anything you wanted to do, would you choose to be Jardin's PA?" Carrick asked her.

Um. Loaded question.

"You can be honest," Jardin told her.

"Uh, no."

"What would you like to do?"

She gripped her hands together. "Photography."

"Yeah?" Carrick asked.

"I loved it at school. I used the school camera. I never had money for my own. But I think I was pretty good."

"Then we'll buy you everything you need. You take what courses you need. And you concentrate on that," Jardin told her firmly.

Tears entered her eyes. "Just like that?" Could this all be real?

Carrick leaned across and cupped her face with his hand. "Just like that. It's important to love what you do."

"Thank you."

"That's something you never need to thank us for."

She shifted around on his lap. Her ass still hurt a bit from that spanking.

"What about my job here? I'll have to give notice."

"What have you been doing?" Carrick asked.

"Cleaning businesses and houses."

"You don't need to be doing that anymore," Jardin stated arrogantly.

"But I have to give notice."

"Who are you working for?" Jardin asked.

"Marcy."

"I'll square it with her."

"But, Jardin—"

"I'll fix it, Thea. Don't worry. And if she doesn't like it, I'll just buy her business from her. I think she's been wanting to retire."

She gaped at him. He was unbelievable.

"You'll get used to him," Carrick murmured.

Yeah. She wasn't so sure.

"Now, the rules."

Carrick grinned. "Something else you probably won't thank us for."

"No going anywhere without telling us," Jardin told her. "And I do mean anywhere out of the house."

Jesus. "Seriously?"

"Yes. Seriously," Jardin told her.

"But when Silvers is no longer a problem—"

"I'm still gonna need to know where you're going and when you're coming back. It's a safety thing. Is that a problem?"

She thought it through. "I guess not."

"No putting yourself down is obviously one," Jardin continued.

"No lying," Carrick added. "That one is for all of us."

"Yes, communication and honesty are important. If someone has a problem, they speak to the others about it rather than try to solve it on their own or hold it in." Jardin looked pointedly at Carrick who nodded.

"Anything else?"

"Safety first," Carrick said. "Always wear your seat belt, stick to the speed limit, no texting or calling while driving, no going out after dark without us."

"And you tell us if someone threatens you or is a problem. Whether it's Derrick Silvers or one of those bitches at the boys' school."

Her mind swam.

"And I don't think I need to remind you what will happen if you break the rules, do I?" Jardin asked, patting the side of her ass.

No, he didn't.

"There is something else," she whispered. "I don't know if I'm just imagining it, but I've had this feeling like someone was watching me."

Jardin frowned. "Could have been Maddox. He's been watching you since he called us."

"He has? I never saw the rat."

"Someone needed to keep an eye on you," Carrick told her.

"This was before I saw Maddox in the diner, though."

Carrick looked to Jardin. "Could Silvers have found her?"

"I don't see how. Thea, is there any way he could have put a tracker on you? Did he ever have possession of anything of yours?"

"I don't think so . . . oh God, my handbag. The first night I met him, his goon took my handbag. I got it back later."

She grabbed her handbag off the desk. Jardin took it, searching through it. He pulled out a small square object. "A tracker. They must have tucked this in one of the pockets."

Thea felt ill. "They knew where I was all along? I was never going to get away from him?"

"Fuck, we're lucky they didn't snatch you already," Carrick said.

"More difficult to do that than it seems in Haven. The men here watch over all the women. Even this motel has good security. My guess is the perfect opportunity didn't come up yet."

"What do we do with the tracker?" she asked. "Should we leave? Oh God, the boys! What if he tries to take the boys?"

"Calm down, baby," Jardin soothed. "I'm going to bring in some reinforcements. We'll keep you all safe."

25

Reinforcements came in the form of the Malone family. And there were a lot of them. Carrick had rushed off to the school to grab the boys while Jardin helped her back their stuff. By the time they'd been ready to leave, Maddox had skidded his way into the parking lot. He'd taken her car and the tracker, leaving them with his truck.

They'd met up with Carrick and driven here to the Malone ranch.

"Thea, we're so glad you're here," Flick told her with a grin. "We women need all the help we can get to corral these guys."

"There is no corralling these guys," Mia countered, turning from where she was cooking something that smelled delicious at the stove. Apparently, Mia had been a chef before she'd come to the Malone ranch to hide from a mobster who'd been trying to kill her.

Alec Malone had agreed to keep her safe and he'd fallen in love with her. He was terrifying, stern, and abrupt. And West, Flick's boyfriend, was even more gruff. She'd wondered what the other brothers were like. Alec and West had been waiting to greet them when they'd arrived.

After settling the boys into the living room with some video games, Carrick and Jardin had gone off with Alec and West, while she'd been dragged into the kitchen for some girl talk.

"I should go check on Ace and Keir."

"They'll be fine." Flick waved her hand. "I need your help deciding how to propose to West."

"Don't do it, Flick," Mia warned. "Do. Not. Do. It."

Flick pouted.

"Maybe you should, uh, try to sound him out first," Thea suggested, feeling sorry for Flick.

"Hmm, good plan. But how?" Flick asked.

"Perhaps Thea could ask at dinner how everyone feels about women proposing?" Mia suggested.

"Yes!" Flick cheered. "That's a great idea. Please, Thea."

She wrinkled her nose at Mia. She should say no, but it was nearly impossible to refuse Flick. "Okay, I'll try. But before dinner I really have to go talk with Ace and Keir."

With her problem solved, well, temporarily, Flick let her go. Thea wandered through the big house, which had a happy, lived-in feel, until she got to the living room where she'd left the boys. She paused in the doorway, watching with surprise as Jardin sat with Keir looking at something on Keir's tablet. While Ace and Carrick played some kind of video game.

They'd obviously finished their meeting with Alec and West.

"Hey, Thea!" Ace cheered. "This place is so cool! And they have Kingdom Hearts III!"

"I take it that's a good thing," Thea said dryly.

"It's the best!"

"Well, I've got it at home too," Carrick told him. "Along with NBA2K20."

"Awesome." Ace gave him a look of hero worship. "Hey, Thea,

can I go play at Carrick's house when we get home."

"Don't be a dork, Ace," Keir said condescendingly. "Carrick is Thea's boyfriend. He doesn't want to have a playdate with you. Besides, we're not going back home, are we?"

"Do you want to?" she asked. "And don't call your brother a dork."

Keir shrugged but there was something vulnerable in his gaze that told her this was more important than he was letting on.

"It's okay if you want to," she said gently.

"I miss home. I mean, I like it here," Ace said. "But I have friends back home. Not that dipshit, Arthur, though."

"Ace," she reprimanded. "Don't call people dipshits."

"Even if they are," Jardin added.

She glared at Jardin. He just shrugged unrepentantly.

"Can we go home?" Keir asked. "I mean, is it safe?"

"Jardin's brother is going to make it so that we can," she told him gently. "We'll have to stay here until he does that, though."

Keir gave Jardin a surprised look.

"So, you're both Thea's boyfriends?" Ace asked, getting to the heart of things.

"They are. That okay?" She was tense, waiting for their answer.

"I think it's cool," Ace said. Keir just shrugged. That was as good as she was going to get from him.

"When we go home, where are we gonna live?" Keir asked.

"You'll all move in with me," Jardin said before she could reply. "My family home has the best security. Once things are settled, we can talk about our own home. I live with my brothers and sister."

"Can we play video games?" Ace asked.

"Of course."

"Will we have our own rooms?" Keir inquired.

"Yes," Jardin affirmed.

Both boys seemed happy at that. Well, that went easier than she'd thought it would be.

26

T hea thought she might be in shock.

She probably looked like a fish out of water as she sat at the huge dining room table. It could easily seat twenty, but somehow it seemed like there were twice as many people in there. The Malones were loud, expressive, and blunt.

And hilarious.

For so long, it had just been her and the boys. When their dad wasn't around, things were quiet. This was the opposite. Food flew around the table. She was sandwiched between Carrick and Jardin with Keir next to Jardin and Ace on Carrick's other side. Alec Malone sat at the head of the table with Mia to his left. West at the other end with Flick next to him.

She saw that both men filled their women's plates first before taking food for themselves. Then she noticed Jardin and Carrick doing the same. They helped the boys with their food then made her plate up. When Carrick went to add another spoonful of mashed potatoes, she had to cover her plate with her hand to get him to stop.

He scowled at her. "You need more."

"I don't need more."

Jardin turned and gave her a firm look. "You'll eat more, Thea."

"I can't eat that much. My plate is too full as it is."

"You will," Jardin said stubbornly.

"I won't."

Jardin opened his mouth, but Tanner gave a whoop of glee from across the table. "You tell him, Thea! Don't let him boss you around."

Jardin scowled across at his youngest cousin, who grinned back unrepentantly.

Thea blushed. How could she have forgotten her audience?

"You want, Thea, we'll get rid of him for the night," Butch offered.

"Raid needs to practice his knots," Maddox said. "Jardin would make the perfect practice dummy to use. I mean dummy in the nicest possible way, of course."

She stiffened. Had they just offered to hog tie Jardin? She looked over at Jardin, who appeared exasperated. Then she looked at Carrick on her other side, who was grinning.

Obviously, it was all a joke.

"No hog tying anyone and leaving them outside," Mia stated firmly.

They all groaned except for West, Alec, and Jaret.

"Mia, you're no fun. One night won't kill him," Butch wheedled.

Mia gave him a firm look. "No. Leave Jardin alone."

"It's no fair," Tanner said. "Ever since Mia came along, we all have to be nice to Jardin."

"That's because I'm her favorite," Jardin drawled, surprising her.

And by the looks everyone gave him, he'd surprised them too.

"He is," Mia agreed with a grin. Her eyes twinkled. "The rest of you should really work harder to be my favorite."

"I'm your favorite," Alec stated firmly.

"Of course you are," Mia replied, leaning over to kiss him. "But after you, it's Jardin."

Jardin gave them all a smug smile. Then he turned to Thea. "Eat."

She blinked at him then looked over at the boys. Ace was busy eating and chatting with Jaret. While West was nodding at something Keir was saying. Happiness flooded her at the sight. She knew they were missing good, stable male influences. And they were lapping up the attention now.

"Eat," Jardin whispered in her ear. "Or you'll sit on Carrick's lap while I feed you."

She shivered, knowing the threat was real and if they'd been on their own, she might well have enjoyed that.

Jardin gave her a knowing look. But she picked up her fork. It was way more food than she could eat, and she'd normally stick to salad or veggies, but it was so good half the plate was gone before she realized it. She sat back, her tummy full. It seemed the Malones took eating seriously as most of the food was already gone.

Mia was a miracle worker, feeding this group every night.

"So, does this mean you're gonna help us with our problem, Jardin?" Raid demanded.

Jardin sighed. "This isn't my specialty."

"But you know someone who could help?" Butch asked.

Jardin nodded. "I'll make some calls."

As Thea looked around, she saw Flick staring at her. She waggled her eyebrows up and down.

What? She didn't speak eyebrow.

Oh. She wanted Thea to ask that question. Shit. Why had she said she'd do that?

"Thea, can we go play Kingdom Hearts?" Ace asked.

"Take your plates into the kitchen first," she said.

Mia made to stand and collect the plates, but Alec gave her a firm look. "Mia, sit. Rest. Tanner and Raid are on clean-up."

The two men got up without a word and started picking up plates.

After the boys left, she looked over at Maddox. "What did you do with the tracker?"

He grinned. "I made sure it went on a nice bus ride to Oklahoma."

"And my car?"

"Afraid we had to get rid of it," Jardin told her. "We couldn't take the risk that there was a tracker on it."

She called bullshit on that. She narrowed her gaze at him. "You had my car destroyed?"

"It wasn't safe."

"Jardin!"

He just gave her a calm look. "Did you seriously think I would allow you to drive around in something unsafe?"

She rubbed her forehead. Okay, she guessed her car situation was the least of her worries right now. *Tackle one thing at a time, Thea.*

"Don't worry, we'll get you something much safer," Carrick told her.

"I don't want you guys buying me things." Especially something as big as a car.

"Why not?" Jardin asked. "If the situation was reversed and we needed something that you could easily give us wouldn't you do the same thing?"

Well. Crap.

She sighed, giving in. "Okay, but nothing too expensive."

Oh, Thea. You are fighting a losing battle.

Flick gave her another look. Shoot.

"So, um . . ." Shit. What if Jardin and Carrick thought she was going to ask them to marry her?

Mia took pity on her. "Flick, Thea and I thought we'd watch a chick flick tonight. There's this new one about a woman who asks her boyfriend to marry her and he says no."

Alec grunted. "As he should. A man should ask a woman."

"Don't you think that's awfully old-fashioned?" Mia prodded.

"Nope. If you'd asked me, I'd have put you over my knee."

"West?" Thea managed to ask the gruff man, who'd barely spoken a word during dinner.

"Agree with Alec. Man's job."

Flick looked crestfallen, and Thea's heart reached out to her. She saw Jardin watching Flick as well.

"Sometimes, a man just wants to wait for the perfect moment. We're not always romantic. We don't always see what's right in front of us. But when we find that woman who is a part of our soul, we will do whatever it takes to keep her."

Flick gave Jardin a small smile at his words. West turned to stare down at her thoughtfully.

Maybe he got the message.

THEA PULLED her pajamas on in the bathroom. She couldn't believe how huge this house was. Probably a good thing with how many Malone brothers there were. Even though most of them lived out in the bunk house. Ace and Keir were already fast asleep in one of the bedrooms.

All the Malones treated the boys, and her, like they were family. And they teased Jardin mercilessly. But he'd given back as good as he got. And not one of them found their relationship odd. Or looked twice at them. But then, it did seem to be almost the norm in Haven.

She walked into the bedroom and slammed to a stop as she saw the two of them lying on the bed, kissing.

Holy. Shit.

Jardin pulled back and looked over at her. "Shut and lock the door then strip and get your cute butt over here."

She cleared her throat, her clit throbbing already in anticipation.

"Maybe I should sleep with the boys," she said.

Both men froze and the look Jardin gave her was enough to have her heart racing. Oh, Lord, he didn't want to hear that.

"And why would that be?" he asked calmly.

"In case they need me. They're in a strange place, and I—"

"They know which room we're in," Jardin told her. "I also pointed out West and Alec's rooms to them. If they need one of us, they can find us."

"They'll likely sleep like the dead," Carrick added. "But if makes you feel better, I'll check on them in the night."

"I couldn't ask you to—"

A growl escaped Carrick, something she was more familiar with coming from Jardin. "You're not asking, I'm offering. Now I'm telling you. Let us help you for a change."

Her mouth dropped open as she closed the door. "Help me for a change? You're always helping me."

Carrick frowned. "You barely let us help. You try to do everything yourself. That's going to change. It's not just you anymore, Thea. You've got us now. Let us carry the load."

Tears entered her eyes and she blinked, looking away. "That's going to take some getting used to. I've never had someone want to help me."

"You do now," Carrick told her warmly. "And we're not going to let you get away with trying to do it all yourself."

She gave a short nod.

"After all, that's what you do for someone you love," Carrick told her.

She gasped at him. "Did you just ... are you saying ..."

"I love you, Thea," Carrick said.

"I love you as well," Jardin added.

Tears dripped down her face. "I love you guys too."

Carrick grinned at her while Jardin gave her an arrogant nod. These two men, along with Keir and Ace, were everything to her.

Jardin sighed long and loud. "Go get her, Carrick."

"No, wait! I'm coming. I'm coming."

She walked over to the huge bed.

"You're forgetting something," Jardin reminded her. "That's five."

"Five! You can't spank me."

"I can't? Hmm, I feel sure that I can," he countered.

"I'm not breaking a rule."

"You're not obeying your Doms when they tell you to get naked and into bed. Actually, that's worth ten."

"You can't spank me here. What if someone hears?" she asked, horrified.

Jardin grinned, shifting position so he was leaning against the headboard. All that delicious skin was on display as well as his firm, thick cock. Lord help her. "Do you seriously think you're the first woman to get a spanking in this house?"

Carrick chuckled. "Not even close."

Carrick swung his legs over the bed and stood. And she was struck dumb once more. How was her brain supposed to function with these two around?

Shit.

He strode to the door and locked it. Then to her shock, he picked her up and swung her onto the bed. Jardin immediately pinned her down, straddling her body and reaching for her pajama top. "Let's get this off."

She held her arms up to help him because really, she didn't want to put up too much of a fuss and have them completely back off, now did she?

"Such pretty breasts," he crooned. "What do you think, Carrick?"

"I think they look lonely." Carrick laid next to her then leaned in to suck one nipple into his mouth. Jardin moved to lay on her other side, taking her other nipple in his mouth. They suckled on her, their hands roaming her body. Carrick's hand slid down her tummy and under the waistband of her pajama bottoms, while Jardin's hand crept up her thigh.

She whimpered. She was stuck between them, held by them, tortured.

And she never wanted to leave.

Jardin sat up then grabbed the waist band of her pajama bottoms. "Let's add some lingerie to the shopping list. A red, silky nightgown."

"One of those teddy things that will show off her breasts," Carrick added.

"Yes. We also need some toys for her. Too bad I didn't bring my play bag with me."

"It was an oversight," Carrick agreed. "We could be stretching her ass."

"I'll have a play while I'm spanking it."

Her heart raced as they talked about her like she wasn't even there. But every word seemed to set her desire soaring.

"Tonight, you can take my ass instead," Jardin said almost casually as he placed her pajama pants and panties on the floor, leaving her bare to their gaze. Carrick stiffened beside her. And when she glanced over at him, his face was filled with hunger as he stared at Jardin.

"My fucking pleasure."

Jardin smiled then leaned over her to kiss Carrick. She groaned. They were killing her. Jardin drew back to wink down at her. "But first we need to take care of our naughty girl. I'm thinking since she's so worried about making noise while I punish her that you should help her out."

What did that mean?

"Happy to," Carrick murmured while leaning down to kiss her.

How would they punish her while she was on her back? Then Jardin grabbed her legs, pushing them back against her chest. Her knees were bent, her ass on display.

Oh, hell no.

She wrenched her mouth away from Carrick's. Although that wasn't easy.

"Jardin, you can't!"

"What? I can't spank you? I think you'll find I can. What were we up to? Fifteen?"

"Sounds right," Carrick agreed.

"Not like this!" Jardin was already staring down at her ass, his gaze greedy.

"Why not?" Jardin asked.

"Because . . . because you can see everything!"

"But I want to see everything. No part of you should be hidden from us, should be forbidden to us. Understand? Carrick, take her legs so I can explore."

Her face went so red she probably looked like a tomato as Carrick wrapped one arm under her knees, pressing them to her chest while Jardin lay on the bed and kissed his way along her ass. He ran a finger down her slit between the two cheeks, pressing the tip inside her asshole.

"Now, this is very, very pretty." He sat up and she breathed a sigh of relief. But he simply stood and turned to the bedside drawer and rummaged inside it, pulling out a small bottle of lube and an anal plug still in its packaging.

"What . . . how . . . why is there lube and an anal plug in the bedside drawer?" she asked.

"Because my cousins are assholes. They're always sticking crap in these drawers. I'm the only one who ever stays in this room. I've found ben-wa balls, anal beads, cock rings, even a strap-on once."

She gaped at him, but he grinned at her. "Can't say I'm upset about it now. Have you ever had anal sex, Thea?"

She bit her lip and nodded.

"Did you like it?" Carrick asked.

She nodded again.

"That's good," Jardin said with satisfaction as he unwrapped the plug and coated it in lube. "We'll stretch you a bit first though, before we both take you."

Holy. Shit.

Her heart went into overdrive imagining one of them in her ass, the other in her pussy.

"Our girl likes that idea," Carrick murmured.

"She'll have to wait, though. Because we won't risk harming her."

"Damn straight," Carrick agreed as Jardin got back on the bed, kneeling in front of her bottom. He ran a wet finger between her butt cheeks before pressing it slowly into her asshole.

She groaned, clenched around him.

"Uh-uh, no tightening," he scolded. "I want you to stay nice and relaxed or I'm going to go downstairs and find a nice piece of ginger to plug you with instead." He wouldn't dare.

Except she knew he would. So, she forced herself to relax, which was really fucking difficult with how damn good it felt to have his finger in her ass as he drove his finger in and out of her. Then he added another finger. She breathed through the burn, her breath coming in sharp pants, especially when Carrick leaned down to play with her nipple. He licked it, sucked, bit down lightly.

Oh. Fuck. Yes.

Then Jardin drew his fingers out and she groaned. But the plug soon replaced his fingers. She writhed on the bed as he pushed it deeply. It was too much. She needed more. She needed them to touch her, take her.

"Please, please, please," she begged once it was pushed in all the way.

"Hold her there while I go wash my hands," Jardin commanded.

"With pleasure," Carrick murmured before kissing her. She was on fire. Nerve endings had been lit and she only knew one way to put them out.

Jardin didn't take long, thank God, and he was soon kneeling next to them on the bed. Carrick drew back from her mouth to suckle on her nipple as Jardin ran his hand over her ass cheek.

"Fifteen. Carrick, help our girl stay quiet."

She couldn't believe they were going to do this. But Jardin didn't waste time, landing two heavy smacks on her ass as Carrick smothered the noises that escaped with his mouth. Each smack that landed made her clench around the plug and drove her arousal higher and higher until she was dizzy. Until she was drunk on lust. Desire.

The sting barely even registered through her haze of need.

"Fuck that's a pretty sight," Jardin said, pausing to massage her cheeks.

Carrick moved back to suck on her neck. Jardin ran a finger along her slit. "How about this, sweetness? You stay quiet on your own for the rest of these and I won't make you wait for your orgasm. But you cry out, make a noise, and you'll wait until both Carrick and I are satisfied."

Fuck. Fuck. She nodded. She wanted that orgasm so badly. Carrick continued to kiss her neck, a spot he seemed obsessed with, while Jardin laid another smack on her ass. She bit down on her lip. Her eyes watered but not from pain.

More. More. It wasn't enough.

Another smack. She managed to hold in her cry.

Another one. Christ, this was so hard, but she could do it. She took in a gasp of air.

Another.

Last one. It landed right over the end of the plug and God help her, it was difficult to hold her cries back.

But she did it. She gave him a triumphant look. Jardin smiled while Carrick chuckled.

"Good girl," Jardin murmured. "Another choice."

Oh. Shit.

They were definitely trying to kill her.

"You can ride Carrick's face while I suck him off. Or you can finger yourself while we both watch."

What kind of a choice was that?

"I'll, um, ride his face."

Jesus. Jardin was good at this dirty talk. She was not.

Carrick let go of her legs then lay down on his back with a grin. She rolled over, feeling the plug shift inside her. Shit.

Jardin slapped her ass. "And don't lose that plug, or I'll make you wear it to breakfast tomorrow."

Christ.

Killing her.

CARRICK WATCHED Thea move over him, her full breasts swaying as she climbed into position, her thighs straddling his face.

"Ride me, Thea," he commanded, grabbing her hips. "Place your hands on the headboard and don't fucking move them. Understand me?"

Her eyes widened and she nodded. He pulled her hips down until her pussy was right over his mouth.

And then he started to feast. Jardin moved his legs apart and Carrick could feel him settle between them. Then the other man's hot mouth surrounded his firm dick and he groaned. Thea moaned as though she could feel that hum against her clit. And she likely could.

Jardin tortured him, running his tongue all over his shaft, cupping his balls and squeezing lightly. The slight sting just heightened his arousal, making him wonder what it would be like to feel a bigger bite of pain.

He concentrated on her clit, running his tongue around it then driving his tongue deep inside her.

"Oh. Oh. Oh. Please!"

"Come whenever you want, Thea," Jardin told her. "Carrick, you need to hold off."

Fuck. Like he didn't know that. It was damn hard though. He continued to drive Thea wild as Jardin took his cock deeply and swallowed.

Shit. Shit. Shit.

Then Thea let out a cry as she came. Thank Christ. He drank her down, gentling his tongue against her clit to help settle her.

Jardin slid his mouth free, and Carrick helped Thea climb off him.

"Thea, grab two condoms, you can put them on both of us," Jardin commanded. "Then I want you on your back on the bed, legs spread."

Thea scrambled to grab condoms from the top drawer while Jardin drew Carrick in for a kiss. "Damn, she tastes good on you."

Carrick grinned then groaned as Thea's small hand circled his cock. He looked down at her as she carefully and slowly rolled a condom onto his shaft.

"She's fucking killing me."

Jardin scoffed at him but then groaned, throwing his head back as she rolled a condom onto his dick.

"Fuck, baby. Stop teasing me and get into position," Jardin commanded.

She sent them both a sassy smile then turned around to crawl on hands and knees into position. Oh, she was getting more comfortable being naked around them.

Thank God. Because Carrick would prefer she was naked all the time. Not possible, but a man could dream.

He ran his hand down Jardin's back then cupped his firm ass cheek. "You sure about this? We can wait."

"I don't want to fucking wait. I want to feel you taking me while I take our girl."

Carrick grinned then leaned in to nip at Jardin's lower lip. "Stop fucking teasing me," Jardin told him.

Oh, but it was so much fun.

JARDIN PRESSED Thea's legs apart so he could kneel between them. Holding his weight up, he leaned in and sucked first one nipple then another into his mouth. He wasn't nervous about Carrick taking his ass.

This was meant to be.

"I need a taste of you first," he told Thea, kissing his way down her stomach. He noted the way she sucked it in. He didn't like that and gently bit her, just below her belly button. "You do not hide from us, Thea. And I will not have you thinking badly about yourself."

He moved to kiss the inside of her thigh as he felt Carrick part his ass cheeks and prod at his hole with a finger slickened with lube he'd obviously found in the top drawer. Oh, fuck yes. He had to pause as Carrick slid one finger in deep.

Christ.

"It's hard to just stop," she said.

"We'll help you," he told her. "Even if it means we need to keep you naked for a week, while constantly praising and touching and licking every inch of this delicious body."

She shuddered at his words.

Carrick moved up to two fingers as Jardin bent down to run his tongue along her wet slit. She groaned, pushing her legs further apart as she thrust her hips up at him. He tongued her clit as Carrick drove his fingers in and out of his ass. He was far rougher than he would be if it were Thea.

But Jardin wanted it rough.

"I need to be inside you," Carrick said in a low, gruff voice. "Before I blow my load just from fingering you."

Jardin slid up Thea's body and grabbed a pillow, shoving it under her hips before he slid his cock deep inside her. She was tighter because of the plug in her ass and it was all he could do to stop himself from coming then and there. He held himself still while Carrick positioned himself. He nudged at Jardin's entrance then slowly pushed forward.

Jardin let out a deep breath, relaxing as he pushed past the ring of muscle. Felt so good. Damn. Christ. A groan escaped him as he got impossibly harder.

"Fuck. I'm not going to last," he groaned.

"Me either," Carrick muttered. "Fuck, you're tight."

They started to move. Carrick driving deep inside his ass, while he fucked their girl. Leaning in, he kissed her, his hand moving down between them to toy with her clit.

"You're coming with us, Thea," he told her.

"Oh. Oh!" she cried as she clenched around him. "Please."

"Fuck! Fuck, I'm close!" Carrick called out before he roared his release.

So much for keeping quiet. But Jardin didn't care. The boys were far enough away not to hear. Still, he reached down to capture Thea's cry as she came. He drove himself deeply one last time before following them over, coming inside their girl. Sandwiched between them.

Nothing had ever felt so right.

27

"**S**heriff is coming up the drive," Tanner yelled into the family room where they were all squished in watching a movie.

Apparently tonight was family movie night. She wasn't sure if it was something they'd come up with for the boys or if they did this every week, but she kind of loved how much these guys did together. Even if they were all flipping nuts.

Mia had made buckets of popcorn with lots of different toppings, Flick had dragged in extra pillows and blankets. Now they were all sprawled out on the floor sofa and chairs, watching an action film.

Until Tanner's phone had buzzed and he'd gotten up to check on something.

Jardin and Carrick shared a look. She gazed over at them. Did they know why the sheriff was visiting? Were they leaving her out of something? She hadn't left the house at all today. Neither had Flick or Mia. She thought it was probably a precaution in case whoever was watching her was still around. She just hoped she wasn't putting anyone on the ranch in danger by staying here.

Jardin stood and reached out a hand to her, pulling her up. Carrick stood along with Alec and West.

"Keep watching," Alec said. "We'll be back soon. West, go grab Jake and bring him into my office."

She let Jardin lead her into the office, looking behind to ensure Carrick was following. He sent her a reassuring smile.

Jardin settled her onto the sofa and both men flanked her, each holding a hand.

Alec sat behind his desk and West leaned on the wall behind him.

"Come right in here, sheriff," Tanner said, leading the way into the office.

She'd only seen the sheriff in passing. But he was a hand-some man, tall with dark hair. He gave Tanner an exasperated look.

"Thanks, Tanner," was all he said.

Tanner walked out, shutting the door behind him.

"You found him?" Alec asked.

"Hello to you too." Jake pulled off his hat then smiled over at her. "We haven't met. I'm Jake."

"Thea." She shook the hand he held out. He had a nice, firm grip but it wasn't too harsh. She looked over at Alec. "Got who?"

"The thug sent by Derrick Silvers to watch you," Jake told her.

She sucked in a breath. "You found him?"

"Pretty hard to hide in a town like this. Even though he wasn't staying in any rented accommodation, people around here notice outsiders. He's been skulking around. But we've kept an eye on him. Today we got him on a minor traffic violation. He was trying to leave town. Turns out he's got a warrant out for his arrest. Name's John Mathers. Long rap sheet. He's not talking, but he's a known associate of Silvers. He'll be transported back to New Orleans."

Oh thank God.

"He'll probably just send someone else, won't he? If they find out I'm still here and not on my way to Oklahoma."

"He won't get to you here," Alec said firmly.

"And remember, Regent is dealing with Silvers. Soon he's going to have bigger problems than you," Jardin added.

Jake nodded. "You're fairly safe here. I'd still be careful until Silvers is dealt with. Don't go anywhere alone. But then, I'm sure that won't be a problem anyway."

She looked from Carrick to Jardin. No, she guessed she wouldn't be going anywhere alone for quite a while

"I don't know about this."

She leaned into Carrick and looked up at the building. It didn't look like what she'd expected a BDSM club to look like. However, she had no idea what she'd been expecting. Flashing red lights? Images of naked men and women having sex painted on the walls?

It was just an ordinary looking building but it didn't make her any less nervous about going inside.

Carrick moved her in front of him and started massaging her shoulders. They'd parked around the back. It was well lit and already filled with cars. Busy place considering it was a Tuesday night. She'd been going out of her mind wondering what was happening with Silvers these past few days. Jardin had finally snapped and told her they were going to find a way to take her mind off things.

Hence, how they'd ended up at Saxon's.

But to say she was nervous was an understatement.

To her surprise, Jardin moved up beside her and took her hand in his big one, running his thumb soothingly over the back of it.

"Are you sure it's safe to leave the ranch?"

"No one else has been spotted in town and nobody gets into

Saxon's who isn't a member. Plus, we're not leaving you alone. We thought you might like the chance to get off the ranch," Carrick told her.

He wasn't wrong. It was nice to leave the ranch. The Malones were awesome, but overwhelming.

"If you don't like it, we can leave," Jardin told her. "I'm more than happy to play at home."

She bit her lip, wondering if that was true. She didn't want him to deny something he needed because she was chicken shit.

"Hey." Jardin grabbed her chin raising her face. "I don't lie. Never to you. Never to Carrick. I did need this for the longest time. It was the only time I felt alive. But now I have the two of you. And you are both more than enough."

He looked from her to Carrick, who continued to rub her tense shoulders. Damn, the man was sure talented with his hands.

"I want to try it," she said with determination.

"That's my brave girl," Jardin praised. "What are the rules, again?"

"I have to stay with one of you at all times. No talking to any other Dom without permission. No making eye contact with them. Jardin is Sir. Carrick is Carrick." Her lips twitched as Carrick snorted. "I don't have to do any play if I don't want to, but if I do then my safe word is red."

"And we've gone through your limits if you decide to play," Carrick confirmed.

She nodded. "Let's do this."

~

Saxon's was a whole new world. She looked around in wonder at all the scenes being played out. Carrick had a firm hold of her hand while Jardin went to the bar to grab them all drinks.

"Want to sit down over there, rocket?" Carrick asked, pointing to a seating area. It was off to one side, but still allowed a good view of what was going on. A big man dwarfed one of the chairs. Beside him knelt a woman dressed in a red halter top and matching skirt.

They'd gone shopping for her earlier. Apparently, Haven had a shop filled with all sorts of toys and fet wear. She'd chosen a black corset and a short skirt.

She nodded. Might as well.

"Remember to use your words," Carrick reminded her, patting her ass.

He led her over to chairs. The man looked up at him with a nod. The woman gave her a sneaky, small smile.

Carrick sat and pulled her onto his lap. She smiled at him gratefully. She wasn't so sure about kneeling like the other woman.

The big man's eyebrows rose as he looked over their shoulders. "Jardin, how's it going?"

She looked back to find Jardin giving the other man a nod of greeting. "Duncan. Good to see you. This is Carrick and Thea."

Duncan nodded at them both. Then he looked down at the woman and patted his lap. "Come sit here, sugar, so we can all have a chat."

Jardin sat beside Carrick and handed her a bottle of water, undoing the top first. She gulped some down. She was sitting with her back to Carrick's front. He reached down and grabbed the bottle from her, finishing it off.

"Carrick, Thea, this is Duncan Jones and his wife, Laken. Duncan is a deputy sheriff."

"How do you like Saxon's?" Duncan asked.

She looked to Jardin, not sure if she could answer.

"You can speak freely, baby," Jardin told her. "Thea's never been to a club before. She's testing the waters to see if she likes it."

Duncan nodded. "Well, welcome, Thea."

"Thank you." She gave them both a shy look.

"I think I've seen you around town," Laken said. "You're working for Marcy, right?"

"Oh, uh, I was." And she felt terrible for letting the other woman down. Although Jardin had told her that she'd completely understood when he'd talked to her.

Laken gave her a confused look.

"We've decided to go back to New Orleans," Jardin said easily.

Before they could ask any more questions, a gorgeous man dressed in a white shirt and dark dress pants approached. Power filled his every move and, around him, people gave him deferential looks.

"Saxon," Jardin greeted.

Duncan sent the other man a sharp nod. Saxon looked amused at that.

"Jardin, Duncan, Laken." He turned that gaze to her, and she had to suppress a shiver. This was the owner? Wow. "This must be Carrick and Thea. It's a pleasure to meet you both."

"Same," Carrick said, squeezing her thigh lightly.

"Um, hi, Sir." That felt weird.

Saxon smiled. "She really is new. Hope you all enjoy yourselves. Jardin, since you're here I wondered if you'd take care of a few issues that have arisen."

What did that mean?

"Don't you have another Dom to act as punisher?" Jardin asked.

Punisher. He'd told her about his role at Saxon's when he was around. However, he'd also told her that if she wasn't comfortable, he wouldn't touch anyone else.

That rock in her stomach told her she was pretty damn uncomfortable.

"He's not in tonight. And you're so good at it."

Jardin reached over and grabbed Thea's hand, studying her

face. Then his gaze moved up to Carrick. "Actually, I'm afraid I'll have to say no. I don't think I can fill that role when I'm here anymore."

She tensed, expecting Saxon to be angry. Instead he just grinned. "Well, good. It finally happened, huh?"

He slapped his hand down on Jardin's shoulder then strolled away.

"Manipulative bastard," Duncan muttered.

"Duncan!" Laken scolded.

"It's the truth. Come on, a spanking bench is free. I'm in the mood to redden your ass."

Arousal flooded Laken's face.

"You didn't have to do that because of me," Thea said when they were alone.

"I didn't. Well, not just because of you." Jardin looked to Carrick.

She glanced up at their big, quiet man. He sent her a wink, but there was relief on his face. "Turns out, I wasn't so keen on him touching someone else, either."

She gave him a small smile and Carrick kissed her gently.

"But what about your needs?" she asked Jardin worriedly.

"Hmm, maybe I should secure one of you to a cross and take a strap to you."

Um. No thanks.

"I'd give it a go," Carrick said, shocking them both.

"Really?" Jardin asked. "I was joking."

"I'm not," Carrick tried him. "Truth is, I think I might like a little pain with my pleasure."

"It will be more than a little."

"Well, maybe I need Thea's mouth on my cock to help me suffer through." Carrick winked at her.

"Are you sure?" she asked.

"About your mouth on my dick?"

"No," she gave him a firm look. "About trying this."

He tucked her hair behind her ear. "I have a safe word. And I want to try this. I want to know."

"All right, then we try." Jardin rose and held out his hand to her. "First, though. I think we should give Thea a bit of a taste."

JARDIN LED Thea to a free St Andrews Cross in the corner of the dungeon. It was quieter back there, more secluded. Which was perfect.

He'd held a small bag that contained the stuff they'd bought today. Not for the first time, he wished he'd brought his play bag. But this would do for now.

"Carrick will you restrain her for me?"

Carrick leaned in to kiss Thea gently then led her over to the cross, getting her into position and securing her ankles and wrists.

"Did you do what you were told and go without panties, Thea?" Carrick crooned to her as Jardin coated a new butt plug in lube. Tonight, they were taking her ass. He'd reserved a private room for them upstairs.

He had no wish to fuck either Thea or Carrick in front of an audience, even if they wanted that.

"Good girl," Carrick praised Thea as he raised her skirt, tucking it up high into the waistband and baring her firm ass. "How are you with this, rocket?"

She'd stiffened slightly but as he rubbed her bottom, she gradually started to relax. She still had some hang-ups about her body they were going to need to work through. This was one small step.

"Okay, Carrick."

Carrick smacked his hand down on one cheek. Then the other. "You're owed some punishment, aren't you? For running when you should have come to us. For not confiding in us. That's going to result in a very hot ass for you. We're going to plug you, punish you, and, later on, we'll fuck you."

"Didn't you punish me for that the other day?" She pouted.

"No, that was for talking bad about yourself," Jardin told her.

Carrick gave her another ten or so smacks before moving around the front of the cross. He gently kissed her, watching her closely. "Beautiful girl."

His hand reached between her legs to tease her clit. She gasped. "Carrick!"

They'd already discussed this scene between them, each of them knew what the other was doing. Carrick would keep an eye on her to make sure she wasn't freaking out while Jardin pushed her.

"How are you doing, rocket?"

"Good. Green, Carrick," she cried out as Jardin pulled her ass cheeks apart and slid the firm plug inside her. They'd been plugging her each night, so she knew to relax and let him push it inside her. He watched it disappear, his cock straining against his black pants.

Christ. So hot.

Leaning in, he kissed her neck, the back of her shoulders. "Want to try the crop, baby?" he asked her.

"Yes, Sir." she murmured.

"That's my good girl. Just relax for me."

Luckily, there was a shop in Haven with a good range of implements and toys. He was just going to use the lightest of touches with her.

He grabbed the crop from the bag as Carrick continued to play with her pussy, kissing her, driving her wild. Jardin smacked the crop down on her ass, loving the red imprint it left behind. He gave her three smacks in quick succession.

"How's that, baby?" Jardin asked.

Carrick pulled his lips away from hers so she could answer, but his hand remained between her legs.

"Good, Sir. Green. Oh hell."

"Here are some more then." He landed five more on her ass. Arousal filled him. Having her bound, the fact she was accepting his discipline, it just fucking did something to him.

"Two more, rocket," Carrick told her. "Still, green?"

"Yes, Carrick."

Jardin gave her the last two right as Carrick drove her up and over the edge. She cried out, her body shaking on the cross as she came. Jardin moved quickly forward to undo her wrists. Carrick dropped down to release the restraints around her ankles. Then Jardin picked her up and carried her to a chair that was next to the cross for this reason. He sat, holding her on his lap with her ass over the edge of his lap so she wasn't resting her weight on it. He held her tightly, rocking her slightly as Carrick came to kneel in front of them. He pushed back her hair, smiling down at her.

"How you doing, Thea?"

"Great, Carrick." She smiled at Carrick then up at him. "More than great."

Jardin chuckled. "I think I might have created a monster."

"Hmm," she murmured. "Carrick's turn next. Can't wait."

CARRICK WASN'T sure he was doing the right thing. He only knew he wanted to try. At least Jardin didn't have his whip with him. For this scene, they'd agreed on a belt. He'd stripped off his clothes already and, naked, he moved to the cross.

Jardin secured his wrists and ankles to the cross as Thea moved around in front of him, in the same position as he'd been in before. Then she wrapped her cool hand around his cock. He groaned.

Fuck. Him.

Jardin warmed him up with his hand, smacking it against his ass. And it became almost hypnotic. It was a dull thud. A heat that built gradually. His head started to swim. Desire flooded him.

"Where are you at?" Jardin asked him.

"Green," he replied.

"Good. What's your safe word?"

"Red."

"Use it if you need to. Here comes the belt."

Thea kept moving her hand up and down his shaft. Fuck. If she kept doing that he was going to come and they had plans for her later.

"Thea, stop," he commanded. "I don't want to come."

"Yes, Carrick." She remained kneeling there, staring up at him with love in her eyes as the belt landed.

Holy fuck. Yes.

The belt packed a sting. The heat burned. And his need grew. Soon he found himself high on the pain. He wanted to come. Shit. He needed to come.

The belt had stopped he realized as he came back to himself. Someone pressed against his back. Their heat surrounded him. Safety. Love.

"How are you doing, Carrick?"

"Green."

"Very good. I'm going to undo the restraints then we'll get you wrapped up in a blanket and Thea will hold you while I tidy up. Is that acceptable?"

"Yes. Fuck. Yes. Want to fuck her."

Jardin chuckled. "We will. As soon as you come back to yourself."

It was a bit of a blur. Moving away from the cross, being held by Thea. His ass throbbed, but in a delicious way. A bottle of water was pressed to his lips and he drank it down, the coldness chasing away the last of his daze. He blinked, looking up into Jardin's face. He was staring down at him with a mix of love and concern.

"Hey, you back with us?"

"Yep."

"Up to more?" Jardin asked.

"If by more you mean fucking my girl's ass, I'm so there."

Thea groaned but when he turned to her, she was smiling. "Hey, rocket."

She leaned in to kiss him. "Hey, yourself."

"Let's fucking go."

THEA HAD to giggle as they made their way upstairs. Carrick hadn't bothered to put his clothes back on, stating there was no point. Jardin held an arm around his waist while holding her hand to guide them up to a private room.

Inside, it looked like any bedroom, except the bed was enormous and everything screamed wealth.

"Carrick, on your stomach on the bed. I want to check your ass. Thea can you get the cream out of my bag."

Carrick grumbled something about Jardin being a bossy bastard, but he laid himself in position. "I don't need any damn cream."

"Well, you're going to have to suck it up because I'm putting it on you." Jardin inspected every inch of his handiwork, lightly rubbing some cream that would help with pain and any bruising. "Fucking beautiful."

Carrick rolled onto his back then winced. Jardin kissed him gently then laid back on the bed. "Thea, grab the condoms from the bedside drawer, you know what to do. You're going to put them on us both then ride me while Carrick takes your ass."

Her gaze went from a smiling Carrick to an intense Jardin. She made short work of getting the condoms on. She was getting good at that. Then she straddled Jardin's hips. He drew her down to kiss her, his finger going to her clit to tease her until she was thrusting her hips against him, wanting more.

Needing it.

Then he guided his dick inside her. So full. So good.

He pumped inside her a few times before holding her still, his hands around her hips.

Then Carrick moved in behind her. She caught her breath as he tugged at the anal plug, drawing it slowly out of her ass.

"Fucking beautiful." He squeezed one of her ass cheeks, then ran a finger over her back hole. "Take a deep breath in for me, Thea."

She felt him position the head of his cock at her entrance. Then she let her breath out as he breeched her. There was a bite of pain, a sense of fullness, and then he was inside her. Filling her. Both of them taking her.

Pure bliss.

They started moving. She was tossed between them. A ship at the mercy of the raging sea and the stormy winds. And she wouldn't have it any other way.

"Fuck, I'm not going to last," Carrick groaned.

"Neither am I," Jardin agreed. He reached between them to play with her clit. Her breath caught in her chest. She needed to come so badly, yet she didn't want this moment to end.

"Fuck. So tight. I can't . . ." Carrick roared as he came.

Jardin thrust up, deep inside her. "Come, baby. Come with me."

She screamed, clenching down around their dicks as she reached that crest then fell over. Jardin yelled as he came soon after.

They collapsed together. Sated. Fulfilled. One.

JARDIN'S PHONE BEEPED, and, with a groan he disentangled himself from Thea to grab it. She shifted over and slipped into Carrick's arms. They were back in their bed at his cousin's house.

He opened the message from his oldest brother.

You're welcome.

That was all it said. He clicked on the link he'd sent and a video clip from a news station came on.

"And in breaking news, Derrick Silvers has been arrested for allegedly conspiring to commit murder, human trafficking, as well as manufacturing and selling drugs."

He texted his brother back.

Thank you.

28

I f the Texas Malones' house was complete chaos, the New Orleans Malones' could only be described as icy calm. The house was enormous. And intimidating. A stern-faced butler had greeted them at the door to help them with their bags.

Thea walked in with Ace and Keir, looking around her with wide eyes and wondering how the hell she was going to keep the boys from breaking anything.

"Is any of this stuff super expensive? One-of-a-kind? Priceless?" she asked Carrick.

"I imagine most of it is. Intimidating, huh?"

She nodded. Jardin turned to look at them. Then he glanced around. "I grew up with it all, so I don't take much notice. Cold, isn't it?"

She couldn't imagine him growing up there. "I'm sure we'll get used to it."

Ace and Keir turned to give her incredulous looks. "Just don't touch anything," she told them. "Or run around in here. Definitely no water fights inside."

"Actually," a masculine voice stated from behind them. "That sounds like a lot of fun. Perhaps if we'd been allowed water fights, this place might have more of a lived-in look."

They all turned toward the man standing there. He looked like an older version of Jardin, with streaks of gray in his dark hair. He was polished and nicely put together, his slate-gray eyes cold.

Regent Malone.

The man she had to thank for getting rid of Derrick Silvers. Apparently, there was no way he could wriggle out of the charges. There was too much evidence against him, and all witnesses were being protected. Which she guessed was also Regent's doing.

Soon after Jardin had broken the good news, they'd packed up to drive back to New Orleans, stopping for just one night in Lafayette so they could retrieve her mother's necklace. She still welled up thinking about the fact she'd gotten it back.

"Thea, Ace, and Keir, this is my brother Reggie."

Regent sighed. "It's Regent, not Reggie. But I'm pleased to meet you all." He gave them all a small nod. "I trust you'll all be at dinner."

"Yep, we'll be down as soon as we've unpacked," Jardin told him.

"Good. Gerald has prepared something special for all of you."

God, she hoped it wasn't foie gras. As though he could read her mind, Regent sent her a small wink. She was so shocked she just stood frozen there as he turned away.

"I'll have Gerald put away all the priceless artifacts and buy some water pistols in preparation for this water fight," he called back.

She turned to Jardin. "He won't really, will he?"

"Get water pistols, sure. Actually participate? Likely not. Couldn't see Regent Montclair Malone actually operating a water pistol. But I will."

"Me too," Carrick said.

Ace and Keir stared at them, then a big smile crossed Ace's face. "Awesome!"

She hoped Gerald really would put away all the priceless stuff.

"Don't worry, rocket," Carrick told her, placing his arm over her shoulders. "We're not living here forever. We'll find an equally stuffy place to call our own. It's the New Orleans Malone way."

"I heard that!" Jardin said.

To her relief, dinner was hamburgers. Regent sent her another of those knowing looks. The boys dug in excitedly. To her surprise, they were taking all these changes better than her.

Dinner was nothing like it had been in Haven. Nobody yelled over each other or tried to steal their food. And Regent and Victor ate their burgers with knives and forks. She'd had to nudge Ace to stop him from staring.

It did look pretty bizarre, though. Especially since they, along with Jardin, were all wearing suits. Only Carrick and Maxim were dressed more casually. Maxim reminded her more of his cousins. There was a teasing grin on his face and his eyes danced with amusement whenever he looked over at her.

"So, Thea, you worked for Jardin?" Maxim asked.

"Um, yes."

"It was an office romance then?" Maxim sent Jardin a look.

"Nothing happened until after she left," Jardin said.

"Ran from you."

"She didn't run from me." Jardin scowled at his brother.

"We were running from that asshole, Silvers," Keir spoke up. That shut Maxim up.

"Keir, don't say asshole," she whispered.

"That's what he was, though," Keir replied.

"Keir is quite right," Regent said, wiping his mouth with a

cloth napkin. She was glad she didn't have to do the laundry. "He was an asshole and more. But you don't have to worry about him any longer."

"Thank you," she told him sincerely. "For taking care of him."

"He threatened our family," Regent answered, taking a sip of red wine. "That will never be allowed."

"We couldn't find your father though," Victor said.

That was the first time he'd spoken.

"Oh." She frowned, wondering where he was.

"Our dad?" Keir asked. "What's he got to do with anything. Wait . . ." Keir turned to her. "Did he have anything to do with this asshole wanting you?"

She bit her lip. "He, um, owed Silvers money."

"Bastard," Keir muttered while Ace stared at her solemnly.

"Keir," she scolded again

"He's not wrong, Thea," Jardin said.

"Maybe we should all talk about something else," Carrick suggested.

"I'm sure Dad is fine," she reassured Ace.

"I don't care," he said. "He's not our real dad. So long as we get to stay with you, Thea, I don't care about him."

She reached over and pulled him close to her. Then she gave Keir a smile. He just gave her a nod back as though in agreement with what Ace had said. Her heart lightened.

The door to the dining room opened and a slim-built, dark-haired woman entered. She was pale. And thin. Too thin. There was something almost ethereal about her. She was wearing a flow-ing, dark blue dress.

Charlotte.

The sister who'd been kidnapped. She paused and looked around the room, her eyes wide. Thea's heart broke at the heartache in her eyes.

Regent immediately rose and slowly, carefully walked toward

her, as though she were a wild animal who could take off with a wrong move.

"Lottie, darling, are you hungry?" he asked her.

"Not really," she murmured, glancing along the table. All of the Malone men had stiffened, watching their sister.

Carrick reached over and slid his hand into Thea's, giving it a reassuring squeeze.

"You're having hamburgers? I love hamburgers."

Regent offered her his arm and she slid her hand into the crook of his elbow. He led her very carefully over to the table, to the seat across from Thea. The way he treated her brought tears to Thea's eyes.

Like she was precious. Delicate and fragile.

"Hello, I'm Lottie." She gave Ace and Keir a smile before looking at her then Carrick.

She blinked a few times. "Carrick? I didn't realize you were here. Did I know Carrick was here?" she asked Regent.

"I mentioned it the other day, darling," he said as he fixed her a burger, placing it on her plate and cutting it into quarters.

"Oh, I'm sorry, Carrick," she said.

"It's all right, Lottie. I'm so glad to see you."

Lottie smiled then looked down at her plate. "Regent, you made it just like when I was a kid. Excellent. Well, if we had burgers more often maybe I'd come down for dinners."

"We'll have them every night if that's what it takes," Regent murmured.

Lottie just patted his hand.

"You're all living here?" she asked Thea.

"Thea and Carrick are mine now, Lottie," Jardin told her. "As are Ace and Keir. They're Thea's brothers."

"Oh, it will be nice to have some children around. This old place could use some laughter. I suppose you won't stay long, though."

Thea made a quick decision, seeing Lottie's sad face. "We're staying for a while."

Carrick stiffened beside her, but when she looked over, he gave her a smile and a wink. She glanced at Jardin, who gave her a grateful look.

"That's good."

"Yeah, once Gerald moves all the fancy stuff, Reggie said we can have a water fight," Ace informed Lottie around a bit of burger.

"Ace, swallow before you talk," Thea scolded.

"Sorry." He swallowed. "You wanna have a water fight with us, Lottie."

She swallowed more delicately. "You know, I might just do that. If Reggie thinks it's okay."

Thea expected Regent to object to his nickname, but he just gave Lottie a gentle smile. "Of course, darling."

"What about you, Vicky?" She turned to Victor. Oh, he definitely didn't look like a Vicky.

But he didn't even flinch. "Oh, I'm in. I'm going to whip Maxim's ass."

"Hey!" Maxim pouted. "I'm always picked on 'cause I'm the youngest."

"No, it's because you're the ugliest," Jardin told him.

Keir and Ace snickered. Oh, dear Lord, she gave up trying to teach them good manners. This was going to be hopeless.

"What school do you boys go to?" Lottie asked.

Keir answered her.

"And you like it?"

"Our teachers are nice," Keir answered. "And we have some friends, but some of the moms are mean to Thea."

She stiffened. She hadn't thought they'd paid much attention to that.

"And some of the kids don't like us 'cause we're poor. I don't see why that matters. Arthur Pincher's family has money and he's a jerk face," Ace added. "Plus, the principal and teachers always side with him when he says Keir and I did something to him."

"Al Pincher's kid?" Regent asked.

Jardin nodded with a scowl.

"Well, that won't do, will it," Lottie murmured looking to her oldest brother.

"I don't think you'll find that a problem anymore," Regent said. "With the amount of money I've donated to the school lately, I basically own it. Including the teachers and the principal."

He what?

She gave Regent a shocked look. "What? You . . . you didn't need to do that."

"Regent always protects his family ferociously," Lottie told her. "He's very good at it."

"Most of the time," Regent muttered darkly.

"Well, thank you." She owed the man a lot.

"Still, a show of force might be needed, don't you think?" Lottie said. "Boys, how would you like your new uncles to come visit your school?"

Keir sat up straight and Ace danced around on his chair. "Hell, yeah! That'll show Arthur Pincher."

It certainly would.

29

Thea glanced down at her phone with a frown as she drove, surprised to find the school's phone number come up.

Shit.

Things had been going so smoothly this last week since they'd returned home. Sure, living in the Malone mansion took some getting used to. As did the Malones themselves. But she had Jardin, Carrick, and the boys. She was also growing closer to Lottie, who was kind and funny. And she was smart. Super smart.

On their first day back, all the Malones except for Lottie had come to the school with the boys. They'd gone in an actual limousine which Ace was still talking about. Even Keir had boasted about how awesome they'd looked walking in flanked by the scary, handsome Malone brothers.

Okay, those were her words not his. But, still, she'd been in awe of them all. Even with Maxim cracking jokes about checking out the teachers.

The principal had practically fallen over herself trying to get on Thea's good side.

Good luck with that, bitch.

Still, Thea kept things civil for the boys' sake.

"Hello?" she answered the phone.

"Ms. Garrison, it's Ms. Mackerly here. I was just wondering if you could come back to the school for a moment?"

"Is there a problem?" She'd just dropped the boys off and she'd been driving to Jardin's office. His latest PA had already quit, and he needed some help, even though he insisted he didn't.

"Um, yes. Ace has been involved in another fight."

"I'm on my way." She turned the car around, ignoring the honking horns.

She kept one eye on the road as she hit Jardin's name on her phone.

"You better not be driving and talking on the phone, Thea," was how he greeted her.

Oh shoot.

"I'm using the Bluetooth!"

"Yes, and I've seen how badly you drive even while using the Bluetooth, which is why I told you not to drive and talk at all on your phone."

"I didn't have an accident, and that other car came out of nowhere."

Jardin just grunted, unimpressed.

"I just got a call from the principal. She said Ace has been fighting." She deliberately didn't confirm that she was driving. But her ass tingled because she knew he'd know. And, later, her butt would pay the price.

"That's odd. I told her to call me first if there were any problems."

"Jardin!"

Damn it, he was unbelievable.

"It's called sharing the load, Thea."

Actually, it was called being overbearing and unbelievably arrogant.

"I'll call Carrick, he's closer," Jardin told her. "He can meet you there."

"I don't need any help, I'll be fine."

"I'll call Carrick," he said firmly. "And Thea?"

"Yes?"

"Your ass is toast tonight."

The call ended and she shook her head. Yep. Arrogant and overprotective. Those were Malone traits. Not that Carrick couldn't be just as protective. He just tended to be more reasonable.

As she pulled up outside the school, her phone rang. Carrick.

"Hey," she said. "You really don't have to come with me."

"I'll be there in fifteen," he told her. "Wait for me."

She let out a sigh. "I can't wait for you."

"Thea, wait for me or I'll be adding to that spanking Jardin is giving you tonight."

"Fine. See you soon."

Christ almighty. She climbed out of her car. Her very new car. With the highest safety rating possible. Jardin had presented it to her the day after they arrived.

She leaned against her car to wait for Carrick. It was ridiculous.

"Thea."

She froze at that raspy voice. A racking cough filled the air. She turned to find her father stumbling toward her. He looked like shit and his stench reached her before he did. She stepped back from him, not wanting him to touch her.

"What are you doing here?" she demanded.

"Came to see you. Thea, I need help."

She shook her head. "I've tried to help you in the past. All I got in return were bruises and a broken arm."

Regret filled his face. "I'm sorry about that, really I am. But I'm sober now, sweetheart."

Sure, he was. That's why he was breathing bourbon fumes all over her.

"Go away. I don't want to talk to you."

"But your brothers might," he told her. "I still have custody of them, don't I? What if I demanded you return them? The cops would like to know how you kidnapped them."

She turned on him. "I didn't fucking kidnap them and you know it. And you go to the police, they'll laugh their asses off. You don't have a leg to stand on. But go if you want. I have the weight of the Malones behind me now. I'm their family. Ace and Keir are their family. And they don't take kindly to threats."

"Please, just a bit of money. Thea!"

Swinging around, she stomped into the building. She wasn't going to be a pushover anymore. How often had he stolen from her? Hurt her? She didn't owe him anything! Although that didn't stop her from feeling guilty.

Reaching into her handbag, she pulled out her phone and sent Carrick a quick text.

Gone inside. My dad was here. Had to get away.

She walked into reception, surprised to see it empty. But she didn't wait for that awful receptionist to return. She just wanted to deal with whatever was going on with Ace.

Knocking on the office, she stormed her way in. She was beyond caring what the principal thought of her at this point.

And she came to a screeching halt at the sight that greeted her.

"J-Jenny?"

30

C arrick read the text message as he drove.

Yes, he knew he was being a hypocrite considering he'd spank Thea's ass for doing the same. But he didn't have time to pull over. He swore as he read it. Then his swearing became a groan of frustration as he rounded the corner and came into a line of traffic. What the fuck?

Quickly, he hit Jardin's name.

"I'm twenty minutes out," Jardin said.

"I've just hit traffic. Hopefully, I'll be there at about the same time. But Thea texted me to say her father turned up outside the school."

"What the fuck?" Jardin snapped.

"She said she was going inside. She'll be safer in there at least."

"Damn it! Fuck."

"I know. I know." He understood the other man's frustration. "I'll meet you there."

～

"WHAT ARE YOU DOING, JENNY?" she asked.

"It's not Jenny! It's Jennifer, you bitch!"

Jenny, who was looking decidedly worse for wear in a dirty pants suit, with her hair all wild around her face glared at Thea from manic-filled eyes.

What the hell?

Jenny also held a gun to Ms. Mackerly's head.

Thea did a quick sweep of the room, making sure no one else was in there and breathed a sigh of relief to find it empty. So, obviously, Jenny had made the principal call her to get her to come back by saying Ace had been in a fight.

She eyed the gun warily.

"You need to put the gun down before you hurt someone, Jenny," she warned.

Carrick would be here soon. She just had to keep the other woman calm. Except what would Carrick do when he arrived? He could get shot trying to protect her.

"I've been waiting for you," Jenny told her with a crazy laugh. "Been watching you. Waiting for the right time. But those men you're with keep you close, don't they? Do you have a magical pussy or something?"

Ms. Mackerly let out a shocked cry as Jenny thrust her away. She fell to the ground. "He should have been mine, you know. Jardin. He was meant to be mine."

She stalked toward Thea, holding the gun up.

Thea took a step back, wishing she hadn't closed the door behind her. What was she going to do?

Jenny's hand shook wildly as she aimed the gun. Ms. Mackerly lay on the floor, weeping. No help there, that was for sure.

Thea tensed, fear flooding her.

Suddenly the door opened behind her.

"Thea, if you'll just listen to me . . . hey, what's going on here?"

her father demanded. "Why are you holding a gun on my daughter?"

Jenny turned to look at her father, just as he pushed Thea to one side. The gun fired and she screamed. Her father fell to the ground and Jenny just stood there, looking shocked.

She could hear loud voices yelling. People flooded the room. Someone tackled Jenny, not that she was putting up much resistance. Thea crawled toward her father, sobs wracking her body.

"Dad. Dad."

She rolled him over. His chest was covered in blood, his eyes open and unseeing. Tears fell down her cheeks as she shook.

"Thea, oh, God, Thea." She was aware of Carrick pulling her back against him, holding her tightly.

"He saved me," she mumbled. "He saved me. He's dead, isn't he?"

Jardin moved to the other side of her father, reaching out to try and find a pulse. He shook his head at her. "I'm so sorry, baby."

She sobbed hysterically, barely aware of Carrick picking her up and carrying her away, of Jardin's softly murmured words. Of Jenny's screams.

It all faded away.

LATER THAT NIGHT, she sat on the edge of Ace's bed, watching both him and Keir sleep. They each had their own room, but they'd opted to sleep in the same bed tonight.

Although they seemed to be taking their dad's death pretty well. They were having a tougher time with the fact that she'd nearly been shot.

"Come on, rocket," Carrick placed a hand on her shoulder. "It's time you rested."

After the shooting, she'd been checked over by paramedics.

Then she'd had to go get the boys and explain what had happened. Then there had been interviews with the cops. All the Malones had turned up except Lottie at one point.

When they'd come home, they'd found that Lottie had ordered pizza. She'd held Thea for a long time, it was obvious she was having a hard time as well.

Thea let Carrick pick her up and carry her out of the room. Jardin closed the boys' door behind them and led them to their bedroom. They walked into the attached bathroom, where the huge jetted tub had been filled with water.

Carrick stripped her while Jardin pulled off his clothes. Then he carried her into the water and sat with her on his lap while Carrick took off his clothes then climbed in. They held her together, running their hands over her as though searching for any missed injuries.

"That's it, I'm hiring you a permanent bodyguard," Jardin stated. "I'll get Maxim on it in the morning."

She sighed and leaned her face against his chest, too tired to fight him right then. She knew it was Jardin's way of saying he'd been worried. And that he loved her.

"Maybe I should quit work and stay with her all the time." Okay, that was a surprise. Carrick was usually the sensible one.

"Or maybe you should both lock me in a tower like Rapunzel," she snarked.

Oh, look, she did have some energy to fight back.

"That idea has merit," Carrick said.

"Thought you'd object to that," Jardin told her. "But if you'd rather, we can arrange it."

"My dad died saving me," she said numbly. "From Jenny. She hated me because she thought I stole Jardin from her."

"She's got more than a few screws loose," Jardin muttered darkly. "Cops found all these creepy photos of me in her apartment. And more photos of you. She'd been watching you for a while."

"And here I thought I was in danger from Silvers," she muttered.

"Our girl seems to be a magnet for psychos and nut jobs," Carrick commented.

"Not fair, Jenny was after Jardin."

Jardin grumbled something under his breath.

"He wasn't a good dad. Not even close. But, in the end, he saved me, so I guess that counts for something."

Carrick cupped her face between his rough hands. "I don't like the way he treated you or the boys, but I will forever be grateful to him for saving you. Because I couldn't live without you."

"You mean everything to us, Thea," Jardin added. "You're the very air we breathe. Nothing can happen to you."

"I love the two of you as well," she told them.

"Good," Jardin said firmly. "Now about this tower . . ."

EPILOGUE

Five months later . . .

THEA LOOKED out at the sign welcoming them to Haven. It hadn't been an easy five months. She still had nightmares of Jenny shooting her father. The boys had had a few nightmares as well. But all of them were slowly healing—with the help of Jardin and Carrick.

The boys were now hers. Forever. Jenny's trial date was coming up and Thea was nervous as hell about testifying. She hadn't been granted bail, but had been remanded to a psychiatric unit instead. Silvers trial had just finished. He'd been given life in prison.

She finally felt like she could breathe easier.

"Here we go," Jardin said from the driver's seat.

Carrick sent her a smile from the front passenger seat.

The boys had both abandoned them, choosing to go in Maxim's mustang. Because, apparently, it was far cooler.

Regent and Vincent were in Regent's Bentley.

Unfortunately, they hadn't been able to convince Lottie to come. But some friends of the family were with her, keeping her company. And Thea had promised to send her lots of photos.

Of the wedding.

Her phone dinged and she looked down at it with a grin. "Flick said to hurry our asses up. She wants all her bridesmaids there for her shower." Which included her. She could scarcely believe it when Flick asked her to be her bridesmaid.

"All six of them," Jardin scoffed.

"Well, she probably thought she needed them with West wanting all his brothers to stand up for him," she pointed out.

"West didn't want his brothers to stand up for him," Jardin countered. "He was forced into it."

"I'm just thankful he finally got a clue and proposed," she said. "Giving her only four months to prepare for the wedding was just mean."

Although, Flick had managed it. She'd become a small dictator according to Mia.

She leaned forward. "So, tell me, what do you guys think about a woman doing the proposing?"

"Hell, no!" They both yelled at her.

Sitting back, she giggled as both of them glared at her, Jardin doing it through the rearview mirror.

"You propose, baby, and you're going over my knee every night for a week," Jardin promised.

"And then the next week you're over my knee," Carrick told her.

Oh, but it would totally be worth it.

LET'S KEEP IN TOUCH!

Don't miss a new release, sign up to my newsletter for sneak peeks, deleted scenes and giveaways: https://landing.mailerlite.com/web-forms/landing/p7l6g0

You can also join my Facebook readers group here: https://www.facebook.com/groups/38683042506991l/

Printed in Great Britain
by Amazon

35807805R00157